# A BLANKET
# OF STARS

## AJ Milnthorp

# TABLE OF CONTENTS

CHAPTER ONE.................................................................................................1

CHAPTER TWO............................................................................................. 15

CHAPTER THREE........................................................................................ 31

CHAPTER FOUR........................................................................................45

CHAPTER FIVE...............................................................................................59

CHAPTER SIX ............................................................................................ 73

CHAPTER SEVEN ..................................................................................... 83

CHAPTER EIGHT........................................................................................95

CHAPTER NINE...........................................................................................109

CHAPTER TEN ...........................................................................................117

CHAPTER ELEVEN......................................................................................133

CHAPTER TWELVE .................................................................................. 143

CHAPTER THIRTEEN ............................................................................. 149

CHAPTER FOURTEEN ........................................................................... 163

CHAPTER FIFTEEN.....................................................................................177

CHAPTER SIXTEEN ................................................................................ 195

CHAPTER SEVENTEEN ......................................................................... 209

CHAPTER EIGHTEEN.............................................................................. 219

CHAPTER NINETEEN................................................................................227

CHAPTER TWENTY....................................................................................239

CHAPTER TWENTY-ONE .......................................................................257

CHAPTER TWENTY-TWO ..................................................................... 269

CHAPTER TWENTY-THREE...................................................................285

CHAPTER TWENTY-FOUR ....................................................................301

CHAPTER TWENTY-FIVE.........................................................................315

CHAPTER TWENTY-SIX............................................................................329

CHAPTER TWENTY-SEVEN .................................................................. 341

EPILOGUE ....................................................................................................355

ACKNOWLEDGEMENTS..........................................................................367

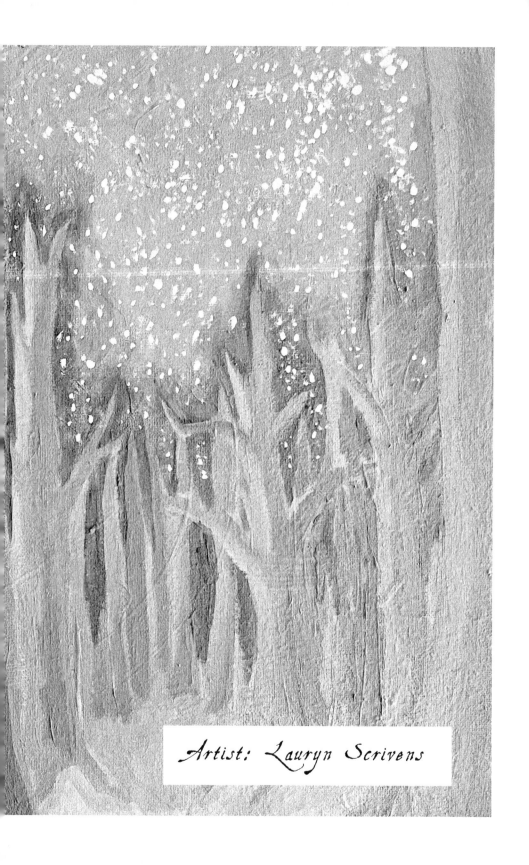

Artist: Lauryn Scrivens

*"She looked up at the moon which had now made its way to the center of the sky, to the blanket of stars that kept it warm and safe."*

—AJ Milnthorp

CHAPTER ONE

THE WARMTH OF EMBERLY'S mom's skin soothed her. Curled up next to her mom made Emberly feel protected and happy. She could hear the soft clinking of crochet needles as her mom weaved a stuffed animal out of dollar store yarn. She took a deep breath, inhaling the sweet smell of her mom's favourite peach perfume. A fragrance she rarely smelled unless her mom was around. Which, since the passing of Emberly's father eight years prior, was a rare occurrence.

Emberly was never one to enjoy silence nor to sit still, but something inside made her stay, making her think she wouldn't be alone with her mom forever. The twins, Eve and Zayne, were taking advantage of the day's warmer weather and were outside playing in the sprinklers. Their joyful laughter filtered in and echoed throughout the house like music. A slight disruption to the current silence she was enjoying, but in truth, Emberly didn't mind the noise. As long as she could hear them, she knew they weren't getting into trouble. And it was good to see them having fun, especially fun that kept them outside of the house. It would be all too soon that the twins would eventually grow tired of playing in the sprinklers and would venture inside looking for some other activity to pass the time, completely disrupting Emberly's silence. So, she wasn't about to start complaining. She never did anyways.

"Sorry honey. It's eleven o'clock. I have to go to work," her mom said as she got up from the couch. "Cook won't be happy if she has to make my first few meals for me again."

"No, you don't. You can stay here with me. Please," Emberly pleaded.

"If I don't go, that means I can't bring us back home food to eat tonight, and I don't think you want to see your sister hangry again. Do you?"

Emberly pondered the question for a bit before giving in. "Fine. But please don't be too long. Maybe you can make them close early tonight!"

Her mom laughed.

"Okay, I'll try." She leaned down and kissed Emberly on the forehead. As she did, the chain of the silver arrow necklace that she always wore brushed across Emberly's face, tickling her nose. "Can you go tell the twins I'm leaving? I still have to get into my chef wear."

"Yep." Emberly jumped up from the couch and ran to the back door, calling out that their mom was leaving for work. It didn't take long for the twins to come running into the house, spraying Emberly with water droplets as they passed her to say bye to their mom. Their mom rewarded each of the twins with a quick kiss on their foreheads and gave one final goodbye to Emberly as she walked out the front door.

Emberly grabbed her book from the coffee table and settled on the couch while the twins headed back outside. Emberly loved to read. It was the only time she could escape from the real world. She could imagine herself as a knight or an astronaut, or even the ruler of her own country. With reading, the possibilities were endless and the escape it gave her was always welcomed.

It wasn't long before Eve's cry of anguish punctured through Emberly's moment of peace. Figuring the situation would only get worse if she ignored it, as she was tempted to do, she ran outside and found Eve laying on the ground crying with Zayne nowhere to be seen.

"Eve, what happened?" Emberly asked as she rushed over. Just as she reached her sister's side, Eve sprang up and bolted away. Zayne popped out from where he was hiding on the side of the house, holding the water gun the twins had received on their birthday two years prior. He sprayed Emberly with a blast of water, causing her to fall to the ground. Both twins collapsed to the ground in fits of laughter.

"Okay, okay. You got me," she chuckled. She looked over at Zayne, who was still lying on the ground, wiping the tears of laughter from his eyes. Emberly's eyes travelled to the abandoned squirt gun—still half full of water. She smiled to herself and before they even realized what she was doing, she darted over and picked it up. "Don't ever let your guard down," Emberly cried and pelted them with the remaining water. Soon, all three were on the ground, clutching their sides as they laughed, completely drenched from head to toe.

"Okay, okay. We should never have tried to prank the master," Zayne said, after they finally calmed down and caught their breath. "But you've got to admit, that was fun."

"Oh, yeah," Emberly replied with the hint of a smirk on her face. "Getting soaked to the bone is a blast!" Emberly tried laughing at her own joke with her siblings but the hunger eating her insides stopped her and reminded her that she hadn't eaten anything all day. "Who wants lunch? I'm getting hungry."

"Me!" Eve shouted and took off towards the house, not even stopping to properly dry off before going inside. Zayne, always the more responsible of the pair, threw Emberly a towel to use before they followed Eve inside.

Emberly rummaged through the fridge, looking for something edible to eat amongst the barebones contents of the fridge. With the small salary coming from their mom and their dad no longer with them, it wasn't always easy feeding four bellies. Finally, she gave up and pulled a frozen pizza out of the deep freeze that was supposed to be left for special occasions, but Emberly was too hungry to care.

"Don't tell Mom we took the last pizza, okay?" The twins nodded enthusiastically. Emberly threw the pizza into the oven and filled three glasses to the brim with milk.

"Speaking of Mom, is she coming home for dinner tonight?" Eve asked.

"I think so. She said she'd bring something home from the restaurant again." The twins groaned. "Hey, don't do that. You both know that we wouldn't get to eat as much if Mom wasn't able to bring home leftovers from the restaurant for us. We're lucky they let her do that. Not to mention, your birthdays are tomorrow. Do you guys want a cake for your birthday or not?"

The twins looked at each other and frowned.

"Yes, we want a cake for our birthday," Zayne huffed and looked away.

"Then it'd be wise to remember that every bit of money Mom saves from having to buy food is money she can put towards things like buying a cake for our birthdays," Emberly scolded. Their mom had been saving up any extra money she could over the past couple of months so she could afford to buy presents and a cake for the twins' birthday. This, unfortunately, meant eating the leftovers she brought back from the restaurant each night. It was neither Emberly nor the twins' favourite as it was often the same type of food night after night, but it was better than starving.

The twins hung their heads in shame. "Sorry, Em," Eve whispered.

Emberly reached out and gave each of their hands a gentle squeeze. Wanting to lift the mood, she shifted the topic, "Speaking of birthdays, what do you guys want to do to celebrate? You're finally going to be eight. We have to do something special!"

"We just want cake and gifts," Eve said straight-faced. Emberly chuckled.

"I think we can do that, but is there something else the three of us could do for fun?" she asked. They sat there talking about the twins' birthday and all the crazy activities the twins came up with until the timer on the oven beeped, signalling that the pizza was ready.

The three of them didn't even wait for the cheese to cool before they each grabbed a piece and took a bite. They hadn't eaten anything since dinner the night before, and the pizza tasted like heaven. They finished their meals in silence, no one wanting to take a break to talk.

Once done, Emberly told the twins to go watch TV while she cleaned up. She knew her mom would be tired when she got back, and Emberly didn't want her to come home to a dirty house. Even though there wasn't much of a house to clean— just two bedrooms, a small kitchen, and an even smaller living room— it was something she enjoyed doing. And truthfully, what else was there to do besides go outside or read?

Emberly filled the sink with water and started to wash the floors, the noise from the TV keeping her company as she worked. She liked it that way. With sound on in the background, she wasn't buried deep in thoughts that would have otherwise made her go nuts. She could just shut her mind off and focus on the task at hand.

By the time Emberly finished, the sun was beginning to set and her back was starting to ache. Emberly put the cleaning supplies away then opened their small kitchen window to allow fresh air into the house. She welcomed in the gentle Connecticut breeze and closed her eyes and smiled as she breathed in its familiar smell.

After a few breaths, she opened her eyes and looked at the clock. *Oh crap*, she thought. *Mom will be home any second.*

"Eve, Zayne, let's get the table set for dinner," she called out.

"Things were pretty quiet the past hour. What were you doing?" Emberly suspiciously asked as she handed them plates and a bundle of cutlery.

"We got bored of watching TV, so we decided to draw," Zayne replied. Emberly's eyes widened.

"I hope on paper." Emberly gave them the look.

"Yes, on paper. We learned our lesson the first time." Eve chuckled deviously, thinking back to the time they had decided to decorate the end table with elaborate designs in permanent marker.

They finished setting the table just in time to hear their mom come in through the front door. The twins ran to greet her while Emberly stayed in the kitchen, making sure everything was clean and ready for dinner. Eve soon dragged their mom into the kitchen by her arm, talking her ear off about their day and the trick they had played on Emberly earlier.

"Wow. Emberly, you cleaned! Thank you so much, sweetie." She leaned in to hug her oldest daughter.

"It was nothing. I didn't have anything else to do," Emberly said, happy to take on watching her siblings and tending to the house while their mom worked. It was easy enough to do and she knew her mom appreciated the help.

They shared stories about their day as they ate, enjoying each other's company. *Even if we don't have much, we always find a way to be happy*, Emberly thought to herself.

An hour later, they finally got up from the table.

"Why don't the three of you get into your pyjamas. I'll stay and clean up. You all have done so much today," their mom smiled and Emberly followed the twins to their shared room.

"Sure, Mom," Emberly said. "Eve, can you get dressed by yourself?" she jokingly asked as they walked into their room.

"Yes, Em," she chuckled. "I think I can manage."

"Just checking. How about you, Zayne? Need any help?" she turned to Zayne who just raised an eyebrow in response. "Okay, okay. Just trying to help." Emberly smiled and turned to her side of the room. Of the two bedrooms, theirs was the largest, considering all three had to share it.

A dresser and a rickety old bunk bed that their mom had purchased years ago from a garage sale and a dresser filled up the twins' half of the room, while a single bed and a closet took up Emberly's side. Their shared nightstand sat under the window between their beds. Its surface was littered with books and various odds and ends that the twins had found and claimed as "treasures" on their many adventures. It wasn't much but it was all they needed.

Emberly's gaze lifted to the wall above her bed and she smiled. It was plastered with photos that she had taken over the years. Most of which were either nature shots from when her dad used to take her into the forest behind their house, or pictures of the twins. The latter offered many different toothless smiles or grins with purple-dyed lips from over the years.

Emberly used to love taking pictures, but rarely did so anymore. She had hardly picked up her camera since her dad had passed away, only ever doing so to make a point of capturing moments of the twins as they grew. Emberly had been seven when their dad had passed away. He had missed the birth of the twins by only a day.

On lonely nights, Emberly liked to look at her collection of photos and remember the days from before, when things were happy and easier. She often tried to imagine what it would have been like if her dad was still around—the adventures he'd take the three of them on, the family dinners the five of them would have enjoyed together, or the trips to far-away lands they might have even been able to afford.

Emberly heard something crash and hit the floor, and she turned and found Zayne lying on the ground, thrashing from side to side, grunting as he tried to pull up his pants.

"Are those pyjama pants getting a little too snug for you, buddy?" she joked.

"No, they're good. I do this every night," Zayne replied as he continued to roll on the ground until he finally managed to yank his pants up. It was true that he needed new pants—new everything for that matter—but she knew that he didn't want to ask. Like everything else, Zayne would just have to deal with those pants until there was absolutely no chance of him fitting into them.

He got up and the pant legs barely went past his knees. The sight caused Emberly to chuckle. But Zayne, who was always the most practical and level-headed of the three, just looked down at his pants, gave her a lopsided smile, and walked out of the room with his head held high to go find Eve who had already left the room. Eve's clothes were always a lot easier to put on considering her entire wardrobe used to belong to Emberly. If anything, they were still a little too big for Eve, but she used an array of belts or knots to tie them up to better fit her. She loved to be creative.

Emberly sighed as she looked through her closet. She needed to take a page out of Zayne's book and not get bothered by things that couldn't be changed.

Emberly's attire consisted mainly of black articles of clothing with a few pieces of blue and grey mixed in. You would be lucky to spot a vibrant colour in her closet. She grabbed a large grey t-shirt that had once belonged to her mom and threw it on. While her mom was slightly shorter, they were close enough to the same size that they were able to share clothes. This made shopping much less expensive. She completed the look with a pair of old black shorts and left to join the others in the living room.

Zayne was sprawled across the armrest on one side of the couch while Eve was sitting on a cushion on the floor in front of their mom. As usual, the curtains had already been pulled tight and the lights were off. The blue glow from the TV was the only source of light that illuminated the room. Emberly curled up on the couch and laid her head in her mom's lap. She breathed out a sigh of relief. Again, she was safe and protected in her small, but happy, family home.

*"After sixteen years of being in prison, today, the two Marley Terrance gang members have escaped from jail ,"* the news reporter exclaimed. The clicking and clacking of her mom's knitting needles stopped abruptly and their moms body stiffened.

"Are you okay, Mom?" Emberly asked as she glanced up at her mom.

"Yes, baby. Just hoping they find those two gang members and take them back to jail before they cause any trouble," her mom responded, her eyes still glued to the TV screen, but her crocheting never stopped.

"I'm sure they will," Zayne piped in.

"Me too, honey," their mom replied.

But the weak smile and tiny nod their mom gave didn't fool Emberly. She assumed though that her mom didn't want to talk about it. She likely didn't want to get the twins worried, so Emberly rested her head back onto her mom's lap and tried to concentrate for the rest of the news segment. Emberly would talk to her after the twins went to sleep and figure out what was bothering her.

When the news ended, their mom announced that it was time for the twins to get to bed and ushered them to their room. After fifteen minutes had gone by, Emberly got up from the couch and quietly crept to their bedroom so she wouldn't disturb the twins in case they had already fallen asleep. As she got closer, she could hear talking.

"Mom, can you tell us another story? The one about our names?" Eve whined. Even without seeing her, Emberly could tell she was giving her mom her trademark puppy dog eyes. Emberly crept closer so she was standing just outside of the doorway but remained hidden from view.

"Okay, honey, but this is our last story."

She cleared her throat, like she was about to tell the most important story in history, and began. "I've always loved how names mean something, so I gave all three of you names that I thought would match the person I knew you would become. Eve, I gave you that name because when you came into this world, I could tell that you were full of life and smiles. And Zayne, I knew you would be gracious and kind, as you very much are, but I could also tell that you were wise beyond your years with your watchful eyes and quiet disposition. Even my name means something. 'Belen' means arrow." She grabbed hold of her arrow necklace. "I don't know why my parents chose the name, but I'm glad they did."

"Tell us the meaning of Emberly's name, it's my favourite one," Eve begged.

"Her name means spark or small flame. Someone who is not afraid of starting something on fire with their words," she winked. "I think I picked a pretty accurate one for Emberly, didn't I?"

"Oh yeah," Zayne laughed. Their mom got up from where she had been resting on their bed, kissed each of them on their foreheads and told them to get a good night's rest so they could have a great birthday tomorrow.

"We'll have a great birthday so long as you're around, Mom," Zayne reassured her.

Before she was spotted, Emberly silently dashed back to the couch and pretended as though she had been there the entire time.

Seemingly better after she had spent time telling stories to the twins, Emberly decided to not bring up any mention of the news and her mom's reaction to it, and instead decided to enjoy their extra one-on-one time.

After about thirty minutes, Emberly couldn't stop yawning and decided it was time for bed. She was careful to open the door, so she wouldn't wake her siblings, and crawled into bed and closed her eyes. She had hoped for a good night's rest, but her sleep was soon taken hostage with memories of hiking through the forest with her dad, or when he'd take her hunting. Even though her dad had a bow and quiver of arrows, they couldn't afford to buy a set for Emberly. He had taught her how to make her own, so she had one that was a bit smaller and easier to use. Closer to the morning, those happy dreams transitioned into nightmares of the Marley Terrance gang and the dangerous things they might do around the community.

CHAPTER TWO

"Ahhhh!"

A shout came from outside Emberly's room the next morning. Emberly's heart raced and her eyes shot open. She looked over at her clock on the nightstand, five o'clock on the dot.

Still drowsy from sleep and shaken from the scream, she swung her legs off the side of her bed and ran from her room to see what had happened. But instead of seeing the twins, all she found were five gifts, wrapped in newspaper, sitting on top of the kitchen table. Each tied off with a simple red bow. She began to frantically look around, checking first the kitchen then the living room. Just as she was about to turn to check her mom's room, the twins jumped out from under the kitchen table and screamed in an attempt to scare their older sister. It worked. Emberly's heart stopped and she jumped backwards, almost knocking herself into the wall behind her. They laughed and high-fived each other as Emberly tried to catch her breath.

Their mom walked into the kitchen smiling, knowing damn well what had woken her up. "I see you found the presents," she chuckled. "I also see that you've woken up pretty early."

"It's our birthday! What did you expect us to do?" Eve questioned. Emberly rolled her eyes and chuckled.

"Mom, can we please open our presents? You're torturing us," Zayne whined. Emberly looked at their mom and the two exchanged glances before she walked over to the table and handed them each their first present.

Eve tore through hers in no time, causing a storm of wrapping paper to float down to the ground around her chair, leaving it for Emberly to clean up. Zayne, however, took his time, carefully peeling off the tape and unwrapping the paper without a single rip or tear. Once both presents were finally unwrapped, the gasps began. Eve received the stuffed animal her mom had finished crocheting her the day before and Zayne got a book titled, *My Journey North*. The book seemed like an odd choice of gift for Zayne since the cover showed it as being a horror novel. Emberly frowned when she saw the book. Zayne was only eight. Why would her mom give him, of all people, a horror book?

The second present Eve opened was also a book. Multiple books, actually. Emberly didn't recognize any of them.

"*Into the Forest* is the name of the series. Ari, the main character, is a lot like you," their mom explained. "She's adventurous and prefers action over laying around."

"Oh, Mom, thank you so much. I love them!" Eve ran over and hugged her.

Next, Zayne opened his second gift, taking equal care with this one to find the treasure buried within. He finally got it unwrapped and revealed a pair of pants. Not ones that were ripped, stained, or previously worn, but brand-new ones that were perfectly washed and folded. He lifted them and the smile that shone over his face was brighter than all the stars in the sky.

"Why don't you try them on, bud?" Emberly suggested. He nodded eagerly, the smile still pressed against his lips, and raced to their bedroom. Emberly looked over at Eve who continued to sit in her chair playing with her new stuffed animal. Then her gaze drifted over to her mom, who caught Emberly's eye and winked, before Zayne came bolting back into the kitchen with his new pants on. They fit him perfectly.

"Thank you so much, Mom," he said as he threw his arms around her neck and squeezed tight. Eve got off her chair and joined in on the hug.

"You kids are welcome, but you still have one more present to open," she pointed at the remaining gift in the center of the table. The twins looked at each other, smiled, and ran over to their last present. They opened it together. Eve gingerly held the present in her hands. It was a book.

"What My Name Means," Eve read the book title out loud.

"I know you guys love hearing the story behind your names, so I bought you this book so you could always remember, and to maybe learn about other names."

"Thank you," the twins cheered, and ran to hug their mom again.

She hugged them back with equal enthusiasm. "Why don't you kids get dressed and come back for some breakfast."

Emberly went to join them, but her mom stopped her. "Wait, Emberly, I have something for you too."

*"For me?* But my birthday isn't until December," Emberly replied, more than a little confused.

"I know, but I want you to have something." She reached around her neck and unclasped her arrow necklace. Then she reached down, took Emberly's hand, and placed the silver chain onto her palm, its metal still warm from being around her mom's neck. Emberly gazed at the necklace; its delicate silver chain that was pooled at the centre of her palm and the delicate arrow pendant that hung from the end of it. Its edges were slightly rounded from years of wear, but it still gleamed as if brand new, thanks to the meticulous care her mom had always taken of it.

"Mom. I can't take this, Grandma gave it to you," she said as she tried to hand it back, but her mom refused to take it.

She folded Emberly's fingers around with the necklace. "Yes, and now I am giving it to you. I want you to have something to always remember me by."

"Mom, it's not like you're going anywhere. There's no reason for me to forget you."

"I know, but I still want you to have it. Who knows what could happen to me? Now, turn around so I can put it on you." Emberly looked at her mom to see if she could find any bit of emotion in her facial expression. Seeing none, she reluctantly did as she was told and turned around.

Her mom's fingers slightly fumbled with the clasp until she managed to clip the two ends together. Emberly shivered as the chain fell around her neck. She picked up and held the arrow charm in her hand, touched by her mom's gesture.

Emberly quickly tucked the necklace into her shirt as the twins rushed back into the kitchen to examine their toys.

After a quick breakfast, Emberly and her mom washed the dishes, claiming the twins didn't have to clean up since it was their birthday. Deciding to take advantage of the break from chores and yet another warm June day, Eve and Zayne went outside to play in the sprinklers.

Once the kitchen was cleaned up, Emberly went to her room to get dressed for the day. She opened her closet and grabbed a pair of clean jeans, before deciding that since it was a special occasion, she ought to find a non-black shirt to wear. Emberly found a white one tucked away in the very back corner of the closet. As she pulled the shirt out, her eye caught the end of something peeking out from a pile of her old clothes. She moved the clothes away, revealing her dad's old bow and quiver of arrows.

Her own bow that she had made with her dad as a child broke years ago, but when her dad died, she hadn't had the heart to throw away his old set. Even though her mom refused to let her go out hunting alone, some days she used to practice drawing it in her room. It wasn't as much fun as getting to use it outside, so she eventually stopped and moved it into her closet to keep it out of the way. Years of tossing things into her closet had hidden it from view, until she eventually forgot she had even put it there.

Emberly ran her fingers along the length of the bow, as memories of its use flooded her mind and brought a smile to her face.

She found the bowstring tucked into the side pouch of her quiver and restrung the bow, before examining the four remaining arrows, all of which were still in good condition. She would have to try to sneak out one day to use it, but for now, Emberly tucked the bow and quiver back under the pile of clothes. She didn't want her mom knowing she still had them, and didn't want to risk her mom finding and throwing them away.

She returned to the kitchen where her mom was looking through the window at the twins. Both were jumping around and playing in the water-soaked grass as if they hadn't a care in the world. Emberly couldn't help but laugh.

Her mom's head turned around to face her, but Emberly had already darted out the back door. *It is much too nice to be inside*, she thought.

Even though she was quite a bit older than them, they always had fun together. Being fourteen didn't change the fact that she was still a kid. She splashed around in the water and joined them as they rolled on the ground, not caring as her only nice clothes got covered in grass stains and mud.

They laughed and played in the sprinklers for hours, soon joined by their mom, who sat on an old, rusty lawn chair and watched. But then the wind started to pick up, bringing with it heavy, dark rain clouds that blocked the sun. The wind rustled through Emberly's hair causing the hair on the back of her neck to stand up, and as if out of nowhere, the heavy rain started. Stream after stream of water rained down upon them, leaving nothing but their thoughts dry. The first clap of thunder rang through the sky as if Zeus himself had called out to take cover. Zayne grabbed hold of Emberly for his life and looked timidly up at the sky as a bolt of lightning struck the stained-black sky. That was all it took for the four of them to dash inside for cover.

Emberly grabbed a stack of towels from the bathroom closet and wrapped each of the twins' shivering bodies in one before doing the same to her own. They joined their mom at the kitchen table where the battery-powered radio had been turned on, waiting for what the news had to say. The lights began to flicker on and off, and they placed bets on how long it would take for the power to go out completely. But Eve soon grew restless. She wanted to watch the thunderstorm, but the blinds on the kitchen window had been drawn shut to make it less scary for Zayne who had always feared storms.

"Come on, Eve, let's watch from our room," Emberly said. She grabbed a spare flashlight from one of the drawers, in case the lights did shut off, then held out her hand to Eve.

The only window in their room was small and tucked at the back of the room between their beds, splitting the room in half. All the windows in their house had been tinted, limiting the view inside. It was a feature their mom had saved up for after her father had died. She described it as a way to protect her new babies' eyes from the sunlight. Emberly didn't always believe this to be true, but in that moment, she didn't question her grieving mother.

Emberly cracked the window open a bit so they could hear the roaring thunder, and smell the sweet air of the storm.

"So, how are you liking your birthday so far?" Emberly asked, trying to talk over the thunder.

"I'm not sure. Today feels weird," Eve scrunched up her face.

"What do you mean?" Emberly asked, sneaking a look at her sister who was staring at the storm outside with a look of worry pinched across her face.

"Never mind. It's nothing."

"No, it's not nothing." Emberly didn't understand what she meant. How could her birthday feel weird? It was the only day where you were supposed to feel no worry.

"It really is nothing, okay?" Eve responded.

Emberly could tell that Eve had started to get agitated, but Emberly wanted to know what was wrong.

"You can't just say that and expect me not to ask," Emberly chuckled, trying to break the tension, "and since when do you keep things from me?"

Eve gave her a side-eye glare but couldn't stop the smile from forming. "Okay, fine. You know when you wake up on your birthday and you think to yourself that nothing is going to go wrong today?" Emberly nodded. "Well, when I woke up today, I had this feeling inside me, saying that this was going to be the worst birthday of my life." Eve dared a glance at Emberly, but instantly looked back down.

"Well, you hid your feelings pretty well when you were opening your presents."

"Those feelings kind of went away this morning, but they all came rushing back when the storm started." Emberly pulled her little sister into a warm embrace, trying to comfort her.

"Don't worry, Eve. Everything will turn out just fine today." She stroked Eve's hair, then gently pushed her back, so she could look her in the eyes. "Once the thunder and rain clouds clear, all those feelings inside of you will go away," she poked Eve's stomach causing her to giggle.

"But," Eve stopped giggling. "I have these feelings anytime something bad happens. Like when Granny died, and Papa too. And, now today."

Emberly could tell that her sister was on the verge of tears. "It's okay. Nothing bad will happen to you, ever. Not while I'm around."

"You promise?" Eve stuck out her pinkie.

"I promise," Emberly reassured Eve, as the sisters locked pinkies.

They continued to watch until their mom called them back into the kitchen. When they got there, their mom was pacing around the room with her head down, muttering to herself, almost as if to give herself a pep talk. Her hands ran through her hair, making it messier and knotted. Zayne was sitting at the table looking at his mom, a worried expression painted on his face, not knowing what he should do.

"What's wrong with Mom?" Emberly asked Zayne. Eve grabbed onto Emberly's hand and squeezed tight. Eve's feelings must have gotten worse.

"I don't know. She won't tell me anything," Zayne explained, never taking his eyes off his overwrought mother.

Their mom's head shot up. "Oh, hi girls." The expression on her face, a mixture of pain and sadness. Emberly pulled Zayne up from where he was sitting and dragged him over to stand behind her with Eve as if to protect them from whatever would come next.

"I'm so sorry, babies, but I just got off the phone with the restaurant, and I have to go into work today after all."

"Why? I thought you had the day off?" Zayne whimpered.

"I did, sweetie, but apparently someone quit, so they need me. I'm so sorry."

The radio noise grew staticky and the lights flickered as if they were in the opening scene of a horror movie. Their mom opened her arms up for a hug, but the twins stayed behind Emberly, not wanting to move.

"Just go say goodbye," Emberly told them. She watched their faces as they hugged their mom. Zayne was trying to stay strong, but Emberly could tell he was going to cry the moment she left. However, Eve was looking straight at Emberly with a blank expression, mouthing the words, *I told you.*

Their mom let go of the kids and kissed them both on their heads, hugged each individually and whispered something into each of their ears.

Then she gave Emberly the same big hug and kiss on her forehead, "Honey, I won't be gone long. I'll be back before you know it. Just...take good care of your siblings for me while I'm gone, okay? And be safe."

"I always do, Mom." Her mom gave her a half-hearted smile.

"Is everything okay, Mom? You don't seem like yourself."

"Oh Em, you worry too much. Everything will be fine. I'm just sad that I have to miss the twins' birthday, that's all." For some reason, Emberly didn't think that was the total truth.

"They understand. We'll have lots of fun." Emberly forced herself to smile.

"Good." And with that, she grabbed her purse and was out the door. Emberly turned to the twins. Zayne had finally let go of the tears he had been holding back, and they were now streaming down his face. Emberly wrapped him up in a big hug and allowed him to cry into her shoulder. She hated it when either of them cried. It broke a piece of her heart every time.

"Why couldn't she just stay? Other people work at that place too you know," Zayne wailed.

"I know, buddy, but Mom will be home soon, and the three of us will have lots of fun until then, okay?" Zayne nodded and Emberly ruffled his short, dark hair, its ends still slightly uneven from the cut their mom had given him on the weekend.

Emberly then looked over at Eve, who had a sour look on her face. Emberly had never seen her so mad before. Her eyes were small slits and her lips were pressed together in a straight line. Emberly walked over to her and gently touched her cheek. At the touch of her fingers, Eve's face slowly melted into Emberly's hand and she brushed away the lone tear that had escaped. Emberly could tell that Eve was trying to be tough, but soon Eve couldn't hold them back. Her back caved, and she fell into Emberly, her tears soaking the front of her shirt.

"It's okay to cry you know. You've been through a lot and this was supposed to be a full day with Mom. It's okay to be upset," she pulled both in for a hug. "But you must know that I will always be here, even when Mom isn't."

"Which means you're here 99% of the time," Eve muttered. Sadly, Eve wasn't wrong.

Not wanting this to spoil their birthday any further, Emberly stepped back and placed her hands on her hips. "Okay, now we can check that off our to-do list," Emberly said, earning a chuckle from the twins. "Let's go eat some lunch, and then when the rain stops, we will go jump in the puddles and make a terrible mess of our clothes! How does that sound?"

"Perfect!" the twins shouted, even though they all knew that it was likely the storm wouldn't let up before the end of the day.

They ate left-over chicken, from who knows how long ago, then spent the next few hours playing board games, snacking on crackers and more leftovers when they got hungry. All the while, leaving the radio on to provide a gentle hum in the background.

The girls left Zayne for a little while, in the company of some pencil crayons and paper, and went back to their room to watch the storm play out.

"So, do you still have that feeling?" Emberly asked.

"Yes. I feel like something else bad is going to happen today."

"Okay, Miss Psychic," Emberly smiled. "Since I already promised that nothing bad would happen today, I'm pretty sure you're just feeling sad because Mom left."

"I don't think so. Something's not right. I just know it."

They watched the storm in silence for a little while longer before returning to the kitchen to find Zayne still drawing.

Emberly looked at his picture and saw that there was a small girl, small boy, and a taller girl holding hands at the center of the page. In the far-right corner, there was a small person.

"What's this of Zayne?" Emberly asked pointing to the paper.

"Our family."

"Who are all the people in the picture?"

"That's you," he said, pointing to the taller girl, "And that's me, and Eve." he pointed to the small boy and girl in turn.

"Where's Mom?" Eve asked. Zayne looked at her then pointed to the small person in the corner.

"That's Mom."

"Why is she all the way over there?" Eve questioned. But without him having to respond, Emberly knew exactly why he had drawn their mom in the corner.

"Because she's never home," he whispered.

The room fell silent as if someone had turned down the volume. No one talked for a long time.

"Mom will probably be home soon," Emberly said. But she looked at the clock and saw that it was already nine. Their mom should have been back by then. Emberly tried to stifle her nerves. She didn't want the twins to see that she was beginning to get worried herself and cause them to be even more concerned than they already were.

"Yeah, you're right." Eve agreed, just as the lights flickered to a stop and the power went out of the house completely.

Emberly instructed Zayne and Eve to grab some candles from their hallway storage closet so she could light them, then she turned up the volume on the radio to fill the empty space.

*"...police are still unclear as to how the two members of the Marley Terrance gang escaped from prison yesterday. But the real question is, will anyone be hurt when all of this is over?"*

A loud knock came from the front door, distracting Emberly from the radio. Puzzled, she made her way to the front of the house with a candle in hand. *If that's Mom, why wouldn't she just open it?* Emberly asked herself.

She walked over to the front window to see who it could be. Emberly had a hard time seeing clearly the two figures who stood on her doorstep on a count of that the tinted windows in the dark made it quite difficult. What she did see, though, was the shinning police bag that was clipped onto the belt of one of the figures.

She opened the door rapidly for the officer and their neighbour, Mrs. Vander, standing behind him, a sad expression on her face.

Emberly scrunched her eyebrows, "Hi, Mrs. Vander; Officer. Is something wrong?"

He twisted his hat in his hands and cleared his throat, "Are you Miss Emberly Clove?"

Emberly's heart was beating in her throat. All she could do was nod in response.

"I'm sorry to inform you that your mother was in a serious car accident tonight."

Emberly's stomach dropped, "Is she okay? Do we need to go to the hospital?" She went to grab her coat from the rack, but the officer stopped her.

"I'm sorry, honey, but your mother..." the officer rubbed the back of his neck with one hand as he paused to take a breath. It seemed as though it was a struggle for him to find the right words to tell her. Emberly braced herself for what she knew he was going to say, "She died in the crash."

Emberly couldn't breathe. She felt nauseous. Her head was spinning, and she couldn't see straight. She fell to her knees and barely registered what the officer was saying. He expressed his condolences and proceeded to tell her that should a situation such as this occurred, her mom had arranged for the neighbour, who was their mom's emergency contact, to stay with them until they could be taken into the proper care. He then handed her a card and told her that the person listed on the card would stop by tomorrow to handle arrangements. She slipped the card into her pocket and numbly thanked the officer, then nodded at Ms. Vander who told her that she was going to run back to her house to pack a bag to spend the night.

The twins came to the living room to see who was at the door. When they found her on the ground, her face streaked with tears, they rushed over.

"What happened?" Zayne asked

"Who was that?" Eve looked out the window and saw the cop car pulling away. "Why was a cop here?"

Questions were flying at Emberly's but she couldn't speak. She needed a moment for everything to register. But when she looked up and took in their distraught expressions, everything clicked together. She needed to pick herself up, dry her tears, then tell them what had happened. She didn't know what would come next for them, but she knew that she needed to be there for them right now.

"Mom," she swallowed and took a deep breath, "died in a car accident on her way home from work."

The twins didn't process it right away, but when they finally did, the tears started pouring down their little faces. It was too much for Emberly, and she couldn't stop the tears from running down her own face either. She clutched onto the twins, and they all collapsed to the floor.

Emberly couldn't believe it. What was she supposed to do? They had no living family left, and she knew almost no one. She was only fourteen so nobody would let her take care of the twins on her own. They would have to go to a foster home—somewhere other than here, their home.

They were the only people that remained in their lives. The only ones that hadn't abandoned them. Their only family left.

"What's going to happen to us?" Eve asked.

Emberly didn't have an answer to that question, "I don't know, baby." In a voice that was barely a whisper, "I told you that my feelings are never wrong. Do you believe me now?"

CHAPTER THREE

EMBERLY WAS STILL IN shock the next morning. Her mind was racing. *Where were they going to go? Who would look after them? What would happen if they split us up? How could this have happened, why them?* So many questions, so little answers and so little sleep.

Eve, who usually got up at the break of dawn, was still sleeping. Zayne on the other hand had already gotten dressed and was staring out the window. Emberly yawned and walked over to stand by Zayne.

"Was it all a nightmare?" he asked, looking out the window.

"No, Zayne, it was real." Emberly wrapped an arm around his shoulders and squeezed. "I'm sorry." He pulled back and looked her in the eye. He didn't cry, he just looked defeated. She understood—she had no tears left to cry either.

"That's what I was afraid of," he whispered. Emberly had nothing to say that would make it easier, so she just looked out the window with Zayne and watched the clouds roll around the sky.

They stood there for a while until a soft knock came from their door. Emberly turned her head and saw that Ms. Vander standing there.

"The officers told me last night that the state would be sending someone to pick you guys up today, to take care of you. I'm so sorry. I wish there was more I could do. I've made breakfast and its on the table for when you're ready. I have to leave for work now. I- I'm so sorry." she stammered over her words as tears welded in her eyes. Emberly thanked Ms. Vander as she closed the door behind her. Eve's eyes opened at the sound of the creaking door hinges. Her eyes were red, as if she had been crying throughout the night. Emberly gave her a hug then pulled out some clothes for them to get dressed, grabbing a pair of ripped jean shorts that had once belonged to her mom and a plain, black tank top for herself.

Stuck under a pan of eggs and bacon, they found a note from Mrs. Vander saying the same things she had told them in person. Since Ms. Vander had looked after them over the years, she was well aware of how forgetful Emberly could be.

"I know this is going to be hard," Emberly said over a mouthful of food. "Someone is going to come by at some point today to fill us in on what Mom had planned for us. I want you guys to promise me something, okay?" the twins nodded. "No matter what happens or where we go, stay true to yourselves, please. Eve, I want you to be a ray of sunshine like always. And, Zayne, I want you to continue to be kind and creative. We still have each other. That won't ever change."

"We promise," Eve said. "But then you have to promise to protect us."

"I promise. And I also promise to tell you stories every night. Just like Mom did," Emberly winked at her siblings.

"Yeah, and sing to us too," Zayne added. "Like you used to." Emberly used to sing to the twins when they were toddlers. After their dad died, their mom usually spent the evenings closed up in her room. This meant it was Emberly's job to put her siblings to bed, and to do pretty much everything else for them. Everything was her job but she had grown use to it.

Just after lunch, they heard a loud knock on the front door. This time, they went to the door together and opened it. A man was standing on the other side, dressed in a suit and sunglasses. It was almost like something you would see in a spy movie.

"Are you the Clove family?" he asked. "The ones who lost their mother last night?"

They all nodded.

"I'm really sorry for your loss. Has anyone come for you since then?"

Again, they shook their heads. "Ok. My name is Mr. Zeros, and I'm here to help you"

Emberly chuckled under her breath, "Wait, your name is Mr. Zeros? Like, actually?"

The twins started to chuckle, but the man just sighed and muttered something under his breath about 'kids' and 'heard that before.'

"Yes. I am here to take you into custody. You are not eligible to live by yourselves, so you have to pack up all your clothes and personal belongings and come with me." He reminded

Emberly of a robot. Probably having to do this type of work for years would squeeze the emotion out of someone.

"We don't have anything to put them in," Emberly replied.

"Well, then it's a good thing I was instructed to bring suit-cases for you," he responded. "You have one suitcase each and one hour to pack."

"Wait, aren't we going to at least stay here until after our mom's funeral?" Emberly asked.

"Sorry kiddo," he said, trying to sound sympathetic. "There isn't going to be a funeral. You're leaving today."

"No funeral? How is that possible?" Eve cried out.

He shrugged, "Funerals cost money, and you don't have the money in your accounts to pay for one. Besides, the body was burnt when the car caught on fire. There wasn't much left, so the coroner will have her cremated per your mom's instruc-tions. The ashes will be sent to you at a later date to do with as you please." It felt as though a robot had taken over Mr. Ze-ro's body. It sounded like he was reading a prepared, heartless script.

Emberly closed her eyes and took a deep breath. This wasn't fair. They deserved to say goodbye to their mom one last time; to have at least more than an hour to sort through and try to pack up what they could of their lives. "What about the house and the rest of our things—our mom's things?"

"Grab what you can to fill your suitcases, and the rest will be boxed up and shipped for you to sort through once you've settled into your new place. As for the house, since you were renting it, the owners will put it back up for rent." He placed a hand on Emberly's shoulder. "Look, I— "

"Don't touch me," she growled as she pushed his hand off her shoulder. "Just give us our suitcases and let us get on with packing."

They took their time packing, ignoring the one-hour rule. Emberly couldn't imagine saying goodbye to her place in less than an hour, let alone try to sort through and pack up what she might need.

They grabbed whatever clothes, books, toys, and mementos of their own, along with some things of their mom's, that they could fit into their bags. It passed by Emberly's mind a few times to grab all the jewelry but she knew too well that their mom's jewelry was worthless. Her mom had already tried to sell it many times and was only offered a few dollars, so Emberly trashed the idea. She did make sure, however, to grab the photos from her wall and stuff them, along with the note from Ms. Vander, into a small box that she had found in her closet. She stared for a moment at her dad's bow and arrows still nestled away in her closet. She knew she couldn't leave them behind. They meant too much to her. She also knew she couldn't exactly walk around carrying them. She took out everything that she had already packed into her large suitcase, put the bow and quiver of arrows at the bottom, and piled everything else back on top.

She grabbed her stuff and did one last walk through before saying a final goodbye. Pictures can tell a lot of things, but not everything.

The three of them climbed into the back seat and buckled their seat belts. It made for a tight squeeze, but Emberly refused to sit with that robot up front. Her feelings had morphed from sadness to anger. She no longer felt sad. She was angry and upset. She wanted to stay with the twins in their home, where they belonged. But most of all she was mad at her mom. She didn't have to go to work on the twins' birthday. She could have stayed home like a normal parent would have. Emberly knew it was wrong to blame her mom for this, but it was all too much for her to deal with.

Less than two hours later, they were no longer in East Granby, Connecticut. Instead, they were now entering the town of Hampton, or at least that's what Emberly had read on the sign when they drove past the city line. They drove a little further, making their way through the city, before the car finally parked in front of a large, ominous bungalow on the outskirts of Hampton.

Emberly took in the house with its faded, salmon-coloured paint, it's porch with missing boards, and the overgrown front lawn. The yard itself was massive, making the size of the house appear almost tiny in comparison, even though the house was far from small.

"Hey, Mr. Negative-One," Emberly said as they got out of the car. The man sighed and the twins snickered. "What are we doing here? Is this some sort of cult house? What is this place?"

"*This* is where you will be staying," he replied in his emotionless, uncaring voice.

Eve gasped and Emberly's eyes grew wide.

"What?" Eve asked. "Here?"

"Yes, *here*," he mimicked. "This is where your mom arranged for you to stay should something ever happen to her. The lady who runs it is almost one hundred years old, but is quite nice. Her daughter on the other hand—" Mr. Zeros was cut off by the screams of a small child that could have pierced someone's ears all the way back in East Granby. Zayne covered his ears. He hated loud noises.

"So, you're just going to leave us here?" Emberly was mad.

He shrugged and opened the trunk to retrieve their suitcases. "I just do what I'm told."

She followed him, determined to get more answers. "So, you were told to leave us here, at a place where the actual structure of the house is falling apart and kids are screaming? With a stranger whose name we don't even know—someone we haven't even heard our mom mention before?" Emberly was practically yelling at this point. She couldn't control it.

"Okay, just calm down there, stinker." he bent down to be at eye level.

"Stop calling me stupid names. I know how to have a real conversation, so stop talking down to me!" Mr. Zeros straightened and stared at her. A slow smile spread across his face.

"I see we have a girl who can talk for herself. How great. Ms. Margot will love that. Yes, you are staying here. Your mom wanted you guys here if anything was to happen. I don't know why, but this is where I was told to drive you. So here we are."

He handed them their suitcases and ushered them to the front door, taking care to avoid the loose and non-existent floor boards on the front porch. He knocked on the door and it swung open to show a middle-aged woman with a cigarette dangling from her mouth. She smelled horrid, as did the house. Emberly angled her head to peek further into the house, and saw four kids standing in the living room. One looked like she was a couple years younger than Emberly, and the others seemed to be around the twins' ages. They all looked miserable—and hungry.

"Hello. I'm Martha Margot," she stuck out her hand to shake theirs, but Emberly just stared at it in disgust. She pulled it back and frowned. "My mom owns the place, but I run the show. You must be the Clove family."

"Yes, they are, and I have to run. Nice meeting you guys," Mr. Zeros said before winking at Emberly. She just glared at him in response, but it was a look that he never saw because he had already turned to rush back to his car. Martha kept a smile plastered on her face until he drove away. The moment he did, her face drooped into an ugly scowl.

"Get your bags," she barked at them. They jumped, and did as they were told. They followed her through the twisted hallways of the house, walking by many small rooms. While the house didn't exactly look tiny from the outside, it was even larger on the inside. Its space seemingly never ending. They followed Martha into a room smaller than the one they had back at home. "You'll stay here. Unpack quickly."

"Yes, Martha—"

"You will refer to me as Ms. Margot," her tone was harsh and sharp. "My mother isn't going to be here for long, but you will be, so get used to addressing me properly. In thirty minutes, you will be needed in the kitchen for dinner. If you are not there in thirty minutes...well, let's just say you don't want to be late." She gave them a menacing smile and walked out of the room, slamming the door behind her.

The three of them huddled together into a tight hug as the reality of their new situation began to sink in. Between the shabby house, the hungry-looking kids, and the sharpness of Ms. Margot, Emberly almost wanted to make a run for it right then. She stopped herself, hoping she was just exaggerating the situation.

"It's going to be alright. I'm going to protect you. Nothing will happen as long as I'm here," Emberly said before she released the twins and told them to quickly unpack. They didn't want to know what would happen if they were late for dinner.

There wasn't much room to put anything. There was hardly enough space in their room for the two beds, a small wooden wardrobe, and a narrow closet. The only decorations in the room were a set of grey curtains that were filled with holes, and an old metal clock that had been hung on the wall with a rusted nail. The faded grey wallpaper was peeling off in places, and the ceiling looked like it would collapse at any given moment.

Emberly took a steadying breath and tried to refocus. They collectively decided that their clothes would be stored in their closet, and the wardrobe would be for everything besides clothes. There were three drawers, so they would each get their own.

The only thing Emberly didn't unpack was her bow and arrows, which she kept hidden inside her suitcase and tucked under her bed. It's not like they were to be kept a secret, but she didn't want to chance what would happen if Ms. Margot saw them. She didn't know much about the woman, but knew enough not to trust her.

They left for dinner and walked hand-in-hand down the twisted hallways. Their room was in a little nook at the back of the house, which made it hard to navigate . After a few wrong turns, they made their way to the kitchen at the front of the house.

The four kids they saw earlier were lined up on one side of the table while Ms. Margot was standing at the head. Everyone stared at them as they timidly entered the kitchen. The other kids shared a look of pain and sorrow on their little faces, while Ms. Margot's look was one of anger. Her arms were folded against her chest and a cigarette was, again, dangling from her mouth.

"Sit!" she shouted at them. She pointed to three chairs on the empty side of the table. They scurried over and took their spots, "You are one minute late. I don't tolerate lateness here. Who was to blame for this?" she spat.

"It's just one minute. We just got here half an hour ago—only hours after leaving our home from where we had to rush to pack because our mom had died. How could you possibly blame us?" Emberly questioned.

Ms. Margot's face tightened, and you could have heard a pin drop in the moment of silence that followed. *"What* did you just say to me?"

She walked slowly over to Emberly.

"I was just saying that we—" she was cut off by the force of Ms. Margot's hand against her bare cheek. Emberly clutched her face and blinked away the tears that threatened to fall. She heard the twins gasp quietly beside her, but she silently willed them to keep quiet. Emberly kept one hand on her stinging cheek and grabbed her arrow necklace with the other, drawing upon its comforting strength.

*"That* was a warning," Ms. Margot said before she turned and walked back to her spot at the head of the table. "Don't you ever talk back to me and don't ever be late again. Next time, it will be worse. Trust me."

Emberly wanted to say something but she couldn't form any words. Her brain was a mess. *How could she do that,* she thought. *How were they supposed to live with this lady?* Emberly looked over at Eve and Zayne who were staring back at her, their lips quivering. She wanted to rush over and give them each a hug to comfort them, but she somehow knew that it would be something Ms. Margot wouldn't stand for. So instead, she just gave a tiny nod and sat in the seat closest to Ms. Margot, hoping they'd follow her lead and leave it alone.

They ate their dinner` of bland potatoes and rock-hard bread in complete silence. It was a far cry from the livelier family dinners they used to have. Emberly knew things were going to be hard, but she never imagined it would be like this. Emberly looked over at Eve, who was sitting beside her, and grabbed her hand under the table. She gave it a little squeeze. Eve then grabbed onto Zayne's hand and gave it a squeeze as well. They didn't need to talk to communicate. For now, this would be enough.

Emberly just hoped that tonight's events wouldn't become a regular occurrence.

After dinner, Ms. Margot got up from the table and looked around the room.

"Get your chores done before I fall asleep. I don't want anything waking me up and if it does it won't be good for anyone," Ms. Margot threaten and left the room.

One of the kids left and soon returned with some rags and a metal bucket that he filled with water to wash the floor, while the others began to clear the table and wash the dishes. The Clove kids joined in wherever they could help.

"Is she always like that?" Emberly asked the older girl as she grabbed another dish to dry.

"Who—Ms. Margot?" the girl asked. Emberly nodded. "Oh yeah. She's terrible. We have to do this every night, plus we have a list of chores that we have to complete every day. You haven't seen the backyard yet, but it's practically a zoo. Her mother, who legally is meant to care for us, used to own a zoo, but when she got sick a couple years ago, she went bankrupt.

Her daughter convinced her, in her weak state, to start a foster home," she motioned to the other kids.

"So that she could get money," Emberly muttered in disgust.

"Exactly," the girl nodded. "But instead of hiring proper workers, her daughter Martha decided to use us for labour and pocketed the money without her mother knowing."

"So why didn't she just sell off all the animals?" Emberly asked the obvious question.

"You would think there is a big market for exotic animals, but that is not the case. So, they built an enclosure in their backyard to house the animals. At this point they are just waiting for the animals to die. Plus, Ms. Margot thinks it's too much work to sell them."

"How is that even possible?" Emberly asked. "Wouldn't she need a license to keep animals on her property?"

The girl just shrugged, "In case you didn't notice, Ms. Margot does what she wants and doesn't exactly respond well to being questioned."

"It sure seems that way," Emberly scoffed. "Well, now you have a few more helping hands. My name's Emberly. I'm fourteen. These are my twin siblings, Eve and Zayne. They just turned eight."

"Hey. I'm Imani. I'm twelve," she pointed to the little girl cleaning the table, "and that's my sister, Amilia. She's nine. We've been here for about two years now. And those two are Wyatt and Verity," she added as she pointed to the two that were washing the floor with Eve and Zayne, "Wyatt's also nine, and Verity is eight. They're not siblings but they've been here together for so long they might as well be brother and sister." Emberly smiled at the thought of having some friends at this place. Maybe it wouldn't be so bad after all.

When they finished their chores, Amilia and the others led them back through the halls to their room. They had to use a candle to guide their way since they weren't allowed to turn on the lights past eight.

Once in their room, the three readied for bed. Emberly tucked the twins in one bed and kissed them both on their forehead. As she turned to get into her bed, she was stopped by a tired, petite voice.

"Emberly, can you sleep with us tonight?" Eve asked. Emberly turned back around and smiled.

"Of course," and with that, she crawled into their bed and settled between Eve and Zayne. They hardly fit in the cramped bed, but they managed to squeeze together into a tight, little ball. Emberly breathed a sigh of relief knowing that no matter what, they at least still had each other.

CHAPTER FOUR

THE SUN CREPT THROUGH the tattered old curtains, and the light spilled onto Emberly's face. She slowly opened her eyes, but sighed as soon as she took in her surroundings. She hadn't dreamt it. They really were in that old house with the chipped paint, peeling wallpaper, and Ms. Margot.

"Em," Zayne whispered.

"Ya, bud?"

"When Ms. Margot slapped you, she said she could have done a lot worse. What will she do to us that would be worse?" Zayne asked.

"Nothing, Zayne. Because I won't let her lay a finger on you or do anything to the two of you," she promised.

"Thanks, Em," Zayne smiled.

They forgot to ask what time they were expected for their morning chores, so Emberly figured they better play it safe and get up and head to the kitchen as soon as possible.

When they arrived, they found it empty. *That's odd*, Emberly thought. *It's almost seven, where is everyone?* She told the twins to wait there while she went to search the house for the others. She looked through each of the rooms—including the master bedroom, of which she was pretty sure that if she were to get caught in there, she would find out what Ms. Margot deemed worse than a slap. Finding no one, Emberly returned to the still-empty kitchen.

"Let's check to see if they're in the backyard," Zayne suggested.

They walked through the back door, that was not-surprisingly held on with one hinge. Once their eyes adjusted to the morning light, they saw that Imani had not been lying when she referred to it as a zoo.

The backyard was enclosed in a ten-foot-tall white fence. In the corner of the yard closest to the house, there was a pen with pigs inside. Right next to it was a cage filled with chickens. And next to that was a gated area for cows, then one for horses, and finally, one for zebras. Across the yard was a set of cages that housed bears, lions, tigers, bobcats and cougars. They began to walk the length of the yard, looking at the animals crammed into their tiny spaces. Whether it was a cage or a pen, and no matter what animal was inside of each, the space was clearly too small for the poor animals they housed. Each barely had enough wiggle room, let alone space to roam freely.

Emberly looked at one of the bears, and it looked back at her as if it were begging to be let free. That was one thing Emberly and the animal had in common.

Once they reached the end, Emberly spotted Imani's dark, wavy hair. They ran over to her and the other kids, but stopped when they heard a voice that had already begun to make Emberly's skin crawl.

"Oh, look. If it isn't the family who can't tell time? You're two hours late," she spat. They slowly turned around to find

Ms. Margot staring down at them. She wasn't much taller than Emberly, but she sure made Emberly feel small.

"We are very sorry. We didn't know when chores were supposed to start. Please don't punish us," Emberly pleaded.

Ms. Margot's eyes went to slits and her lips pressed tightly together in a thin line, showing off the wrinkles around her lips, "Fine. I won't hurt you," she smiled. "But I am still going to punish you. All three of you will work four more hours today. Which means you will finish at nine tonight."

"Oh, please don't make us do that," Eve pleaded. Ms. Margot went to raise her hand, but Emberly quickly pushed Eve behind her back.

"What if I make a deal with you instead?" Emberly suggested.

"I don't make deals." she started to walk away, but Emberly stopped her.

"I'll do two extra hours for three days so Eve and Zayne don't have to."

Ms. Margot turned around slowly. She pondered the question for a bit, not taking her eyes off Emberly.

"Fine, but the three of you don't get breakfast since you were late."

"Deal," Emberly said as she stretched out her hand to shake on it. It wouldn't be the first time they went without a meal.

"Just get to work!" Ms. Margot yelled at them, and Emberly quickly pulled her arm back. "You, with the messy purple shirt," she pointed to Eve, "Go help Verity get the feed. And you, boy, help Amilia and Wyatt with the weeding. And you, the girl who can't keep her mouth shut, go help Imani with the water," she snapped before she turned and went back into the house.

Emberly walked over to Imani who had already laid out more than a dozen metal buckets beside the well. Imani had a beauty like no other. Her eyes shone in the heat of the sun and were so kind they made Emberly smile as she looked at her. It had been something she hadn't noticed the night before in the dark kitchen.

Emberly began handing one of the buckets to Imani who attached it to the hook and began to lower it down into the well. As she turned the crank with her arms, Emberly took in the patchwork of bruises, burns, and scars that covered Imani's gorgeous, dark brown skin on her arms; some fresher than others.

"Hey, are you okay?" Emberly asked, pointing at Imani's arms.

Imani looked to her injured arms and winced as if remembering the pain, "Yeah, I'll be fine. Last night, when everyone was asleep, I snuck downstairs to grab something out of the panty because I couldn't bear to hear Amilia's stomach growling anymore. But I must have made too much noise because Ms. Margot found me," she pointed to three large welts on the backside of her hands. "Let's just say, it didn't end well."

"So she what, whipped you because you were getting some food for your starving sister?" Emberly asked in confusion.

"Yeah. It's not uncommon though," she pointed to bruises on her forearm. "These are from the rocks that she had thrown at me because I didn't put something back in its correct spot," then she pointed to a set of scars on her left shoulder, "And this was from when she threw pieces of a plate at me after I accidentally dropped it on the floor and broke it."

"That's ridiculous! How do you just let her do that? Isn't she just a step-in for her mom that's sick?"

"Yeah, but it's just a matter of time before her mom dies and Ms. Margot gets full control," Imani pulled the bucket back up and swapped Emberly for an empty one.

Emberly fell silent. She didn't know what to say. She felt like she was in a different era or a different world altogether. Almost no one whips or beats kids anymore; and she could only imagine the story of the burns on Imani's hands. They continued their job in silence until there were no more buckets to fill. The girls placed the buckets on a rusted out red wagon and began to pull it towards the cages. At Imani's instruction, they stopped first at the cougars' cage.

"Okay, now we have to take the water into each cage for the animals to drink," Imani explained.

"We don't have to go in though, right?" Emberly nervously asked. Imani laughed.

"Of course, we do," she said simply, as if it was odd to even be a question.

Emberly's eyes grew large, "What?!"

"Well, I don't see Ms. Margot offering to do it. Do you?" Imani looked around jokingly.

"Alright, fine. But you have to show me first. I'd rather not get eaten on my first day," Emberly chuckled.

"Sounds fair, but don't worry, it's not that hard," she said as she grabbed two buckets. "You just have to know how to handle them," Imani unlocked the door and slowly slipped into the cage. Emberly's heart was racing, and she wasn't even in the cage.

Yet.

As Imani made her way through the cage, the cougars started to walk alongside her. Emberly's heart jumped into her throat, but Imani just kept walking as if she was merely taking a casual stroll through the park. Once she got to the other end of the cage, she emptied the buckets into the low trough at the far corner and turned around, coming face-to-face with all four cougars. But instead of running and screaming in terror, she did what Emberly would never dream of doing. She reached out and scratched one of the cougars behind its ear. That cougar purred as she scratched it then made its way over to the trough to have its fill of water. The remaining three also stopping by for a scratch as they walked by Imani. After all four cougars had left, there was a clear path for Imani to walk back to the front of the cage.

Once Imani slipped out of the cage, Emberly couldn't do anything but stare at her in mere shock.

"How...what..." Emberly was too confused for words. Imani couldn't help but laugh.

"Here," she handed Emberly a bucket. "It's your turn to go in the bobcat cage now," Emberly's heart dropped.

"That is a terrible way to start a sentence," Emberly replied.

"No, I promise it's fine," Imani said as they walked over to the bobcat cage. "After being in those cages for so long and being so badly mistreated and malnourished by Ms. Margot, the animals know that we're the only ones willing to take care of them, and that we'd never hurt them. They're all really just glorified house pets at this point...for us, at least."

Emberly peered into the cage. Luckily there were only two bobcats in this cage, but that was still worse than just one—or none.

"I'm here if you need me, but I promise you will be okay," Imani reassured her as she handed Emberly a bucket. "By the way, each of the animals are branded on their left side with a different number so Ms. Margot can keep track of them, so don't be alarmed when you see that."

Emberly nodded then took a deep, deep breath and clutched the handle of the bucket tight in her hand as she unlocked the cage door. She walked in and heard Imani close it behind her. *There's no turning back now*, she told herself.

While she walked through the cage, she could see the bobcats walking up slowly, curious at who the newcomer was. Emberly's heart rate doubled with every step they took towards her. Emberly turned around to look back at Imani and saw that she was no longer the only one watching her. Everyone, including Eve and Zayne, were standing outside of the cage watching her.

She couldn't chicken out now that the twins were watching. She had to be strong and persevere. Meanwhile, the bobcats kept getting closer and her heart rate became even more erratic.

She continued walking until she reached the big water dish at the end of the cage and filled it up with water as Imani had done. When she turned around everyone was still watching her, as were the bobcats.

With her eyes wide, she looked to Imani for help. Imani moved her hand in a scratching motion. She hadn't wanted it to come to this, but since it had she had no choice. Emberly knew cats could smell fear, or she at least thought they did, so she tried to swallow her fear and reached out her hand. The first bobcat to stepped forward was branded with the number seven on its side. It had a scar running across its right eye and half of its right ear had been bitten off. Emberly grew even more terrified as she took in the features of the fierce creature.

The cat was clearly a fighter, which she supposed she could relate to. She smiled at the comparison, and before she could really think further on it, the bobcat sniffed her hand then rubbed its head against her open palm. Her fears almost immediately dissolved as she grew bolder and started to pet the bobcat along its head and neck. After a few moments, her new friend made its way over to have some water, and Emberly soon found herself doing the same with the other bobcat, this one a little less rough-and-tumble looking than the first, before it to went for some water. Emberly eyes grew wide as she realized what she had done, but her feet were too fast for her brain and before she knew it, they had already carried her outside the cage.

Once the door closed behind her, Eve wrapped her arms around her. Zayne quickly followed suit.

"Guys, I'm okay. It wasn't even that scary," Emberly lied.

"Good," Eve said pulling back.

"Alright, guys, we should all get back to work. Don't want to get in trouble," Amilia warned them. The twins gave her another quick hug before they all parted to continue with their chores.

Once the girls finished giving the animals their water, they met up and sat on the rickety picnic table at the back of the yard to wait while everyone else finished their chores. Eve and Verity had put feed into metal pails and were hauling them onto the red wagon they had used for the water earlier, while Zayne, Amilia, and Wyatt were finishing weeding a large patch of dirt that Emberly assumed was to eventually be planted as a garden.

"So, what now?" Emberly asked as they each guzzled a glass of water.

"Well, right now," Imani looked up at the sun and tilted her head. "It's about half past eight, which means we get to drink something before we have to go and feed the animals. This and lunch are our only breaks. Plus, maybe some water in the afternoon if we're lucky."

"Okay, three questions. What did you do in the morning before we came outside? Do we have to do these chores every day? And lastly, how were you able to tell the time just by looking at the sun?" Emberly said, bewildered.

Imani laughed, "Well, every morning I water the grass with a watering can." She motioned to the entire fenced-in backyard.

"You do this all with a watering can?"

"Yeah. For some reason, Ms. Margot can afford to buy a nice car and another house in Portland, but she can't afford to install sprinklers in the back yard. To answer your other question yes, we have the same set of chores to do every day. Except for on Sundays. That's our day off—well, depending on Ms. Margot's mood and whether her family comes to visit. She usually doesn't like us in the house when they are here because she's scared we'll say something or whatever. As if we are stupid enough to say something. We know the repercussions of that later. Anyways, today we also have to go into the forest behind the house to get more wood for the fireplace," Imani explained.

"Oh, that sounds fun," Emberly replied sarcastically. She hadn't even started the second part of the day and she already wanted to fall to the ground and sleep.

"It is actually," Imani replied with a smile. The other kids started to show up to take their breaks, and Imani hopped up from the picnic bench. "You and I should probably get back to our chores. I'll answer your last question later in the forest."

Emberly heard the all-to familiar voice of Ms. Margot booming through the air, calling out for Amilia. They all stopped and watched as Amilia trudged towards the house, her shoulders curved forward. Amilia hadn't been the only person that was called into the house that day either, Verity had been called in earlier as well and came out looking like she was holding back tears.

"Why is she calling the kids into the house?" Emberly asked Imani as they made their way to the wagon to feed the animals.

"Ms. Margot has what she likes to call 'Monthly Correctional Days'. That's where she calls you in for no apparent reason and beats you. Some beatings aren't as bad as others, and some don't all happen on the same day. It usually happens once or twice a month, but no one knows the schedule." Imani took a deep breath and Emberly tried to picture what Ms. Margot would do to her sister or brother. Neither of the kids spoke another word as they finished their morning chores then shared a measly lunch.

At the back of the fence, there were two axes, a pair of dirty gloves, and a basket. Imani handed Emberly an axe and one of the gloves. Emberly slipped it on and looked around, but frowned when she couldn't find an exit.

"How do we get out?"

Imani winked, "Watch," she walked a little way down the length of the fence, to where some pieces of wood had been nailed onto it to form a make-shift ladder, and started to climb. Emberly followed Imani up the ladder and sat beside her at the top of the fence. She gasped as her eyes took in the view of the forest. It was breathtakingly beautiful. Filled with trees as far as the eye could see, the forest was endless. She closed her eyes and listed as the birds chirped and the leaves rustled in the soft breeze. Sitting up here, it felt as if the fence and anything inside of it didn't even exist.

"Earth to Emberly," Imani laughed. "You're practically giddy. What's up?"

"I've never seen something this beautiful before," she smiled. "It's unbelievable."

"Well get used to it because you're going to be spending a lot of time here gathering wood. And on most of our days off, if the weather is nice, there's a small lake a little way into the forest that we like to go swimming in."

"That sounds amazing," Emberly breathed.

"Come on, I'll show you. That's usually where we get the firewood anyway," Imani said, opting to jump off the top of the fence rather than taking the ladder that was built onto the other side. Emberly jumped as well, but instead of landing it perfectly as Imani had done, she took a dive and rolled on the ground, almost cutting herself with the axe.

"I'm good," Emberly declared as she took off running into the forest, Imani right on her tail.

Imani was right. The lake was amazing. They hurried to collect wood, looking for small, dry branches that would burn easily, and used their axes to cut the larger ones into more manageable pieces for carrying.

After they grabbed as much wood as they could carry, they took a break and sat on a couple of rocks at the edge of the lake. Since the lake was quite large, it left an equally large opening in the canopy of the forest, allowing for lots of light to shine down upon the lake and its surrounding edges. Emberly soaked up the sun and watched as water spilled into the lake from the connecting creek that extended deep into the forest. The water flowed effortlessly and gentle. Emberly took a deep breath and smiled. She hadn't seen anything this beautiful since she and her dad had stumbled across a lake like this one on one of their hikes. The forest had always felt like home to Emberly because it always reminded her of her dad.

"Hey dreamer," Imani joked.

"Oh, sorry. I got lost in thought again," Emberly said. "Are you ready to go?"

"Yeah, let's go."

"What were you going to use the basket for?" Emberly asked pointing at the basket that was laying on the ground.

"Oh shit, I forgot. Come on, you can help with this too."

Emberly followed Imani as she walked towards a clump of bushes near the lake and started picking the small white flowers growing in front of it.

"What are those?"

"These flowers are called 'chamomile'. They can be brewed into a tea or made into a paste and used as medicine for pain and inflammation. And since it's pretty much the only source of medicine we have at the house, I like to make sure we never run out."

On the walk home, Imani taught Emberly how to tell time based on the location of the sun. If it's closer to the east that means it's in the morning, but if it's in the west, then it's the afternoon. Then, based on where it is in proximity to the mid-point, she showed Emberly how you could figure out the hour mark.

After a few more trips to the forest to gather wood, they finally returned to the house to wash up for dinner; though Emberly knew she still had two more insufferable hours left of chores.

When dinner was finished and the dishes washed, Ms. Margot gave Emberly her orders for the night. She was to go outside and wash the side of the house. It seemed liked a meaningless task since no amount of scrubbing could ever make the house look nice, but she found the night air refreshing and the darkness peaceful. And at least for this moment, when she knew Ms. Margot would be fast asleep, she could pretend that it was just a normal night back at home.

CHAPTER FIVE

DAYS BECAME WEEKS, WHICH turned into months. It was always the same—early morning wakeups, long days of chores, and the occasional beating. The routine of everything seemed almost programmed in its repetition – almost like a dream.

No.

A nightmare.

Emberly was slowly shaken out of her sleep by a hand at her hip.

"Hey, sleepy," Imani whispered. "Time to get up."

They had made a deal that Imani would wake the Clove family up every morning for as long as it took them to get used to the new schedule. So far, they still weren't used to it. "Yeah, I know," Emberly grumbled, but Imani just chuckled.

"I better get the twins up as well," Emberly added. "They were reading until eleven last night. They're going to be tired."

As usual, the sun had yet to come out and, per the rules, they weren't able to use any electricity from eight at night to six in the morning, so they were forced to navigate their way through the house by the light of a candle. By now though, they had grown pretty accustomed to the house, even though Eve said it still reminded her of a haunted house they used to visit on Halloween each year with their mom. They barely had to rely on the candle light, their bodies remembered which steps to take and what turns to make without having to think to hard.

They walked into the kitchen to find the other kids already waiting. The others usually beat the Cloves down for breakfast, but today, there was an excited and jittery air about them that made things feel different.

"Happy two-month anniversary!" they cried. Emberly's mouth fell open in surprise, and she started to laugh.

"What are you talking about?" Zayne asked, equally surprised.

"Well, you've been here for a while, so we decided to do something fun today," Verity replied.

"Yeah. We asked Ms. Margot if it would be okay if we switched our Sunday free day to today and work on Sunday instead," Wyatt explained excitedly. "And she said yes!"

"When we first got here, the older kids that were here before never acknowledged our existence," Imani said, once again taking center stage. "But with you guys, we really feel like we've become close friends—or even a family of sorts. So, we wanted to do something special for you today and thought we could spend it at the lake. How does that sound?"

"Awesome!" Eve and Zayne exclaimed in unison.

After a quick breakfast, the kids rushed to gather bathing suits, towels, and anything else they'd need for a day at the lake, then they hurried to get out of the house as fast as possible. No one wanted to spend a single moment longer in the house than they needed to that day.

The second they arrived, Eve and Zayne both stopped in their tracks and stared at the lake in awe. Since they had not yet been given a day off, despite supposedly having Sundays off, and it was always Imani and Emberly's job to gather wood, this was the first time that either of the twins were seeing the lake. Emberly laughed. She knew they would love it.

"Can we go in?" Eve asked, her eyes wide in amazement.

"Of course, but I bet you can't beat me in!" Wyatt challenged. All seven of the kids stripped down to their bathing suits and raced each other into the water, splashing the others as they went.

The cool water was the perfect balance for the already hot temperature of the day. They splashed around for hours, floating along the surface, having swimming competitions, or even seeing how far the little ones could walk before their toes no longer touched the ground.

Eventually, when the sun came up over the treetops and reflected off the water, making it look like it was dancing, Emberly announced that it was almost noon and that they should head to shore for a break.

"Do we have anything to eat?" Verity asked.

"No, but I thought we could catch something to eat," Imani answered as she went to a bush near the lake and pulled out a pair of small fishing rods from its underbrush. "Why don't we have a contest to see who could catch the most fish?"

"Where did you get those?" Zayne asked.

"I found them one time when I was cleaning out the shed in the backyard. They were buried under a pile of junk, and I don't think Ms. Margot even knew they were there, so I snuck them out and hid them by the lake one time I went to gather wood."

"Aren't you scared she'll find out?" Eve asked, eyes wide in concern.

"It was a year ago, and she hasn't said anything yet and she *never* comes to these woods, so I stopped worrying about her finding out months ago."

"Well, fishing sounds great," Emberly said. "Let the competition begin!"

They took turns using the rods, and within an hour, they had managed to catch a total of five fish, with Verity—who caught three of the five—winning the game.

Claiming that since it was the Cloves' special day and they shouldn't have to do any work, Imani volunteered to clean and gut the fish while Wyatt and Verity gathered wood to build a fire to cook them on.

"So," Imani said, starting the conversation as they ate. "We've been so busy working that we still don't really know you guys that well. Tell us some stuff about you," she looked at Emberly.

"Well, there's not much to know. We're from East Granby, as you already know we aren't going anywhere soon," she chuckled slightly and took a bite from her piece of fish. It tasted amazing. Along with fishing rods, Imani had at some point managed to sneak out some spices and spare cooking gear and hidden them amongst her stash to use whenever they were able to cook a meal out here.

"My dad used to take me on a lot of camping and hiking adventures in the woods near our house when I was younger," Emberly continued. "But he died the day before the twins were born—when I was seven—which was a pretty tough time for our mom. She ended up spending most of her time in her room and never felt comfortable with us being away from the house on our own. From that point on, other than having to go to school, we rarely got to leave the house. So, this whole making friends thing is kind of new to us."

"It's new for me too," Verity said. "For a long time, it seemed to be just me and Wyatt that were the only ones that stayed while other kids would constantly circulate through the doors. Until Imani and Amilia came and we built a friendship with them, it felt like it was just the two of us. And now, we have you guys to count as friends as well," Verity smiled shyly as she fiddled with her fish in her hands.

Imani smiled and reached out to squeeze Verity's hand, "We've been here together for just over a year now. We're like one big family—going through everything together."

"Especially when it comes to Ms. Margot," Amilia added with a shudder.

"She is quite scary," Zayne confessed.

"She really is," Wyatt chuckled, and everyone laughed.

They spent the afternoon exploring the forest, running through the woods like freed prisoners, which in a way, Emberly supposed, they were. They laughed as they ducked under branches filled with vibrant green leaves as they raced each other. They jumped out from behind warted tree trunks and tried to tackle one another into the piles of pine needles that littered the forest floor. They ran until their legs couldn't carry them any longer and decided to rest near a group of American beech trees. Before long, they were up on their feet racing each other up the thick branches.

Thanks to her dad who had taught her to climb trees all those years ago, Emberly was the first to reach the top, quickly followed by Imani then the remaining little ones. The view from the top of the trees was nothing short of breathtaking. It provided the perfect vantage point of the forest floor and the animals that crawled along it as well as the creek that continued to flow throughout the forest, and it allowed them to see above the trees to the sky above.

Emberly looked to the birds soaring high above the tree line and sighed, "I'm envious of their freedom."

No one dared a response, for their silent agreeance spoke louder than anything they could have said.

They stayed at the top of the trees for as long as they dared; until eventually, the sun's departure below the tree line marked their time to leave. Despite knowing they had to make it back in time to cook dinner, they were slow to gather their things and head back to the house. For the first time in a long time—for all of them—they had felt safe and happy. Emberly looked to the others on their walk back. She knew that from that moment, none of them would ever be alone again. After everything they'd been through together, the seven of them had formed a bond of comradery, and it had been a long time since Emberly had met a person she could trust, let alone four of them. She would do anything to protect them, and she knew they would do the same for her.

Fully expecting to receive a tongue lashing from Ms. Margot when they got back, even though they did technically make it back in time, they were surprised to find the kitchen empty. They looked around the house, confused, until Zayne finally found Ms. Margot in the living room. She was sitting on the couch, her eyes fixated on a spot on the wall across from her. Everyone cautiously stepped forwards, but no one dared speak.

"Um, Ms. Margot?" Emberly finally whispered after minutes of uneasy silence.

Ms. Margot slowly turned her head, a horrible grin on her face, like an animal who just found some easy prey to pounce on or a clown in a horror movie. Emberly took her quiet as a signal to keep talking, "We just got back from the forest. Do you want us to get started on making dinner?"

"Oh, you want to have dinner, do you," she asked in a weirdly sarcastic tone. "Well guess what, you're not getting any. And you want to know why? Because my mom just died, so I don't feel like eating, which means that none of you will either." Everyone's eyes went wide. Ms. Margot's mother, the owner, had died? What did that mean for them? So far, her existence was the only thing somewhat keeping Ms. Margot in line. If she was gone, how much worse were things going to get for them?

No one dared move or make a noise as Ms. Margot slowly rose from her spot on the couch and walked over to them. Then as fast as lightning, she rose her hand and slapped Eve across the face. Eve fell to the ground and started crying.

"What did you do that for?" Emberly yelled at Ms. Margot, as all heads turned her way. "Don't you ever hit my sister again," she yelled, threateningly.

Ms. Margot slowly walked over to Emberly and looked her right in the eye. Emberly could feel a chill of anticipation run down her spine but she stood tall knowing everyone's eyes would be on her. Ms. Margot's gaze grew colder and a sly smile appeared across her face.

"I was hoping you'd say something," Ms. Margot said as she drove her fist into Emberly's gut. Emberly doubled over in pain and fell to the floor. It was all she could do to weakly try to cover her body as Ms. Margot rained punches and kicks upon her entire body. Out of the corner of her eye, she saw Zayne make a step towards her before Imani, who was trembling with restraint of her own, reached out and pulled him close to her. Emberly was grateful for it. She didn't want anyone to jump in and try to help her. She knew that's what Ms. Margot wanted— for others to join in so she could unleash her anger on them too. Emberly could handle it. For the others, she *would* handle it. She only hoped she could hold out as long as possible, until Ms. Margot would eventually grow tired and leave.

After a few more kicks to her stomach and a final one to her head, Emberly could barely make out Ms. Margo's instructions to "get her out of my sight and clean up the blood."

Emberly tried to get up, but her body refused to obey her commands. All she could do was lay there as six sets of hands gently picked her up and began to move her. To where, she didn't know. Didn't care. All she did know was that everything hurt.

Then her mind went blank and everything dark, bringing with it the sweet reprieve of pain.

Emberly's eyes twitched open and she could barely make out the silhouettes of six people standing over her. Her ears were still ringing, so she could hardly make out any of their words, but she got the gist of what they were saying—they wanted to know if she was okay. She tried to sit herself up but someone— Imani? — placed a hand on her shoulder and gently lowered her back onto the bed, "It's too soon for you to sit up, take your time," the person, who was indeed Imani said as she resumed dabbing Emberly's forehead with the damp cloth.

"Emberly, how are you feeling?" Imani softly asked. Now that she was more awake, the ringing in her ears had mostly stopped, but Imani was still kind enough to keep her voice down.

"What happened? Where am I?" Emberly asked, trying to recall the events that led her to this moment.

"Let's just say that you're in an extra room—far away from Ms. Margot's room—so you don't have to worry about her popping in anytime soon," Imani chuckled. "I looked you over before, and I don't think anything's broken, but you took a pretty good kick to the head. Are you feeling okay?"

"I think so. Is Eve okay? I need to see her." Emberly's memories were beginning to come back, so she no longer cared that her entire body was in pain. She just wanted to see Eve and know that she was okay. She tried to sit up, but Imani once again just lowered her back onto the pillow.

"Ya, Em, I'm okay," Eve responded, calming Emberly's fears. "But Imani says you need to stay here. You won't heal overnight, and it won't do you any good if you stand up right now so just try to relax."

"How bad is it?" Emberly asked, knowing it couldn't be good since her body felt like it had been dragged behind a truck over a pile of rocks and head felt as though it were being set on fire by miniature people throwing flaming spears.

"You can look for yourself if you want," Imani replied as she handed Emberly a small mirror.

Emberly gasped as she took in her reflection. Her face was already covered in bruises, and had a nasty gash that ran from her right cheekbone to just above her jawline. She quickly put the mirror down before she threw up. She already felt nauseous enough, and she didn't need the mirror to know that her body was likely covered with bruises and cuts of its own.

"It's a pretty deep cut, so I'm going to need to stitch it up. Unfortunately, all I have are a regular sewing needle and some thread." Emberly's eyebrows shot up, the movement causing her to wince in pain.

"Don't worry," Imani chuckled. "It's not my first time. My mom was a doctor, and Amilia was always hurting herself, so Mom taught me how to use a needle and thread to sew up larger cuts when she wasn't there to do it herself." Imani turned and nodded at Amilia who took the kids out of the room, each giving Emberly a shaky, but reassuring, smile as they left.

Emberly tried to calm her nerves. She knew it'd have to be done so the cut wouldn't get infected, but she wished there was another way, "Is it going to hurt?" Emberly asked.

"Do you want the truth?"

"Yes?" Emberly wasn't sure if that was a question or an answer.

"Well, it won't feel great," Imani smiled, "but I'll make it as painless as possible. These will also help," she reached over and grabbed a small brown bottle and a larger clear one from the nightstand beside the bed. "I stole them from Ms. Margot's stash. This brown bottle is hydrogen peroxide. It will help clean out the cut. And this..." she added as she poured some of the clear liquid into a glass and handed it to Emberly, "is for you."

"What's this for?" Emberly asked as she sniffed the glass.

"It's vodka," Imani replied matter-of-factly. "It will help numb the pain."

"Wow, sneaky *and* smart," Emberly said. Then she downed the vodka, but quickly scrunched up her nose and coughed. It tasted horrible.

"I know it's gross, but it will make all of this hurt a lot less," Imani reassured her.

After a few minutes, and a couple more shots of vodka, when Emberly could feel the warmth of the liquor settle in her stomach, she took a deep breath and relaxed her shoulders. "Okay, I'm ready."

"Here, bite on this," Imani handed Emberly a small piece of wood. At Emberly's confused expression, she added. "It will muffle the noise. The kids are likely still standing outside the door, and I don't want to scare them in case you do scream."

Emberly put the chunk of wood in her mouth and laid back on her pillow with her eyes closed.

"Amilia," Imani turned to her sister who had come back into the room, "Come and wash Em's cut with the peroxide while I get the needle and thread ready."

Luckily, the peroxide didn't burn as she had expected. Still, Emberly took a few calming breaths and tried to gather her courage as Imani's cold hands gently touched her on her face, signaling what was about to come next.

"You've got this, Em," Imani whispered as she readied the needle for its first stitch. Her steady confidence lending some to Emberly's nerves. Imani nodded to Amilia who placed her hands on each of Emberly's shoulders, firmly holding her in place. Then, Imani inserted the needle.

Even after drinking the vodka, the pain of the needle was near unbearable. Emberly tried her best to not scream out. She bit down hard against the piece of wood in her mouth and was grateful for Amilia's firm grip that held her in place and prevented her from thrashing about, but the pain was unlike anything she'd ever experienced before. She didn't know if the beating or this fixing of it was worse. Eventually, Emberly passed out from the pain.

Emberly woke to a familiar pair of hands gently rubbing something onto her wound, and winced. "It's some chamomile that I ground up," Imani said by way of explaining. "It will help keep the swelling down and will speed up healing."

Emberly took the mirror that Imani held out to her and inspected the wound. She counted a total of ten stitches. "It will unfortunately leave a bit of a scar, but I tied each tight enough to help reduce the amount of scarring."

"Thank you," Emberly whispered. "For protecting the others from Ms. Margot earlier, and for taking care of me. I owe you one."

"It's nothing," Imani smiled. "That's what friends do. For now, all I need from you is to rest. You can sleep in here tonight. I'll leave some candles and a match by the bed in case you wake up. And don't worry about tomorrow either. I'll talk to Ms. Margot and ask for another day off for you and one of the others. Someone needs to take care of you since you probably have a concussion and you shouldn't be alone."

"Okay, so long as that won't get you into trouble."

"It won't, I promise." Then with a wink, she added, "I'll just explain to Ms. Margot that one more day of rest means that you will be able to do that much work that much earlier."

Emberly chuckled.

"And don't worry about the twins, I'll check on them on my way back to my room to make sure they're okay. Now go to sleep. I'll stop by in the morning to see how you're doing." With a final wave, Imani left the room.

Emberly settled into her pillow and closed her eyes; and exhaustion from the days' events soon stole her away into a deep slumber.

CHAPTER SIX

EVERYTHING HURT. ON TOP of the constant throbbing of her head, and the now pulsing pain that emanated from her cut, Emberly's entire body ached. This morning, it had taken every bit of strength left in her just to sit up and grab the glass of water from the nightstand that Imani had left her the night before.

As she took in the unfamiliar room, Emberly's mind raced at the memories of what had happened the day before. How things could go so wrong, so quickly. She laughed at the irony of the situation—it had gone from one of best days she had had in a long time, to one of the very worst.

A knock sounded at the door, and a familiar head popped in, interrupting Emberly from her spiraling thoughts. "Good morning, how are you feeling?" Imani asked.

"Like I went toe-to-toe with a lion."

"I figured as much. I find the day after one of Ms. Margot's beatings to always be the worst. With the state you were in, you might be feeling pretty tender for a while. Here, I brought you a change of clothes."

Emberly swung her legs off the side of the bed and readied herself to stand. But before she could, Imani rushed over to her side. "Let me help. I don't want to risk you falling and reopening that wound on your face."

The first steps were the hardest. Her legs felt like jelly and the movements, small as they were, highlighted the stiffness still lingering in her body. "I don't think I'll be climbing that fence anytime soon," Emberly wheezed out as she took a few more small steps, thankful for Imani's strong grip.

Imani laughed, "No, and you probably won't be hauling big buckets of food and water either. Don't worry, we'll shift around the chores for when you have to go back to work. For now, why don't I help you get changed so you can get back to relaxing."

Imani slowly guided Emberly back to the bed and handed Emberly a set of her pyjamas with a grin. "I figured you'd probably be comfier wearing these than your jeans in bed," she explained. She then began to help Emberly change her clothes since she was still a little too weak to do it on her own.

As Emberly pulled her pyjama shirt down over her torso, she caught a glimpse of several large bruises on the side of her body where Ms. Margot had kicked her several times. She quickly pulled the shirt the rest of the way down so she wouldn't have to look at them for another second. The pain was reminder enough for her.

Feeling better after a simple change of clothes, Emberly decided she should tackle her hair. She didn't need a mirror to tell her that her hair was a mess. She looked around the room and spotted a hairbrush on the nightstand. *Imani must have brought that too*, she thought. She grabbed it and started to brush through the crusted blood that had matted her hair. Unfortunately for her, the pain and stiffness prevented her from being able to move her arms around enough to properly get out all the knots. Eventually, she threw the brush on the bed in frustration. But Imani, who always knew when to lend a helping hand, simply picked up the brush, positioned herself behind Emberly, and gently brushed her hair. Once she managed to coax all of the knots out, she proceeded to make two Dutch braids in Emberly's thick, dark hair, being careful to keep them loose so they wouldn't pull.

"Now, I know it's your day to rest, but what if instead of staying in this room, I take you to another where you can sit and visit with me while I finish some chores?"

"A day with you sounds lovely," Emberly grinned.

Imani wrapped one arm around Emberly's waist and used the other to hold onto her hand to provide support as they exited the room, and began to make their way down the unfamiliar hallway.

The Cloves had been there for two months now and they were always too busy with their chores to have time to explore. The more they walked, the less things seemed familiar to her. "Where are we?"

"Last night, after everything happened, we brought you down to the basement," Imani explained. "We thought it would be better to have you down here so you were out of Ms. Margot's warpath."

"And where are we going?"

"Well, I sort of got us out of working today," Imani replied guiltily, "We have to make seven black shirts to wear at Mrs. Margot's funeral. We only have three days. I hope you don't mind."

"As long as I can sit—and hopefully eat," Emberly added after her stomach grumbled embarrassingly loud. "I'm fine doing whatever."

"Don't worry," Imani laughed, "I made sure to grab snacks!"

They entered a room at the end of the hall, and Imani led Emberly over to a chair by a table in the back corner that was covered in pieces of fabric in a variety of different shades and material. Another table, closer to the front of the room, held a sewing machine, a lamp, and blessedly—a tray of food.

Imani grabbed the plate of food, along with a second chair, and brought both over to where Emberly was sitting. The girls sat in silence for a few moments as they polished off the plate.

"So," Emberly said as she scrunched up her nose, "I know that *you* can handle a needle and thread," she laughed, referring to Imani's stitchwork on Emberly's face. "But I'm clueless when it comes to making clothes."

Imani tipped her head back and laughed, "It's alright. I've already cut out all the patterns and completed two on my own before I came to get you. Your only job is to hand me things."

"Why didn't you wake me up earlier? I could have been helping you."

Imani just shook her head, "I don't know if you remember this or not, but you did technically get the side of your head cracked open yesterday. Besides," Imani added, "Ms. Margot didn't want to 'waste a lot of fabric' and made it explicitly clear that these were to be basic black long-sleeved shirts with 'nothing fancy about them'. Meaning, they're relatively easy for me to sew."

"Oh, fine, but I owe you another one for this."

The girls finished making the shirts around lunch, Imani doing most of the sewing as promised. "We'll leave the shirts here for now," Imani said. "I'll get Verity to grab them tomorrow when she has to do laundry. Think you can make it all the way up the stairs and outside so we can meet up with the other kids?"

Emberly just nodded, for she could think of nothing better than being outside in the fresh air.

As with before, Imani held onto Emberly as they slowly made their way, allowing Emberly to lean on her for support whenever she needed a break. The walk was slow moving, but with each step, Emberly swore she shook off a little bit of the stiffness still clinging to her bones. Despite the pain, it felt good to move.

They walked through the kitchen then out the back door into the hot, August sun. Emberly blinked a few times as her eyes adjusted to the light. From a distance, she could hear excitement. Emberly squinted to where the noise originated from and could see the twins running towards her at full tilt.

They rushed to her and wrapped her in a tight squeeze. Emberly laughed, even though it pained her.

"Hey. Did you miss me?" she jokingly asked.

The twins both nodded. "We were so worried for you, Em!"

"Well, I'm here now, and I'm just fine. Nothing more than a couple of scratches," Emberly joked.

Imani laughed, "Come on, guys, why don't we take your sister to the table so she can sit down and eat some lunch. We can visit there." They helped Emberly to the picnic table where a plate of sandwiches had been laid out; the twins never strayed further than a few steps from her as they walked. When they grew close, the rest of the kids ran over to her and each gave her a massive hug and expressed how happy they were to see her walking about.

Not caring that everyone else took their time eating their sandwiches, Emberly dove into her sandwich and devoured it in no time. Her body was healing, so there was no time to savour the food. While Emberly waited for everyone to finish their lunch, she turned around and looked at the tops of the trees that were peeking out above the fence. The fence was too high for her to see anything else, but she didn't need to see it to visualize it all—she closed her eyes and remembered the gentle flowing creek that fed into the cool waters of the lake, the small squirrels, rabbits, and other animals that called the forest home. She pictured the tree branches dancing as they got caught in the breeze.

She felt a hand on her shoulder, and she slowly opened her eyes and turned around. The kids were all looking at her with smiles on their faces.

"Sorry, what did I miss?" Emberly asked.

"Nothing," Imani chuckled. "We were just saying that you looked very 'spiritual' just now."

"Ya, very, 'one with nature'," Wyatt joked, causing them all to laugh.

"Real funny, guys," Emberly rolled her eyes and tried to keep the grin off her face, but it was no use and soon they all erupted into laughter.

"Hey!" Ms. Margot yelled out from the distance. The kids immediately stopped laughing and turned towards the voice. "What are you guys doing?" Ms. Margot spat as she grew close. Before she could reach them, the kids got up at once and hurried into a single file line as was expected of them.

"We were—" Verity started, but Ms. Margot interrupted her with a backhand. Verity held a palm against her cheek and kept silent, but Emberly could tell that she was on the verge of tears. Emberly's body began to shake with suppressed rage at how Ms. Margot always treated them.

"Why were you guys laughing? Do we *laugh* when we're working?"

"No, ma'am," the children replied together.

"Do we ever laugh?"

"No ma'am," It was like they were programmed robots or military soldiers. When they talked to Ms. Margot it felt as though what they were saying was scripted.

"And why is that?"

"Because if we laugh, that means we are having fun," they replied. Saying that made Emberly feel dead inside.

Ms. Margot continued to scowl at them, "And why don't I want you to have fun?"

"Because that means we aren't doing our jobs," they finished.

"That's what I thought." She looked over and locked eyes with Emberly. "I see that one of your little friends helped you with this cut of yours," she moved close enough that Emberly could smell the mixture of cigarette smoke and alcohol on her breath and pressed her finger against Emberly's cut. Emberly jerked in pain, but Ms. Margot didn't seem to care. "Just remember, I could do a lot worse," she whispered into Emberly's ear. Emberly stood straight and kept her eyes forward.

"Your *friends*," she spewed, "can't help you forever. Eventually, you will be alone, and then who will protect you?"

Emberly knew it was meant to be a rhetorical question, and she knew that she shouldn't answer it, but she leaned in anyway. "I will never be alone," she whispered back into Ms. Margot's ear. "Even if you and I were the last people in this house, I would still never be alone because, unlike you, I have people who love me and will always love me," she said slowly, sounding out every syllable of the last sentence. Emberly stood up straight with a slight smile on her face, fully expecting the full strength of one of Ms. Margot's famous backhands.

But instead of getting hit or screamed at, something even more terrifying happened. Ms. Margo's half-smile morphed into one of pure evil that sent chills down Emberly's spine.

"You better bank on that," was all she said as she turned and walked back to the house.

CHAPTER SEVEN

THREE DAYS LATER, AS she woke on the morning of Ms. Margot's mother's funeral, Emberly still couldn't shake the sense of dread that had been gnawing at her. The last few days had found the children back in their regular routine - chores, eating, and sleeping. Although Ms. Margot yelled and doled out the occasional backhand or punishment when she felt like it, she never once said anything to Emberly about their exchange. Almost as if she was willing to pretend it never happened. But as nice as that would be, Emberly knew that she hadn't forgotten—that it was only a matter of time until Ms. Margot got her revenge. The question was, what form would it take?

For once in her life, Emberly wished her name meant something other than spark or flame. *Why did I have to say something,* she whispered to herself. *Why do I always have to say something? Why can't I just let some things go?*

But she turned to face the twins who were still fast asleep and she knew why. For them—and the other kids—she would always speak up. No matter what happened to her because of it. Emberly touched the arrow pendant on her necklace for comfort.

Even though it was the day of the funeral, the kids still had to wake up early and work. Not only did they have their regular list of chores to complete, but Ms. Margot had given them an additional list of things to get done before the funeral that afternoon. They only had half day to complete everything in. There would be no time for breaks and no acceptance of "goofing around" as Ms. Margot put it.

It didn't bother Emberly though. She welcomed the work, even if she was still sore. As long as she kept busy, her mind would be kept off the funeral. She dreaded the moment that they would have to lower Ms. Margot's mother into the ground. Emberly knew that all she was going to think about, as they lowered the casket into the freshly dug grave, was her own mother.

The kids rushed about and finished their chores in record time, then hurried to prepare the food and to make sure that the house was completely spotless, inside and out.

They were left with barely enough time to wash up and change before the guests started to arrive. They all retreated to their rooms to change into their funeral clothes.

Emberly was brushing Eve's hair when their bedroom door burst open and in flew Imani, Amilia, Verity, and Wyatt. Not far behind them was Ms. Margot. "Sit," she pointed to Emberly's bed. They obeyed without any hesitation.

"After the funeral, there will be people coming over, so you better be on your *best* behaviour. You will all put little smiles on your miserable faces and act like we're all one big happy family. Got it?"

They all nodded.

"And if any of you make a scene, open your mouths, or make any noise at all..." she said the last part with a pointed look at Emberly, before continuing, "Then you will all find yourselves in a six-foot hole of your own. I will not tolerate any misbehaviour."

No one thought she would.

"Now get the hell out of here!"

They all scrambled to leave the room as fast as possible, but before Emberly could escape, a firm grip on her arm halted her. "Okay, listen up. If you say *anything* about what I did to you," she pointed to Emberly's stitched-up head, "that will be the end of you, and your siblings. Do I make myself clear?" Ms. Margot asked, nostrils flaring.

Emberly stood up straight, still falling shorter than the six-foot height of Ms. Margot. But she mustered up enough strength to give Ms. Margot a gutsy smile and responded, "Yes, ma'am."

"Good, now get out of my sight," she said as she let go of the vice-like grip she had on Emberly's arm.

Not needing to be told twice, Emberly bolted out of the room and headed to the front of the house where the children were already gathered, waiting for Ms. Margot to drive them to the church.

No one talked on the long drive to the funeral. Even though Ms. Margot was in the front seat driving and the seven of them were crammed into the back seats of the van, their close proximity in the enclosed space somehow felt more threatening.

Thankfully, the car pulled up to an old church that looked like it had been built in the early 1800s. The kids jumped out of the car, and Emberly took a closer look at the church. It was tall and had one of those large brass bells at the very top. The siding was made of old, crumbling brick, and the shingles were practically peeling off.

Her gaze slid down to the entrance where she was surprised to find a large group of people waiting to go inside. The crowd was certainly bigger than any of the funerals she had been to, and Emberly had been to her fair share. First, her dad's, then both her Granny and Papa's almost exactly two years later. Then again with her mom's parents three years after that. Of course, her mom had now passed away too, but they didn't even get to have a funeral for her. But for the others, each had very few people in attendance. Making the attendance at this funeral look like it was for someone of the royal family in comparison. Emberly hadn't met Ms. Margot's mother so didn't know much about the woman, but she knew enough about her daughter that she just assumed that there wouldn't be many people showing up.

Ms. Margot's mother must have been a well-liked woman for all these people to show up at her funereal. *Too bad her daughter had to be so terrible,* Emberly grumbled to herself.

The kids followed Ms. Margot into the church to where even more people were gathered, many of whom were crying. Of course, the one person that *should* have been crying was not. Instead, Ms. Margot circulated around, smiling and chatting with people as if it was a gala she was attending instead of her own mother's funeral. Emberly would never understand her.

Not knowing what to do, the seven of them stood awkwardly at the back of the church near the doors until Ms. Margot saw them and walked over, a loving—though they knew it to be fake—smile plastered on her face.

"What are you guys doing?" Ms. Margot whispered angrily through her teeth.

"We don't know where to go," Emberly protested.

*"We don't know where to go,"* Ms. Margot mimicked her. "Just sit in the back, and *don't* say a word," she spat. Emberly rolled her eyes and turned. She knew she'd likely pay for that later, but for now, Emberly couldn't help but enjoy the look of unbridled rage that Ms. Margot was so carefully trying to keep from her face.

They took their places far away from everyone else—just how Emberly preferred it to be—and tried to focus on the small reprieve it gave them from Ms. Margot. When the service finished, everyone piled into their cars and drove in a single file towards the cemetery. Much to Emberly's relief, rather than having to get out and stand by the grave as Ms. Margot's mother was lowered into it, they were told to stay in the car.

So, they sat in the vehicle and watched the large group of people gathered around the gravesite. When an idea came to her, Emberly turned to the others.

"Hey, you know how there is going to be a lot of people at the house tonight?" she said with the biggest smile on her face. It made her stitches throb, but she couldn't help it. Everyone exchanged confused glances.

"Yes?" Imani replied, unsure how to answer.

"Since they're all related to Ms. Margot, I'm guessing they're probably going to stay for a long time and drink. So, why don't we sneak down to the basement after we're done serving and have a sleepover?"

Everyone's face lit up with excitement, and they all agreed. Suddenly, the dreariness of serving everyone for the next few hours didn't seem all that bad.

The only bonus of having a funeral was the free food. The downside, for this particular funeral at least, was that they weren't allowed to touch any of the food until after seven when they were finished serving.

Emberly didn't know the last time she had ever seen so much food. She looked at the trays ladened with food, and her mouth salivated at the prospect of having something to eat that wasn't a mixture of potatoes, stale bread, or eggs. It was all she could do to keep circling the room and passing out snacks and drinks to the guests, instead of running off to a corner and scarfing down an entire tray of food on her own.

Emberly searched the room for the rest of the kids. She found Imani and Verity talking to the tall, raspy-voiced woman that Emberly had met earlier in the evening. Amilia and Eve were flitting about the room, passing out trays of drinks to the guests. The poor girls had the busiest job of the evening. Hardly anyone was grabbing food, yet they all couldn't seem to get enough liquor. Emberly made a mental note for her and Imani to trade jobs with them the next time they passed by. She then found Wyatt and Zayne standing across the room from her. Both looked extremely awkward as the woman who had them cornered, and their trays of snacks, wouldn't stop blubbering Even from where she was standing, Emberly could tell that the woman's words were an incoherent mess through all the tears and booze.

Emberly sighed. *Only two more hours,* she muttered. Two more hours of plastering a smile on her face, serving food and drinks to a bunch of people, many of whom barely acknowledged her or any of the other kids. Only two more hours of making up lies to answer the "what happened to your face" question that everyone seemed so curious about. Then they could grab some food and disappear into the basement for their sleepover.

Finally, when their shift as Ms. Margot's personal servers was over, the kids ran to the kitchen. They stacked their plates full of delicate finger sandwiches and hot hors d'oeuvres. They filled any remaining space with loads of macaroni and other cold salads until their plates threatened to topple under the weight. They didn't care as people watched in disgust at how much they were taking. They were hungry, and they didn't know when their next opportunity to eat would be.

With plates full, they rushed through the kitchen and into the connecting hallway towards the entrance to the basement. They hurried down the stairs, being careful to not to trip, and made their way to the large basement bedroom. Earlier, when they had first got back to the house after the funeral—when Ms. Margot had gone up to her room to "take her medicine", which really meant, to dose up on the various bottles of prescription pills she kept by her bed—the kids ran around and grabbed the supplies they'd need for the night. They then snuck down to the basement and hid the candles, matches, spare blankets, and books they had gathered into the room with the two queen beds for safe keeping.

They set their food down on the small table they had dragged over from the sewing room and started to light the candles. Thankfully, they couldn't hear anything that was going on upstairs, which meant that no one from upstairs was likely to hear them either.

Once all the candles were lit, the kids dove into their food. Most things were familiar to Emberly. Some she had eaten before, albeit years ago. Those brought back memories of family dinners spent at her grandparents' houses. Other foods were new to her. Things like bacon wrapped scallops or coconut shrimp, as Imani had informed her of the names, seemed like they'd be gross at first, but turned out to be delicious. And others, that were still hot from the serving trays, had burnt the roof of Emberly's mouth as she ate. She didn't care though, she wanted to get as much food into her mouth as possible before her stomach tried to tell her it was full. She didn't want to waste a single morsel of food.

"Okay. So, who else thinks they will never be able to go back to stale bread and potatoes after this?" Imani said, her mouth filled with a bread roll she had crammed in. The others couldn't help but laugh and mumbled their agreements through equally full mouths.

They spent the next hour laying in various spots on the beds or the floor and talked as they allowed their food to digest.

"So, we have this whole basement to do whatever we want," Eve said as she rolled into a sitting position on the floor. "Is anyone thinking what I'm thinking?" the corner of her lip twisted up into a smile.

"Hide-n-seek!" Verity shouted, knowing exactly what Eve meant. Because Emberly was the oldest, she counted first. The rest of the kids scuttled from the room in search of hiding places. They played for hours; taking turns counting and hiding. The time spent together had been a blast, but eventually, everyone grew tired. Aside from the time they were at the funeral, they had been doing chores from just after five in the morning to seven that evening, with barely a break. So, it wasn't a surprise to anyone when they found Eve fast asleep in her hiding spot —tucked behind the door of one of the rooms. Emberly gently picked her up and carried her to one of the beds. Not long after, everyone else slowly started to trickle in. They exhaustedly climbed into the beds, their eyelids with barely enough strength to hold themselves up.

"Did everyone have a good night?" Emberly yawned.

"Yes. The last time we got to run around the house was probably..." Wyatt tried to think. "Is it bad that I can't think of a time where we ran around?"

"Yes, it is." Imani answered. "It's terrible here. Ms. Margot is abusive, rude, and smokes way too much," she added. Everyone chuckled but knew she wasn't joking. Emberly looked around and saw that everyone's eyelids were growing heavier by the second.

"We better get to bed. We have to wake up extra early tomorrow so we can sneak back upstairs before Ms. Margot finds out what we did," Emberly reminded them. The kids groaned.

"On one condition," Zayne piped in. "You sing us a lullaby so we can go to sleep."

Everyone nodded in agreement, so Imani gave each of the kids a kiss on their forehead as she tucked them into bed, while Emberly stepped back and started to sing the first song that popped into her head. A song her father would sing to her before bed every night.

Don't fear. Stay near.

You'll be alright.

Sleep tight my baby, until night.

Close your eyes. Listen closely.

You'll always be safe, so long as

You're with me.

Emberly repeated the verse until eventually each of the kids had fallen fast asleep. Then she too crawled into one of the beds with Imani, smiled at her beautiful friend who slept beside her, and fell into a dream-filled sleep of her own.

CHAPTER EIGHT

DAYS AFTER THE FUNERAL, the unnerving smirk was still plastered on Ms. Margot's face. Emberly had never seen such a vile expression. Whenever Ms. Margot passed by Emberly and one of the kids she would chuckle and grin in a way that would make even the Grinch look sincere. Even for her, the behaviour was out of the ordinary.

A week later, Emberly woke up with a pounding headache, but not from the beating that left a scar on her face. No, that had healed well enough that Imani had been able to pull the stitches out the week prior. Instead, this headache was courteous of her first official "Correctional Day" with Ms. Margot the day before. She had been thrown to the ground and beaten until Ms. Margot had grown tired and told to get up and go back to work. She ran her hand over the fresh set of bruises on her legs and arms. Luckily, the beating was still nowhere as bad as the one from weeks ago, and even luckier, the twins hadn't had to endure one of the Correctional Day beatings. Yet.

She sighed and ran a hand through her hair. After two and a half months, she was finally used to waking herself up at the ungodly hour they were forced to. The twins on the other hand were a different story. Like every night, they'd stay up late reading and Emberly would wake to find them sprawled across their bed. Emberly stood over their bed and smiled. They were only eight years old but were already reading books that kids her own age could never finish. Words could not express how proud she was. She slowly removed the books from their bed and woke them up. All three got dressed then walked to the kitchen to begin their day.

Since it was closer to the end of August, with the sun sleeping in later each day now, they had to start their chores while the moon was still awake. It didn't matter much though; after months of doing the same mindless chores, the routine was so engrained into the Clove children that they no longer needed light to know what needed to be done.

The children worked hard until lunch where they were surprised with a spread of bread and vegetables that covered the table. Emberly's mouth watered. The vegetables were from the garden that Wyatt, Zayne, and Verity worked on each day. They were delicious, but of course, Ms. Margot took full credit for the state of the vegetables. It didn't bother them though; they were just happy —though shocked—that she was willing to share any with them.

"I have a question," Eve blurted over the silence. "Do we get go to school in September?" Emberly had wondered the same thing. As far as she knew, Ms. Margot never hired anyone else to do anything around the house and she certainly didn't seem the type to step in and help. So, who would tend to the animals and take care of the house if not them?

"Well, we're technically homeschooled," Amilia explained, "but we still have to complete the same chores as we do in the summer. So, it's double the work."

"Wh—who teaches us?" Emberly asked. She dreaded the thought of it being Ms. Margot.

Sensing where Emberly's thoughts strayed, Imani was quick to ease her concerns, "We teach ourselves. Someone comes by and drops off a set of textbooks for us each year."

"Actually, they should be coming any day now," Wyatt said. "They usually come around the twentieth of August each year."

"Well, that should be fun," Emberly replied sarcastically.

"Yeah, you could say that," Imani shook her head. "It's a pain to have to fit in the extra work, but we have no other choice. Plus, Ms. Margot usually allows us to sit together when we go through our school work, so it's actually kind of fun."

"Better than having to do it on our own at least," Amilia added. The kids nodded.

They ate the rest of their lunch in silence and cleaned up. Once everyone else left for their jobs, Emberly and Imani grabbed their axes and the basket and began to make their way to the back fence.

They climbed the fence and walked to the lake to gather wood. It took an hour or so to get to the lake, but the forest was so beautiful that Emberly enjoyed the time. Forests were her happy place, somewhere she would never stop loving. The setting had always calmed her, no matter the situation. When they got to the lake, they sat on a rock and spent a few minutes watching the water in the lake as it spun and twirled along the shore.

Around two, the wind had picked up and brought with it the darkness of thick clouds that blocked out the sun. Emberly looked up from where she was stacking wood and could instantly tell that they were in for a massive storm. They would need to get back to the house immediately—this wasn't going to be a small thunderstorm. Storms like this in Connecticut, in August, usually turned into tornadoes. And if Emberly's guess was correct, this storm had potential to do some damage.

She called out to Imani, who at first didn't respond. She called again and saw Imani's head reluctantly pop out from a clump of bushes across the lake. When their eyes met Emberly motioned towards the sky. As soon as she saw the dark clouds, Imani knew what she was thinking—they had to leave. Now.

Emberly looked around for something to hold the wood together so it'd be easier to carry as they ran. Despite the storm, Emberly knew Ms. Margot would be irate if they left any wood behind. Emberly quickly grabbed some vines and wrapped them around the wood. She then flung the bundle over her shoulder like a sack of potatoes, and picked up their axes and proceeded to run towards Imani who was still picking Chamomile. Emberly grabbed hold of Imani's elbow and hoisted her up from the ground, "Time's up," Emberly said as she yanked Imani along with her. "What you've picked will have to be enough."

The bundle of wood slammed against her back as she ran, but Emberly didn't care. They were not getting trapped in that storm. Bushels and thorns caught on their bare skin and hair but the girls kept running.

By the time they neared the forest's edge, they were both out of breath and drenched in sweat. Yet still they ran, until a yelp of pain shattered the silence. She whipped around and saw Imani lying on the ground, holding onto her left arm. She ran back and with one hand, picked up the basket Imani had been carrying then helped Imani up with the other hand. Imani's arm hung loose from its socket and she looked like she was in an extreme amount of pain, but the storm was getting worse. "All we have to do is get to the house, Imani, then we can fix your arm. Okay?"

With her mouth twisted in pain, Imani just nodded.

Emberly half dragged Imani the remainder of the way to the fence. Light rain had already begun to fall on them, but it was only a matter of minutes before she knew the sky would open and heavy rain would begin. When they finally reached the fence, she was lucky enough to find Amilia, Eve, and Wyatt still outside. They must have been covering things up around the backyard to protect them from the storm.

"Guys, help!" Emberly cried out over the pounding rain, "help!"

Eve, who was standing closest to the fence, rushed over, "Imani fell, and I think she dislocated her arm. Get Amilia, Verity, and Wyatt to help me get her over the fence," Emberly commanded frantically.

Eve nodded and bolted back to the others who had already started walking back. While they waited, Emberly helped Imani slowly make her way up the ladder. She climbed the latter behind her in case she fell and held onto Imani to provide support since she only had the use of one arm.

On the other side, Emberly could hear the others stacking crates and boxes to make bigger steps that would be easier for Imani to climb down on. When they got to the top of the fence, Imani stopped to take a deep breath before she mustered enough strength and swung her legs over the side of the fence. "Easy now," Wyatt said as he and Zayne helped Imani maneuver her way down the makeshift stairs they'd created.

Imani successfully made it down the crates, followed by Emberly. She then grabbed hold of Imani's non-injured arm and gently wrapped it around her neck. Amilia grabbed Imani's torso on the other side and they all ran towards the house.

"What should we do?" Eve asked.

"We'll go directly to the basement," Amilia called back. "It will be the safest place to wait this thing out."

"Where's Ms. Margot?" Emberly asked to no one in particular.

"I saw her heading into the basement when we rushed inside to grab some boxes," Verity said. Emberly didn't relish the idea of staying so close to Ms. Margot, but there was no other choice. The basement was the safest place in the event of a tornado.

By the time they reached the house, Imani had begun to hang limp in their arms from pain, "Not much longer, Imani,"

Amilia said. "We're almost there. Just a few more steps and then we can fix your arm."

Imani nodded weakly and did her best to stay alert as they descended the stairs.

They ran to the room where they had had their sleepover, passing by a loudly-snoring, Ms. Margot, confirming she was already fast asleep after her afternoon's dose of pills—totally unaware of the disaster going on outside. The boys rushed to light some candles they grabbed on their way down.

Emberly and Amilia gently laid Imani onto one of the beds as the others circled around her.

"What happened to her?" Zayne cried.

"We were running back and—" Emberly bent down to catch her breath. "Imani fell and dislocated her shoulder. I think. Can you guys find something down here that we can use as a sling?" the boys nodded and took off, quickly returning with a bolt of fabric from the sewing room.

"Perfect," Emberly said as she looked at the fabric. "This will work great. Now, Amilia and Verity, you sit on Imani's other side and hold onto her. Try to keep her from moving."

"You ready?" she asked Imani.

A weak smile and a thumbs up from Imani were all she received in response.

"What can we do?" Wyatt asked.

"Stand back, and give us some space," Emberly answered, "and have that sling ready."

Emberly took a deep breath, then firmly grabbed onto Imani's wrist. She had seen this done a couple of times on a TV show, so she desperately hoped it would work. Then, with her next exhale, she pulled Imani's arm straight out and up above her head until she heard the shoulder pop back into place. With credit to Imani, who barely made more than a whimper, Emberly helped her sit up and used the fabric the boys had found and tied it around Imani's neck and arm as a sling.

Once everyone calmed down and realized that Imani was going to be fine, they all settled together in the two beds to wait out the storm; hoping there wouldn't be too much damage for them to clean up that the animals would be okay. Exhaustion soon took them.

A short while later, Emberly woke to find Eve curled up beside her, her eyes as round as pumpkins.

"What's on your mind, Eve?" Emberly whispered, careful to keep her voice down so she wouldn't wake the others.

"Are we ever going to leave?" Eve asked.

The question caught Emberly off guard, "Do you want to the truth, or a lie?"

"The truth?" Eve sounded unsure.

"The truth is, I don't know. I hope we do, but I just don't know anymore. I'm sorry." Eve wrapped her small arms around her big sister. Her protector. Her hero. Her friend.

"What I do know," Emberly added as she wrapped Eve in a tight embrace of her own, "is that we will always be together. No matter what." Eve melted at Emberly's words. They stayed that way, wrapped in each other's arms until Eve eventually succumbed to sleep.

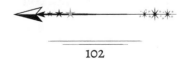

Morning came, or so Emberly thought, and Eve was still fast asleep. Emberly hadn't slept a wink after her conversation with Eve. She just laid there and watched as her sister's chest rose and fell with every breath of the basement's musty air. Trying not to disturb Eve, Emberly climbed out of the bed and headed to the sewing room where she knew there was a clock.

*Five thirty*, she read. *We must have slept through it all.* She turned around to leave the room but was met by a pair of beautiful, ocean blue eyes.

"How's the arm?" Emberly pointed at Imani's arm which was still in its makeshift sling.

"It's much better. I mean it's still tender, but it's better," Imani smiled, "Thank you."

"Well, I *did* owe you one," the girls shared a grin.

"Since your arm is feeling okay, want to venture upstairs with me to check out the damage?"

The yard was a mess. Everything was in disarray. Fence boards had been ripped off, and parts of the fence were missing altogether. Big tree branches had been left in the middle of the yard. Crates and buckets had been scattered throughout. Even the animals' pens and cages had been battered.

The girls went to inspect the animals. Emberly looked in the chicken coop and reached down to take a bucket off one of the chicken's heads. But when she did, she found that its head had been detached. It lay only inches from the chicken's lifeless body. She dropped the bucket in shock and took a few steps back. That's when she realized it. Most of the chickens were dead. Some likely from shock. Others due to injuries gained from things that had been hurled at them during the storm.

Emberly moved to examine the rest of the animals. Many, like the chickens, were dead, while some must have gotten out of their cages and disappeared through the gaps in the fence. Others sat traumatized in their cages. It looked like almost all the bobcats had made a run for it, with their wooden encloser left empty and destroyed. The ten cows they had had to begin with were now three; six dead, and one missing. To Emberly's dismay, everywhere she looked, animals were either dead, missing, or traumatized. Yet, somehow, every single one of the pigs were perfectly fine.

Emberly met up with Imani where the picnic bench *used* to be, when in fact, it was now standing on its side on the other side of the yard. Only one thing could have caused this much damage. A tornado.

"I'm glad we got inside when we did," Emberly said, fully understanding the gravity of the situation.

"I can't believe what these animals went through," Imani's face fell in sadness. "Most of them are dead or escaped. The poor things."

Emberly looked towards the section of the white fence that appeared to be bulldozed, to where multiple sets of tracks led out into the direction of the forest. "Well, at least now they don't have to be stuck here any longer, *unlike us.*"

Imani looked to her and gave a wry smile. She heard what Emberly had said; unlike us.

"Come on," Imani grabbed her hand, "let's go back inside. We can figure out what to do about the yard and the animals after some breakfast."

Thanks to the storm, there were no eggs left, so Emberly and Imani made some toast for everyone while they waited for Ms. Margot to show up.

They didn't need to wait long. Halfway into eating, Ms. Margot stood in the doorway of the kitchen, sporting the same old scowl on her face and cigarette clutched between her two stained fingers, "Why aren't you guys outside?"

The tone of her voice sent chills down Emberly's spine.

"We were waiting for you to tell us what we should do," Emberly replied.

"What the hell are you talking about? You've been doing things long enough to know what needs to get done every day. Or, do I need to teach you again?" Ms. Margot cracked her knuckles loud enough to send shocks through Emberly's veins.

"Well, in case you forgot, we had a tornado come through yesterday. It kind of made our job slightly impossible," Emberly replied.

Ms. Margot's eyes grew wide as she rushed to the window to examine the horror that was her backyard. She took one deep breath and turned back to the kids.

"You're all on cleaning duty for the next week or for however long it takes," she started. "Imani, and the girl who talks too much, you're going to haul everything back into its original place and fix the fence. Boys, you'll be fixing my garden, and you little girls will deal with my animals. If you finish your jobs earlier than everyone else, go help the others. I really don't care. But you all are working an extra hour today since you wasted my time. And I don't want to hear a peep out of you about how your arm is in 'too much pain' to do anything," she finished as she pointed at Imani's arm that was still in its sling—completely uncaring if Imani was okay or not.

Ms. Margot walked out the door and into the living room. Everyone rolled their eyes and headed outside to get to work.

In the end, they disregarded Ms. Margot's separation of tasks and worked together to get the yard in shape. Imani and the younger girls looked for lighter things that they could easily put back on their own, while Emberly and the boys used whatever fence boards they could find to cover the holes in the animal's cages. They'd worry about the fixing the fence later.

"We just have the bobcats' cage left to close up," Wyatt said, "but we've run out of fence boards."

"Alright, you guys go and help the girls move the picnic table back into place so we have somewhere to sit at lunch, I'll go look in the front yard to see if there are any up there."

Emberly slipped through a hole in the side of the fence and made her way towards the front of the house. She found the front to be almost as bad as the back. Tree branches had been ripped off and tossed along the yard. The vines that had once grown along the sides of the house were now lying in a tangled heap on the ground. Shingles had been ripped off and tossed across the yard.

Emberly waded through the junk and made a pile out of fence boards and fallen branches that they could use to finish boarding up the cages and hopefully help close some of the holes in the fence. While pulling a board out of a particularly twisted bunch of vines, she heard the sound of a car coming down the gravel road towards the house.

The car parked in front of the house, and a man stepped out. He walked around to his trunk and pulled out three bundles of books and started to walk towards the house.

Emberly rushed up to the man and coughed to get his attention, "I can take those in for you, sir." Emberly offered, her arms extended.

"Well, okay. But be sure to give them to Ms. Margot. She'll need them for the three of you," he handed the bundles to Emberly.

Struggling under their weight, she adjusted her grip to better balance the pile of books, "Wait, 'three of us'," she asked confused, "but there are seven kids here."

"I was only told there were three, sweetie."

"Number one, don't call me 'sweetie'. Number two, there must have been a mistake. There are seven kids that live here."

"Talk to your foster lady, kid," he said as he got into his car, "I've got to go."

Emberly walked inside and dropped the books onto the kitchen table. Hearing the noise, Ms. Margot came into the kitchen. She took one look at the three bundles of books then smiled up at Emberly.

"Why did he only bring three books?" Emberly asked.

"Oh sorry, did I forget to tell you, my dear?" Ms. Margot replied in a sickeningly sweet tone. "In three days, Imani and her sister are getting sent to a different foster home, and Verity and Wyatt to another."

Then her smile turned to pure evil as she delivered her next bit of news, "But don't worry, you and your siblings," she paused, "will get to stay here with me," she cackled at Emberly's horror-stricken face. "Maybe you should think twice before you speak to me like that again."

CHAPTER NINE

EMBERLY STARED AT MS. Margot In complete shock; her mouth agape, her heart racing, and, for once in her life, speechless. How could Ms. Margot do such a thing? Emberly had known that something was going to happen, it was so obvious from all Ms. Margot's cryptic laughs and malicious smiles she had given over the last two weeks. Still, she never imagined something this cruel could have ever been the punishment.

Emberly was so lost in her thoughts that she failed to realize that Ms. Margot had slipped out of the room, until she had come back in with everyone else in tow.

Eve and Zayne rushed over to their sister's side. They tried to talk to Emberly— to ask her questions—but she wouldn't answer them. She couldn't. Her mouth was frozen. Imani and the other kids had become family to the Cloves. The only people left that she could count on. And Ms. Margot had just stolen them from her.

"You're probably all wondering why our little Emberly is tied up in knots," Ms. Margot snarled as everyone watched Emberly in terror. She bent down to be at eye level with the kids. "Well, she's in shock. And do you want to know why?" Ms. Margot asked in a fake pity tone.

It was the condescending way that Ms. Margot always spoke to the kids that bothered Emberly the most. It was the way she talked to them like they were all of bunch of idiots. It infuriated Emberly. Ms. Margot was so hung up on being miserable that she failed to see the good in others. She never bothered to get to know them or to learn anything about them. Ms. Margot didn't know that Zayne and Eve were reading books at a grade seven level. Or that Imani was a genius when it came to medicinal and natural remedies. She never knew that Verity could name almost any constellation in the sky and that she could navigate her way across anything, so long as you could see the stars. She never knew that Wyatt could memorize and repeat back any sequence of numbers you gave him, no matter how long, or that little Amilia had such an analytical and strategic mind that she could practically her own business.

None of them were idiots, and Emberly was beyond tired of people thinking that they were. It was this, that finally snapped Emberly out of her trance.

"First of all, you evil witch, get the hell out of their faces," Emberly growled. "Secondly, start talking to them like the humans they are. And if you can't, I will."

Not giving Ms. Margot, and her shocked expression another moment of her time, Emberly turned to the kids, "Ms. Margot is moving Imani and Amilia to a new foster home," Emberly took a deep breath, "and Verity and Wyatt to another."

The kids instantly broke into tears. "Well, you got what you wanted," she said as she finally turned back to Ms. Margot. "You wanted to punish me for talking back to you. You've succeeded. Happy now?"

Emberly then stormed out of the room with her head held high, clipping Ms. Margot's shoulder on her by.

She made it all of two steps out of Ms. Margot's eyesight before the tears started to stream down her face. Not the soft, pretty tears that you'd see on TV. No, these were hot, heavy streams that poured down her cheeks and dripped off her chin. She walked into her room and closed the door. She slid down the door and buried her face in her hands, sobbing. She cried until there was nothing left but croaks and hiccups. Her chest felt hollow, yet heavy. Tight, yet weak.

When even the hiccups stopped, Emberly walked over to her bed and pulled the mirror that she'd found in the basement out from under her mattress where she'd hidden it. She stared at her reflection. Her eyes were swollen from the tears, but her face was red with anger. Mostly for Ms. Margot and everything that she had done to them, but also for herself. If she hadn't said anything, then the others would have been able to stay. Though, depending where they went, maybe it wouldn't be the worst thing for them to get to leave this place. But perhaps they wouldn't have had to separate. Either way, they were in this mess because of Emberly's big mouth and her inability to know when to stop talking.

No, actually, it was because of her mom that this had all happened. Her mom was the one that decided to go to work on the twin's birthday, and it was her death that caused them to go here. But even Emberly knew that that wasn't fair to say.

Her mom hadn't planned to die. Still, she had chosen to leave them to this place.

Emberly sighed. *Well, it will do me no good just standing here feeling sorry for myself.* Every second she stood in this room was another second that Ms. Margot got the satisfaction of knowing she had won. She remembered something her dad used to tell her, "Somewhere out there is someone worse off than you. So stop feeling sorry for yourself, and pick yourself back up."

Emberly had lived by that motto her entire life, and she'd be damned if she let Ms. Margot, of all people, make her stop believing in it.

She dried her face, straightened her clothes, and held her head high as she joined the others who were now sitting outside at the picnic table. She was Emberly Clove – stoic, confident, and sometimes revengeful.

That afternoon, everyone was quiet as they continued to clean up the debris that been blown about the yard. Even Imani, who hardly ever stopped talking, barely said a word. The two worked side-by-side for hours until Imani's voice broke the silence, "Why would she do it?" Imani asked through a veil of tears.

Emberly embraced her friend, "Because she doesn't like it when people stand up to her. I told her something true, and sure, maybe it was a *little* mean," she winked at Imani, "and she punished us for what I did."

"It's not your fault. She's just mean," Imani said and turned to face Emberly. "No matter what happens—or wherever we end up—do you promise we'll always stay friends?"

"Always," Emberly promised, hoping against hope that it was one she'd be able to keep.

They worked well past sunset that day. The heat had retreated with the sun, making it easier to work. But still, after working a twelve-hour day and hardly any breaks, even Emberly thought Ms. Margot's voice was music to her ears when she called them to head back inside.

Like most nights, the kids ate dinner alone, as Ms. Margot had chosen her usual potion of liquor and pills that they knew would be followed by a deep sleep.

"Hey, guys," Imani asked in the middle of dinner. "Want to have another sleepover tonight?"

Everyone smiled and silent cheers arose from their faces.

"Won't Ms. Margot get mad though?" Wyatt asked cautiously.

"As long as we're quiet and are back upstairs before she wakes in the morning, we should be fine," Emberly said.

That was all they needed to hear to quickly finish their meals. They cleaned up and rushed to their rooms to gather their things. Imani snuck some snacks out of the kitchen, Emberly grabbed a few candles and matches, her younger siblings grabbed some books, and the others scrounged up spare blankets. They made their way downstairs to their hideout where they lit the candles and curled up under the blankets.

They stayed up late into the night talking, seemingly unable to get enough of each other's company since there was no way to know when they'd see each other next. But looking around, Emberly knew that even though they would be separated soon, there was no way on earth they would ever forget each other.

"Emberly?" a voice asked as if her name were a question.

"What's up, Zayne?"

"Could you read us something? I brought the book Mom gave us. You know, the one with all the names," he pulled the book out from under his pillow and held it out to Emberly.

"Sure, bud," Emberly smiled and grabbed it from Zayne. She opened the book and scanned the pages for their names.

"Alright, our first name is 'Amilia'," Emberly said as though she was the host of one of those old game shows her mom used to watch when Emberly was a little girl. Amilia perked up in her bed.

"Amilia, your name means hard worker," Amilia smiled, and everyone nodded their heads in approval. She was always the one to tell them to get back to work, even though she was only nine.

"Oh, oh! Read my name next!" Verity was practically jumping out of the bed. Emberly chuckled and flipped to the V's.

"Your name means truth or humble," Emberly read. That one was also true. Verity was one of the nicest people Emberly had ever met. She was also the wittiest and had a great sense of humour.

"And while I'm at the bottom of the alphabet, let's search for Wyatt's name," she turned the pages until she came across his name. "Wyatt, the little warrior."

She saw Wyatt wrinkle his nose a little at the description. Wyatt wasn't exactly the type of person to fight anyone off. He was very quiet and shy, which was part of what made him and Zayne such great friends. "Remember, Wyatt, a warrior isn't always someone that fights. They're also the people that never give up, no matter what's thrown at them," she said, referring to everything he had already persevered through. When seen through this lens, it was the perfect description for Wyatt. Emberly knew he believed it too when she saw him sit a little taller.

"My turn," Imani burst out. Everyone chuckled, and Emberly flipped the pages back to the front of the book.

"Imani. Faith, belief, or beautiful soul," everyone's expressions went soft as if they were watching a romantic part of a movie. This description was perfect for Imani. Nothing more, nothing less. Perfect, just like her.

"I like that one," Imani smiled. "Can you read yours?"

"Oh, I don't have to read ours—those I know by heart. Our mom used to tell us what our names meant at least once a week before bed. Zayne's name means gracious, which Mom always said was meant for someone with a creative mind and a giving heart," Emberly winked at Zayne who smiled back.

"Eve's name means life or breath. Which is *perfect* for Eve because she's so full of smiles and laughter, and she has such a bold personality." Everyone looked over to Eve and laughed because they knew that it was true.

"And my name means spark or flame. Mom used to say that it was meant for a person who isn't afraid to start something on fire with their words," and when they heard that, no one said a word. They just smiled and nodded their heads, knowing that it was the perfect name for Emberly. Their friend. Their sister. Their defender. Their leader.

CHAPTER TEN

*The smell of horse was pungent, and the hay that pierced her side were wildly uncomfortable. Emberly lifted her hand and held it to the light of the sun that streamed through the barn's window. Its glow a welcome warmth on her skin. A rustling noise to her left alerted her to the presence of another person. Her head turned towards the noise, where a figure standing in the corner appeared. The figure—a boy, as she could now tell—took a step forward, but the shadows kept his features hidden from her, except for the kind smile that alighted his face. He opened his mouth to speak but then dissolved into nothing. Emberly frantically looked around, trying to find this mysterious boy, but he was gone. So too was the barn and the rest of the surroundings. Everything began to wither away until she was falling into an endless abyss.*

EMBERLY'S EYES SNAPPED OPEN and her heart pounded as she sat up in bed. She looked around the darkened room and took in her tangled sheets, her sweat-drenched t-shirt, and the hay-free floor. *That dream,* she said to herself, *it felt so real.* Emberly closed her eyes and tried to recall its sensations. She could almost smell the horses, and feel the hay beneath her. Her fingers still tingled with the memory of the sun's warmth.

And that boy. The one with the kind smile. Though she didn't see his face, Emberly remembered him most of all.

She opened her eyes again and sat in silence as the remaining strings of her dream drifted away.

Confused and a little groggy, Emberly got out of bed and looked at the clock. It was four. *No sense in going back to sleep*, she rationalized as she threw back the covers and quietly got out of bed. Emberly tip-toed over to the closet to get dressed. She changed out of her pyjamas and threw on the only pair of pants she owned that weren't in desperate need of a wash and a shirt that had become so worn out that she had once mistaken it for a rag.

Once dressed, she went about waking and helping Zayne and Eve get ready for the day. The others were going to leave tomorrow, and they didn't want to miss a single moment with them.

They entered the kitchen and were met with Ms. Margot's snarly grin, "Only one more day," she boasted. "Enjoy it while you can," she added as she left the kitchen.

"I hate her so much," Verity spat once Ms. Margot was out of ear shot. This was the only time Emberly had ever seen her show any negative emotions towards anything. "When we woke up, Ms. Margot came into our rooms just to tell us that we still have to work today. And on top of that, that we have to do an extra two hours' worth of work since we won't be working tomorrow," she huffed and grabbed some eggs. They ate in silence after that. No one knew what to say.

It was still quite dark outside, but the moon provided them with enough light to work. The little kids worked on clearing out the garden and cleaning up the animal cages while Emberly and Imani continued working on repairing the fence. The girls had started patching it the day before, using the fence boards and branches that Emberly and the boys had gathered the day after the tornado, but they had a long way to go until it would be finished. They pretty much had to redo an entire side, so they knew it was going to take a while to finish. Especially since Imani only had one good arm to use after the accident.

Finally, sun peak its head out from behind the horizon and they were able to see more. They could, however, have used the candles for heat since the day was colder and windier than usual. On a positive note, the sun wasn't beating down on them and they weren't dying of thirst, which was a welcome change, but the wind was harsh and unforgiving. Even the thick trees struggled to stay upright under the wind's relentless force.

The wind provided them with another set of challenges. Sometimes, when Imani would try to hold a board in place so Emberly could nail it to the fence, the wind would steal it from her grip and the girls would have to chase after it. Or, when the wind was feeling particularly cheeky, it would blow the jar of nails over, causing them to scatter all over the ground, until the girls found them all and put them back in the jar.

The only thing the wind could not take from Emberly's possession, were her reoccurring thoughts of the boy from the barn. Her focus on him became so singular, that it was almost as though he'd taken up permanent residence in her mind.

Who was he? At one point, she almost nailed Imani's hand to a board when she couldn't stop thinking of the way the corners of his mouth turned up ever so slightly as he smiled. Why was she dreaming of him? She couldn't get him off her mind. Yet when Imani asked her what was wrong, she simply responded by saying that it was nothing. Because it was nothing. He was nothing— or was he? Though, if she was honest, deep in her gut, she knew that her dream had meant something.

She just didn't yet know what that something was.

They spent the entire day working on the fence; hammering boards in place, adjusting poles, and climbing ladders since they were too short to reach the top of the fence. They stopped only briefly for lunch before they were back at it. And when the sun set, they did not miss a beat and continued to work under the moonlight.

Finally, the time came to go inside. Ms. Margot had thankfully already fallen asleep; the only reason Emberly knew this to be true was because the whole house practically shook from the vibration of her snoring.

As the children sat down to eat, it finally hit Emberly that this would be the last time they would all sit down for dinner together. She looked around the table at all their faces, trying desperately to capture the moment before it was gone indefinitely.

"So, this is it, huh. I'm really going to miss you guys," Wyatt sniffed. He looked around the table at all of them and they smiled.

"Yeah, it really sucks. You guys won't be together, and we'll be stuck here with her," Emberly looked deflated. "She is going to torture us beyond repair," she whispered.

"Wait!" Imani held out hand out to stop them. She stopped to think about what she was going to say, then spoke again, "What if you don't stay?" Emberly scrunched up her eyebrows. What did she mean? What other choice did they have? The room filled with whispers and confused faces.

"What are you talking about Imani?" Amilia asked

"I mean, what if they left here—" Imani paused, "or escaped," she finished in a whisper. "Then they wouldn't have to be stuck with Ms. Margot." Imani seemed proud of her idea, but Emberly wasn't so convinced. They couldn't leave, and even if they did, where would they go?

"I'm not sure how that's going to work. In case you haven't noticed, we are almost literally in the middle of nowhere. The only way out of here is by car, and I doubt Ms. Margot would be willing to drive us," Emberly sarcastically pointed out.

"Or if you run through the fence like the animals did," Wyatt joked.

"Wyatt," Imani cried. "You're a genius!" she looked at the others. "You can escape into the forest! Zayne was telling me about the book your mom had given him, *My Journey North*. About how the main characters escaped from a crazy gunman that was chasing after them and ran through the forest, surviving off the food they caught and foraged, until they made it to Toronto, Canada. *You* guys could totally do that."

"Do what? Run through one of the holes in the fence and try to make it to Toronto?" Emberly scoffed.

"I don't see why you guys can't try. Emberly, you said it yourself—the forest is your happy place. You spent years exploring forests with your dad; going hiking, camping, even fishing and hunting. You know the forest better than anyone I've ever known. And Toronto isn't that far. I know for a fact that there is forest line that continues from Connecticut all the way to Toronto. You would just have to walk through Connecticut, Massachusetts, New Hampshire and then Maine. All of which are small states. It seems simpler to just go north but it's the riskier option. It's safer to just travel through the forest even if it takes longer."

"Yes, but why Toronto, of all places?"

"Well, it seemed like a good place to end up for the characters in Zayne's book. It's a big city with a lot of opportunity for someone to start over. And, I know Canada has lots of forests, and we know how you love those," Imani joked. "But really, it's one of the few places you could go and be safe. As long as you're in the US, she would be your legal guardian. Even if you ran away to another state, there'd be nothing stopping her from hauling your ass' back here if she found you or someone else did and turned you in. And you could imagine what kind of punishment she'd hand out to you then. Legally, Ms. Margot wouldn't be able to get hold of you if you made it across the border."

Imani paused for a few moments to let her words sink in, "Em, trust me."

Everyone looked around and started to laugh. In theory, the plan sounded amazing, but in reality, it seemed impossible.

"We're very thankful that you want to help, Imani, but you have to know that won't work," Emberly stated.

"I thought you were brave," Imani challenged.

Emberly sat up straight in her chair and looked at Imani. They hadn't even known each other for three months, but already Imani knew her so well. Emberly never liked to be proven wrong, but most of all, she hated when people thought her to be lazy or weak.

Imani's challenge flipped a switch in Emberly's head. *Could they do as she suggested? Could they really escape—would it work? Then her mind began to turn. Even if it didn't work, what would they lose? Nothing really. No matter their fate in the forest, it couldn't be any more dire than the one that faced them here.*

But if they went, they would be completely alone in the forest. Three children alone in the wild, exposed to all its elements. They would have to sleep outside when there was no warm place to be found. There would be wild animals lurking around, waiting to prey on them. That's not to mention the other challenges of living off the land; no money, no transportation and no guarantee of food or a clean water source. *No,* Emberly thought. *This is crazy. They couldn't survive.*

*But what if it's not crazy? What if we could do it?* Emberly smiled.

"How long have you been thinking about this?" Emberly suddenly asked Imani. Everyone's heads turned to look at her.

"Only just now," Imani admitted.

"And how would we survive?"

"We could steal some food, money, and supplies from Ms. Margot's secret stashes to get you started. I have a good idea of where we could find them. From there, you'd have to be careful to try to find food and water to keep you going until you reached Toronto."

"Say we make it all the way to the border. How are we supposed to cross it?"

"I don't know exactly, but it's not like there'd be a fence running the length of the country. I'm sure there's some place you could slip in during the middle of the night."

"Okay, we can come back to that. When would we leave? Once you guys are gone, there'd only be three of us left, and Ms. Margot would be watching us like a hawk."

"And working us overtime to make up for the difference of work load," Eve added.

"It'd have to be tomorrow, then. As soon as the cars pull up to get us, when Ms. Margot will be distracted with sending us off, you three could head out the back door and through the fence."

It was like Imani had an answer for everything.

"But how would we actually get to Canada? It's almost three states away," Zayne pointed out. "That'd be an awfully long way for us to walk,"

"We could take a train," Eve suggested. "Em, wouldn't it be worth it to at least try?"

Emberly looked to her sister. Her gorgeous blue eyes were impossible to ignore.

"A train," Emberly repeated. She tried imagining what their life would be like in Canada. They'd finally be free from the beatings and the pain that their short time in Connecticut had brought. They could go wherever they wanted and be whoever they wanted. And best of all, they wouldn't be here. She could see them getting on the train and heading to their new life. It was perfect. "Yes, I think that could work," she smiled.

The feeling of hope began to spread across the table.

"If this is going to work," Amilia piped up, "we need a plan." Since this was her area of expertise, she took charge. "Okay, so tomorrow, no one is working because we are supposed to be packing and cleaning our rooms, so Ms. Margot will be watching us like a hawk. That means that we have to gather whatever supplies we can find for you tonight. The four of us will grab food, water, matches, money, and some other things that you'll need on your journey. We'll hide the stuff in our rooms tonight and sneak them over to yours in the morning," the others nodded at their assignment.

"And you," she said pointing at Emberly, "will need to find a backpack as well to carry everything. Only one so you can hide it in your room. I'm sure we can find one lying around here somewhere. You'll also need to pack some clothes, but only the essentials. One backpack means you won't have a lot of space, and you'll want to leave as much room as you can for food and water. So put on as many layers as you can, and stuff the rest in your bag.

"Also, we will have to make sure we say our goodbyes before the cars pull in. You'll need to be ready to leave the second the cars come so you can be long gone before Ms. Margot realizes it.

"For now, we need to finish eating, then get started on our tasks as quick—and quietly—as we can, then get to bed. It's going to be a long day tomorrow."

Once they finished cleaning, they started their assignments. Emberly took her candle and ushered the twins into their room.

"Okay, I'm going to look around for a backpack. While I'm gone, I want you guys to pack your stuff. Two shirts. Two pants. And one extra thing. If the backpack is big enough maybe we can fit more, but we'll have to play that by ear," Emberly was about to turn and leave but Eve stopped her.

"Are you sure we should do this?" Eve's voice cracked.

Emberly's heart was racing and she knew that no matter how planned out they would be, this idea was still crazy and ridiculous. But Emberly also knew that it was the first time in a long time—maybe even since their dad had passed away—that she thought they were going to be okay.

"I know you're scared, Eve. You too, Zayne." She knelt so she could be at eye level with them. "But the idea of staying here any longer is even scarier. She's abused us in so many ways. She split my head open. We're no safer here than by ourselves in a forest. At least out there, we have a fighting chance. If we stick to the plan, we will be fine. I promise." She gave them each a kiss on the forehead, got up and left.

The halls were filled with an empty darkness. She remembered the first day she'd met Imani and how she had welts on her hands from sneaking food for Amilia. Emberly shuddered then tried to put that thought in the back of her mind. She didn't have the time for it, she had a job to do. She walked the hallways and searched through closets and rooms until she found what she was looking for. In the closet closest to the kitchen was a large backpack with lots of pockets and plenty of room for storage. It was perfect for their adventure.

Emberly heard someone come up behind her as she pulled the backpack out of the closet and closed the door. She froze, her heart pounding. Slowly, she turned around, hoping it was Imani or one of the other kids. But she found herself not so lucky when she turned and realized it was Ms. Margot.

"What are you doing up?" Ms. Margot growled.

"I—I..." Emberly stammered. She tried to swiftly move the backpack behind her back, so Ms. Margot wouldn't see it, but Ms. Margot's eyes caught the movement and she snatched the backpack from Emberly's hands.

"What are you doing with this?" she flailed the pack in the air. Emberly didn't know what to say. She obviously couldn't tell her the truth.

"I got it because..." she paused, trying to find a lie, "Eve feels really sick—like's she's going to throw up—so I wanted to find her something to put by her bed that she could throw up into in case she had to during the night. This was the only thing I could find." Emberly was impressed with her quick lie, but she worried Ms. Margot didn't buy it.

Ms. Margot squinted her eyes then whipped the bag across Emberly's face before shoving the bag into her chest and knocking her to the ground.

Emberly could feel something warm trickling down the left side of her face, but she didn't dare move to touch it. She just laid there staring up into Ms. Margot's smug face.

"Fine, have the bag," Ms. Margot said, "but it'll be an extra couple hours or chores for each of you if she throws up in it. And, Emberly," she added, "if I find out that you're lying to me and that you're using this bag not for your sister's puke, but to escape, then you can kiss those twelve-hour shifts goodbye. It will be fifteen-hour shifts, with even less food and water, when I find you and bring you back. And *trust* that I will find out."

Then Ms. Margot turned back towards her room, leaving Emberly lying on the floor with the backpack clutched between her two hands, still reeling over what had just happened.

Emberly thanked whatever gods had been watching out for them; that Ms. Margot had seemed to buy Emberly's lie, or at least had pretended to. Even more luckily, was the fact that she hadn't come across one of the others as they were stealing supplies.

Once her heartbeat calmed, Emberly got up from the floor and walked back to her room, backpack in hand. She opened the door and found Eve and Zayne reading, per usual, as they waited for her. Everything of theirs that was supposed to go in the pack was sitting on the nightstand.

Emberly crossed the room and grabbed the mirror that she had still kept hidden under her mattress and inspected her new wound. Luckily, it wasn't anything big. Just a little cut on her eyebrow. *Likely from the zipper*, Emberly thought. She grabbed an old t-shirt and used it to wipe the blood off her head.

"What happened?" Eve asked worriedly when she saw Emberly's cut.

"Ms. Margot caught me with the backpack. I told her you that you felt like you were going to throw up and that this was the closest thing I could find to a bag. In response, she ripped the backpack out of my hands and hit me with it. She warned me that if she found out we were really trying to escape, that she'd find us and punish us." Emberly looked down. She didn't know what to do. They needed to go. If they stayed any longer, who knew what would happen to them. But how could they leave if Ms. Margot was always watching over them?

"I'm still not sure about this, Em," Zayne went to sit by his big sister. "Maybe we're being a little crazy thinking we could escape."

"That's the thing," Emberly smiled. "We aren't being crazy enough." The twins scrunched up their faces in confusion. "We have nothing to lose. We're already tired and hungry and work twice as long as most adults do in a day. If we leave, we can start over. You guys could even go back to school. So could I."

Eve reached over to hug Emberly, "Okay, Em," she looked at Zayne who nodded. "We trust you."

Emberly hugged them both, "Thanks guys. Now, we don't have much time left. We need to finish packing, then we need to get to bed. We'll need our rest for tomorrow. Eve and Zayne, you guys put your stuff in the bag, and I'll grab what I need."

Emberly found some shirts, a pair of pants and shorts, and some underwear and socks and shoved everything into the bag alongside the twins' clothes. Then she remembered— her photos. There's no way she'd leave those behind. She dug around the closet until she found the box that still had the photos that were hanging in her old room. She smiled and sat on her bed and shuffled through them. The twins joined her as they looked through their memories together.

But one in particular made her remember something else they'd need. It was a photo of her and her dad that was taken in the forest behind their house. They were each holding a bow with an arrow nocked onto the string; Emberly with the one her dad had taught her to make, and her dad with his own bow.

Emberly scrambled off her bed and pulled out the suitcase that she had stored underneath when they had first arrived. She opened the suitcase and pulled out the bow and quiver.

"What's that, Emberly?" Eve asked.

"Dad's old bow and quiver set. I couldn't leave it behind, so I had hidden it in my suitcase. It was made for his height, so it'd be a little big for me. But I should be able to handle it well enough to hunt—or try to at least—to get us food if we needed it." Emberly put the box of photos, along with a couple of the twin's books, into the backpack and shoved it under the bed with the bow and quiver. She put her suitcase in front of them and just hoped that Ms. Margot wouldn't find them.

"Time for bed, guys," she announced. Tomorrow was going to be long, and they had already stayed up later than they should have. After she crawled into her own bed, Emberly's mind continued to cycle through, going over every single detail, so to avoid any hiccups along the way.

She felt like she was in some sort of action movie. They were going to run away, hop on a train, and then somehow try to—illegally—cross the border into Canada. Then from there, create a new and wonderous life for themselves. Simple, right?

She tried to stay positive and remain strong in order to not lose her resolve. To save her family, she'd need to be brave, fearless, crazy, *and* clever all at the same time. It was the only way.

CHAPTER ELEVEN

EMBERLY ROLLED OVER IN bed and looked at the clock hanging on the wall. *Only a few short hours until it's time to leave.* Emberly checked under the bed to make sure everything was there; still on edge by her encounter with Ms. Margot.

Emberly got up and searched through her closet. She needed to find the perfect outfit. Nothing too light, nor too warm; but things that could be worn in layers so she could easily remove them if needed.

She threw on a slightly dirt-covered t-shirt, a pair of stained shorts, and the cleanest pair of socks she could find from the closet. Then she tied a sweater around her waist. Clean clothes were one of the things she missed most about her old life. While her wardrobe had consisted solely of hand-me-downs from her mom, at least she could always count on them being clean.

Emberly turned and walked over to the window. She stared at her reflection in the glass. The cut she got from the zipper had stopped bleeding during the night and her eyebrow looked like a slit had been shaved from it. She thought it made her look tough. She smiled and closed her eyes, going over the plan one last time.

She heard little footsteps as the twins came up behind her. She gave them a quick hug and told them to get dressed. Emberly brought Eve over to the bed and started to double French braid her dark, pin straight hair so it wouldn't be in her face when they ran. She wove her hair in and out, just like her mom used to do for Eve when she was little. Emberly only wished she had some ribbons or bows that she could add to Eve's braids. Emberly sighed.

Emberly then started to tackle her own hair, first by removing the near-constant tangles that seemed to always plague her long, thick hair, then braiding it similar to Eve's. The only hair cut Emberly had received in the last year was a trim that she had done herself over the kitchen sink with a pair of scissors, so its length now extended down her entire back. After securing the ends with a couple of hair elastics, Emberly threw the brush into her backpack and they left for their last meal with their friends.

As they ate, Imani exchanged a worried glance with Emberly, clearly confused as to the origin of Emberly's newest cut on her face. But they couldn't talk about it because Ms. Margot had chosen to eat with them that morning. Emberly knew why. She was going to keep an eye on all the kids that day. All Emberly could do was to mouth the words "my room" to Imani when she was certain Ms. Margot wasn't looking.

Halfway through the meal, Ms. Margot excused herself to go to her room, undoubtedly to have a second—liquid—breakfast. The girls left the table and hurried to Emberly's room.

"Okay, so last night," Emberly started as she closed the door to her room. "While I was looking for the backpack, Ms. Margot found me and asked what I was doing up. I told her that Eve was sick and I needed a bag. She took it from me and hit me with it, which is no real surprise," Imani nodded. "But when she turned to leave, she warned me that we better not think of escaping today."

"No, no, no. That can't happen. Now she's going to watch us like a hawk. You're still leaving right?" Imani asked in concern.

"Yes. We have to. That was just further proof that it's long past the point of being 'safe' here. I don't know how you guys are going to be able to get the supplies over to our room without her noticing."

Imani paused to think before her face lit up with an idea, "Out of all of us, Ms. Margot will have her eyes on your family the most, so after we finish eating, the three of you will offer to clean up from breakfast. The four of us will say we're going to go finish packing, but really, we'll grab the supplies that we hid in our rooms and sneak them over to yours. Sound good?" Emberly nodded, and the girls quickly snuck back to the kitchen before they were caught.

As planned, after breakfast the Cloves offered to clean everything up so the others could finish packing. And as expected, Ms. Margot stayed behind to watch them as they worked, completely uncaring and unaware as to what the other four were really doing. To her, they were already gone—it was the Cloves that she would watch. But that was fine with Emberly. She could put up with the watchful eyes for now. Only a few more hours of Ms. Margot and then they'd be free at last.

She tried to imagine Ms. Margot's face when she went back inside after saying her fake goodbyes to the other kids, only to be greeted with an empty house. Emberly could barely keep the grin from spreading across her face.

Since they weren't expected to do any chores today, Emberly casually suggested they go to their room to make use of the time off and get a head start on studying.

"Fine," Ms. Margot said, "but you're going to stay in your rooms until I come and get you, so you better say goodbye to your little friends now," she cackled.

Again, Emberly fought to keep her emotions in check. She just nodded and took the twins to their room.

When they arrived in their room, the three were surprised with a pile of supplies sitting on top of the twins' bed. They quickly closed their bedroom door and surveyed the items.

From Imani and Amilia, they found a red blanket, a tin of dried chamomile, and a pile of food. In it were bars of all sorts, hard candies, boxes of crackers, and packages of dried meat. Pinned to the blanket was a note, "Some items to help on your journey. Stay safe, and thank you. We'll miss you. – Your sisters, Imani and Amilia Maier."

From Verity and Wyatt, there was a flashlight with an extra battery, a box of waterproof matches, a pocket knife, some rope, and two water bottles, as well as a note, "We hope this will help you. You guys are so brave. Thank you for everything. – With love, Verity Byre and Wyatt Ahuja."

Emberly smiled as she folded the two notes and stuffed them into her pocket. The risk they took to gather these items for them was no small feat. Ms. Margot was like a vulture constantly circling her prey looking for them to slip up so she could dole out a punishment. Emberly couldn't even manage to get a backpack without being caught, yet these four had grabbed food, water, clothes and everything else, just to give the Cloves a fighting chance when they escaped. They weren't able to find any money though. Ms. Margot hardly had enough money to pay bills let alone have money to risk being left out on the kitchen table. But that did mean there was no chance of being able to get on a train. Meaning the journey would be all done on foot which was an option Emberly and the kids had discussed. Even though it wasn't the best option, it would have to do.

"Do you think we'll ever see them again?" Zayne asked as he grabbed the backpack from under Emberly's bed.

"Yes," Emberly promised. Emberly knew deep in her heart that they would one day be reunited. They had formed too close of a bond not to be. She only hoped it'd be sooner rather than later.

With the help of the twins, Emberly packed everything into the backpack. She secured the rope to one of the outside straps, stuffed the pocket knife and matches into the side pockets, then put the water and snacks inside the main pouch, alongside their clothing. She threw the bag back under her bed with the bow and arrows.

A short while later, there was a knock at the door. Quickly looking to make sure everything was well-hidden from view, in case it was Ms. Margot, she crossed the room and opened the door.

"Find everything?" Imani asked as her and the rest of the children entered the room.

"Yes, thank you all for everything—the food, the blanket, the supplies...the notes. We are going to miss—" Emberly choked back tears. "And the risk you took, you all could have been caught and—"

"It's what family does," Wyatt said, with nothing but a confident assurance in his voice. The other three nodded.

"Yes," Emberly smiled. "Family." For there was no doubt that that's what the seven of them had become. They had each lost and gone through so much in their short lives. And yet, in the worst place and point in their lives, they had somehow ended up with the very thing they had all so desperately hoped for—a family.

They shared a round of smiles and tears as they hugged and said their farewells, each wishing each other a safe journey.

"Almost noon," Imani said as she looked at the clock on the wall. Almost time for them to go.

"I was thinking," Amilia said. "Since Ms. Margot is still in her room—likely with a bottle of vodka and cigarette—we should take your stuff now and hide it in the back. We can hide it on the other side of the fence near the hole. That way, it will be easier for you to sneak out of the house later."

"Great idea," Emberly praised her. She grabbed her bag and handed it to Imani, then she reached and pulled out her dad's bow and arrows from under the bed. Everyone gasped when she pulled them out, so Emberly laughed and explained why she had it.

Imani and Verity, the stealthiest of the four, took the bags and ran outside, careful to take the hallways less used by

Ms. Margot, just in case she did come out of her room. Once outside, the girls grabbed a tarp by the side of the house and ran through the hole in the side of the fence that had yet to be boarded up. They then used the tarp to cover the bag, bow, and quiver beside a set of bushes.

The two came back shortly after, closing the door behind them. This time, the happy expressions and joyful laughter had been wiped clean. It was all too soon that they would be parted.

The seven of them spent the next thirty minutes talking, sharing stories from their pasts, and playing games; pretending it was just like the day at the lake.

But all too soon, it was put on pause when they heard Ms. Margot open the front door and talk to someone.

"They're here," Emberly stated. Her nerves were uncontrollable. She took a deep breath and grabbed onto her necklace.

Emberly bemoaned the loss of her friends, but she and Imani had something special. The two fell into each other's arms. Imani cried and cried, and Emberly let her; the same tears fell from her own eyes. Emberly pulled back and looked Imani straight in the eyes.

"We will find a way to stay in touch. This is not the end," Emberly promised. Imani nodded, but the tears continued to cascade down her face. The two just held tighter.

"I'm going to miss you," Imani sniffed.

"I miss you already."

The four left for their rooms and returned with their suitcases, each giving everyone a final hug before they walked to the front of the house.

Emberly took a deep breath and turned to walk back in her room to ready the twins to run. But a voice from down the hall interrupted her movement.

"Don't you want to say goodbye to your friends?" Ms. Margot asked.

"Umm. Yes, but I thought you told us we had to stay in our room?"

"Nonsense, my dear. I would hate for you to miss watching as all of your friends left," she smirked as she ushered them to the front door.

Emberly's heart was pounding in her chest. This was not part of the plan. They were supposed to be making their escape right now, not heading to the front with Ms. Margot in tow. They got onto the front porch and watched as the other kids walked to the cars. Imani looked back towards the house and saw Emberly. Her eyes wide in question. Emberly stood frozen. She didn't know what to do.

But when Ms. Margot went over to the other car where Wyatt and Verity were standing, Imani wildly waved her hands back and forth. Emberly's eyes shot out as she realized what that meant. Imani wanted them to make a run for it. Emberly looked over at the twins and gave them a nod. They understood—Imani was going to make a distraction so they had a chance to escape. *It was now or never*, she thought.

"What's that?" Imani cried out, pointing at nothing in the opposite direction. That was their cue.

Emberly grabbed hold of the twins' hands and they ran off the porch. In the corner of her eye, she could see Ms. Margot turn and start to run towards them, shouting at them to stop, but the three of them just kept running. She could hear people—Imani and the others—shouting and cheering them on, their voices growing softer as they rounded the backside of the house and took off through the yard towards the hole in the fence. She knew Ms. Margot was still in pursuit, but nothing was going to stop them now.

They slipped through the hole in the fence. The hole was barely large enough to allow Emberly to pass through it; there was no way an adult would fit. No, the only way an adult would be able to get to the other side would be to have to scale the fence, giving the three of them extra precious moments to make their escape.

Emberly grabbed the backpack while Eve grabbed the bow and Zayne the quiver of arrows. The twins took off sprinting towards the forest as planned, but Emberly turned back. Through the hole, she could see Ms. Margot getting closer to the fence, the two social workers in close pursuit. But a little further back, she saw her friends cheering them on. Emberly smiled, and with a final wave she turned and ran to catch up to the twins.

Emberly held onto her necklace and her smile widened. It was time for a new adventure.

CHAPTER TWELVE

WHEN EMBERLY CAUGHT UP to the twins, she grabbed hold of their hands and pulled them along. Past trees, through bushes, around puddles, and over fallen branches until she could no longer hear the cries of Ms. Margot. She wasn't sure how far they would follow them, but Emberly didn't want to stop to find out.

The bow that Eve carried slowed her down, leaving Emberly with no choice but to slip it over her back and shoulder, being careful to position it so the backpack wouldn't rub against it. Their first stop would be the lake. Although running was certainly faster than walking, it seemed to be taking forever.

Worries flooded Emberly's head. She doubted herself on whether they were doing the right thing. Three kids alone in the forest, trying to make it to Canada, didn't exactly seem wise. But they couldn't turn back now. If they did, the outcome would not be good for any of them. But, if they continued, where would they go? How would they get to Toronto? Where would they find a train? Maybe they would find a small town along the way where they could grab a map or ask for directions. They had no other choice.

The bushes tore and scratched at their bare legs, but they just kept running. They had no time to stop and fuss over bumps and bruises. They were on the run.

Fugitives.

But soon, the gruelling pace became too much for Eve and Zayne, and they had to slow down. Even under normal circumstances, a run like that would have been too much for the twins.

"Guys, we need to keep going," Emberly encouraged between gasps. They were only minutes away from reaching the lake, where they could take a break. The lake was a place Ms. Margot knew nothing about. At the very least, they knew of enough hiding places from their time spent gathering wood or playing near the lake that they could evade her if need be.

Eve and Zayne mustered up the strength to continue their escape. Emberly pulled up the rear so she was able to encourage the twins.

Finally, they reached the lake. Emberly took the twins to a hollowed out bush at the edge of the forest where they could still see the water and be camouflaged by the green canopy.

No one said a word. They hydrated while they tried to catch their breath and listened for sounds of pursuit. After a period of silence, they realized that they were safe—at least for now.

Emberly looked out at the lake. It was surrounded by tall, leafy trees. The water was clear. Even though there was hardly any sunlight showing through the clouds, the water still managed to find enough tiny rays that made its surface dance and sparkle in the sun. Emberly held her legs close to her body and hugged herself. It made her feel warm and safe.

She couldn't believe what they had just done. It was unfathomable. It was reckless, yet brave. Necessary, but risky. It had been their only chance of refuge.

Emberly looked over at the twins huddled together. Zayne was still partially awake and Eve had closed her eyes and was laying with her head resting on her brother's lap. Emberly smiled. She would let them rest for a bit.

Emberly got up quietly so she wouldn't wake Eve and made her way through the forest to search for some chamomile flowers. Even though Imani had packed a tin for them, Emberly wanted to make sure she'd have enough in case they weren't able to find it later. Emberly came across a patch of the flowers and picked as many as she could and used the stem of one stalk to tie them together in a bunch. She gathered some small branches and returned to their makeshift camp.

Emberly returned to find both twins fast asleep, curled into a little ball to keep themselves sheltered from the now-brisk air. The sun had completely hidden behind the clouds and the wind was starting to pick up. The temperature was dropping. Emberly dropped the wood by her bag and grabbed one of the fishing rods that Imani had hidden near the lake and went to catch some fish.

She was no fishing expert, but Emberly thought she should try. Still, she wished Verity was there with them; she was the real fishing pro. The fish refused to bite at first, but eventually she was able to coax in a few. It would have to be enough for now. She walked back to the shelter and found both twins awake from their nap. They rubbed the sleep from their eyes and joined Emberly at the firepit.

Emberly took one look at the fish and again wished for someone else to be there to help. Imani had cleaned the fish with such precision during their anniversary cookout. Emberly sighed. She knew it was up to her now. Luckily, she had fished enough with her dad that she had a general idea of what to do. She grabbed the knife and dug in. She was careful to toss the guts far into the forest on the other side of the lake so they wouldn't attract any unwanted guests.

While Emberly worked, the twins grabbed the wood she had gathered and carried it over to the pit to make a fire. "Make sure you keep the fire small and use dry wood only. We don't want to give our location away by sending up big plumes of smoke," Emberly warned.

Once the fish was cooked, they put out the fire and huddled back in their make shift shelter and ate their meal. They also took advantage of the nearby freshwater creek and drank as much water as they could.

They watched as the wind grew stronger, and it was around the time that the dark clouds began to roll in that Emberly could feel her panic rising. The night of the tornado flashed through her mind, but she forced herself to remain calm. Emberly knew from the look of these clouds that the storm wouldn't be anywhere near as bad as that night, but the wind—and rain that was soon to follow—would still be a danger to their well-being. They needed to fortify their hideout. On her command, the three of them went into the forest in search of large branches and strong vines that they could use for their shelter.

Emberly found four large fallen branches and dragged them back to the campsite, while the twins had found armfuls of smaller, but sturdy, leafy branches and vines. Emberly began fastening the branches together using the vines, until it resembles a roof. She placed it over the hideout to keep them dry.

Inside, they took some of the smaller, bushier branches and used them to fill the gaps and built an elevated floor to keep them off the ground. The shelter wasn't perfect, but it would do for now.

Between the three of them and their backpack and gear, it was a tight squeeze but that didn't bother them. The smaller the space, the easier to keep warm.

Emberly turned to her siblings who were already huddled together, "Thank you," she said unprovoked.

The twins' heads turned her way, and she smiled. "I know I haven't said much, but it's only because—"

"You don't need to explain yourself to us," Eve interrupted her. "We get it. You needed time to think. So did we."

Emberly was shocked at her eight-year-old sister's intuition. Most kids her age would have been too immature to comprehend or care about the level of danger they were putting themselves into. But not Eve.

Eve leaned her head on her big sister's shoulder and took a deep breath. Zayne then came around Emberly's other side and laid his head on her lap. He too took a deep breath, but he exhaled slowly and cautiously, as if he was afraid he'd make the shelter collapse with too large a breath.

Just as they were starting to relax, a huge clap of thunder made them all jump. The twins grabbed onto Emberly with all their strength. Emberly held them, trying to protect them. To help soften the mood, she sang.

Don't fear. Stay near.

You'll be alright.

Sleep tight my baby, until night.

Close your eyes. Listen closely.

You'll always be safe, so long as

You're with me.

Emberly felt their little bodies relax as Eve and Zayne let go and fell asleep. The rain started to pour down — they would be going no further tonight. At least it would keep Ms. Margot and the others away.

The fresh smell of the falling rain and the clap of thunder brought back memories of the twins' birthday. She remembered the smell of spring and happiness then. Even the thunder was musical—to everyone but Zayne she supposed. And that, in her opinion, was the perfect setting to fall asleep in—and that's exactly what she did, even if it was still early in the evening.

CHAPTER THIRTEEN

EMBERLY AWOKE TO A gentle breath of wind that brushed across her face. The birds were chirping, the leaves rustled, and the sun was pouring in through the holes of their shelter. The twins were still fast asleep, which came as no surprise because they were exhausted—they all were. But they couldn't sleep forever. They had to get moving in case Ms. Margot decided to come after them. Emberly gently shook them awake. Their little eyes opened slowly as they adjusted to the morning light. They crawled out from the shelter and stood up to stretch their stiffened limbs.

Emberly's back was equally sore from the awkward position she had slept in during the night, so she stretched it out before bending back down to retrieve their bag. They had covered the bag and Emberly's bow and quiver with leaves and branches, which thankfully kept most of the moisture away, but everything was still damp. She set the bag on the beach, and the twins crowded around.

Emberly pulled out a protein bar, peeled the wrapper off, and split it into three pieces. Each ate their piece slowly, savouring every bite. They didn't know when their next opportunity to eat would be, so they had decided to ration their food as best they could.

Emberly licked the last traces of the bar from her fingers, not wanting to waste a single bit of it, and waited for the twins to finish. She retrieved the bow and quiver from beside the shelter and gave Zayne the backpack before she knocked the shelter down and dragged the remaining branches back into the forest. If anyone came looking for them, Emberly didn't want to give them any chance of knowing where they had been.

"Okay," Emberly said as she filled their water bottles, "we need to find out where we're going."

"Do you know which way is north? That would help us out a lot," Zayne mentioned.

"Oh, I never thought of that," Emberly joked sarcastically. "Imani taught me a trick on how to do just that." She walked into the forest, with the twins not far behind her. She looked at the base of every tree until she found what she was looking for. Moss. She turned to the twins and motioned to it. "Imani told me that moss only grows on the north side of the tree, which means," she paused for effect, "that way is north." Emberly pointed to the darkest, leafiest part of the forest, to where the creek from the lake wound through its tangled trunks.

The twins exchanged glances and nodded before they took off.

Though the smell of rain still lingered in the air, the wind wasn't nearly as unbearable as in recent days. Emberly looked up at the clear sky and smiled, hoping it would be a good day. They walked through the forest in single file with Emberly at the back so she could keep an eye on the twins. They continued north, making sure to check for moss on the trees every so often to confirm they were heading in the right direction. Emberly told Eve, who was leading, to follow the creek. So far, the creek was continuing north. At best, it would eventually lead them to a town who used it as a water source.

They walked past trees and through bushes; they climbed under low hanging branches and jumped over fallen trees. Within an hour, they were covered in more scratches and the thick carpet of pine needles that blanketed the forest floor had caked the sole of their shoes. But the nearby creek also provided a constant water source for them. The standing trees provided a canopy over their heads and blocked out any unnecessary sunlight from beaming down on them. Both making their hike abundantly easier.

After a few hours, the three decided to stop to rest and eat.

"Where are we going?" Eve asked in an exhausted and slightly impatient tone.

"I already told you, Toronto."

"No, I know that. But where are we going—as in, to stop for the night? We've been walking for years," Eve whined.

"We've got to be getting close to a town," Emberly said— hoped. "We can rest there, and possibly find out when the train might be leaving. We just have to keep walking. Just a little bit further," she encouraged.

Luckily, Emberly's prediction had come true. After another hour or so, they finally came across a small town. The streets were lined with houses on either side. This would be their best chance at finding somewhere decent to stay for the night. The town was surrounded by the forest, almost as if the town had been swallowed whole into the belly of the leafy monster, with only one gravel road leading out. The Cloves walked down one of the lonely streets, trying to look for someone that could be of help them.

To their right, Emberly saw some kids playing basketball on their front driveway. Emberly's mind wandered to a time when she was able to play and have fun. On rare occasions, their mom allowed her to take the twins to the park to play basketball with the other neighbourhood kids. Those days were buried long in the past for her. So much had changed since then.

They turned onto what looked to be the main street. A couple of stores looked promising. The first was a clothing store that appeared as though it had been in dire need of repairs. The fluorescent lights that dangled precariously from the roof flickered; the faded paint peeled off the walls in tatters; and through the dirty windows, Emberly could  make out someone's head poking out from behind the counter.

Against Emberly's better judgement, they walked into the clothing store to look around. But before doing so, Emberly hid her dad's bow and quiver under a pile of leaves behind the store.

The clothing wasn't expensive, but practical. They had no money, so stealing was their only option. Emberly looked around; they were the only people in the store, which usually would have meant the person at the register would be watching them. Instead, she walked into the back of the store, uninterested in their presence. In a move that shocked even herself, she quickly grabbed three thicker long sleeve shirts and stuffed them into the backpack. The twins looked at her in surprise, but Emberly nodded and motioned for them to leave the store before the woman came back.

Emberly hadn't stolen anything in her life, even though it seemed like she was a natural at it. She knew that it was bad to steal, —even if they needed those clothes. It was getting colder, and they had no idea how long they'd have to travel on foot and sleep outside. They needed to be prepared for anything. Which meant it was either steal or freeze.

The next store they came across was some type of general store by the looks of it. It was also in much better shape than the first. They entered the store to see if they could find anything useful. Its shelves were stocked with everything a person could ask for. Everything from grocery items to camping gear. Sporting goods, household items, and tools adorned its shelves. Emberly was tempted to grab a few items that would make things easier on their journey, but the store surprisingly had quite a few people in it. Well, only three, but that was still far too many considering the small size of the store, which meant that it was too risky to try stealing anything. So, they left. They had enough food to last until they found a train station anyways.

The last store on main street was a mysterious, almost ghostly looking, store with the store's only window covered by blinds. Its exterior sign that had once marked its significance to the town had long since gone missing. With caution, they entered the store to see if they could find a map or some information on nearby train schedules. Very quickly they realized that it wasn't a store at all, but a small post office that was attached to the side of the general store, each equipped with their own entrance. Emberly whispered to the twins, "I will do the talking. We can't have our stories crossed, otherwise they will think something's up. So just nod and smile, got it?"

The twins nodded and smiled in response.

Before walking into the post office, Emberly stopped and walked back to where she had hidden her dad's bow and quiver. She picked them up and moved them over to the last building and leaned them up against the wall in the back alley. Then she walked back to the front to where the twins who had stayed standing and they walked into the office.

Sitting behind the counter was a grumpy looking old woman staring at her phone. Emberly walked up to her with a big smile across her face.

"What do you need?" the women greeted them in a curt tone.

"We were just wondering if you could give us a map," Emberly replied. The woman frowned at her and narrowed her eyes, outwardly annoyed that she was being bothered by a young woman. She reluctantly walked to the back room and returned shortly with a map that also had information about the US on it. She handed it to Emberly who promptly looked through it.

Apparently, they were in the tiny town of Traiet, one so small that most maps wouldn't waste their time including it.

Luckily, they were headed in the right direction. But while they had already walked for what seemed an eternity from the twin's perspective, it hardly looked that way on the map. It looked as if they'd hardly even moved.

Emberly flipped through the pages once more before turning around to leave. But the women stopped her before she could get any further.

"You have to pay for that you know," she told them, pointing at the pamphlet that was still in Emberly's hand.

"No, we don't," Emberly protested. "Maps are complementary. If I were to take something more valuable than paper, maybe then I'd pay, but I'm not paying for something as simple as a piece of paper with a map on it."

"Well, then I'm just going to have to call the police." The woman reached for the phone, but Emberly held up her hand to stop her.

"Listen, I get that you're running a business here, but you've got to be kidding me. I'm not paying for a piece of paper, and that's final. Besides, the police have better things to worry about than three kids taking a pamphlet."

"Well guess what? They don't," and she reached for the phone again and dialed out. As she waited for her call to connect, she told the three of them to sit down and wait for the police to come.

But Emberly had another plan. She stuffed the map into her pocket and grabbed the twins' hands and bolted out the door. They ran around back and snatched the bow and quiver from the first store and took off down the back alley. The woman tried to run after them, but she was no competition for their young legs. So instead, she yelled at them to stop, but they didn't listen. They just kept running. It was like déjà vu, except without the cheering from their friends. Emberly thought she could hear sirens behind her so she encouraged the twins to run faster.

They left the back alley and made a beeline for the forest; the twins still keeping up. Thistles scrapped their bare legs as they ran. What was a few more scratches to an already thick patchwork of previous scars, scratches, and bruises?

Finally, they stopped when they knew they were in the clear. Emberly sat down on a tree stump to catch her breath and started to pick the thistles off her legs, one by one. Some were painful to remove, especially those that had burrowed into her legs, but it was nothing compared to pain she had felt in the past. Once she was thistle-free, she did the same for Eve and Zayne's legs.

"We need to stop running from people," Zayne chuckled.

"Yeah. That's probably a good idea," Emberly replied with a smile. "Shall we look at the map?"

The twins nodded.

"Based on this, it looks like we're going in the right direction, so that's a bonus. I think we should continue north until we reach Connecticut. From there we can chart our path forward." Emberly bent down to look at the moss on the tree to find their bearings. She pointed north and they were off once again.

The sun had softened, and the wind had died down, which helped keep them cool as they walked. So far, the day had been a little more adventurous than Emberly had initially planned it to be, but she was beginning to expect that it would be the norm from then on.

The rolling hills provided a different kind of challenge for their endurance. Some hills were quite steep and had a longer ascent, making for a much harder climb. But Emberly reminded herself of when she was little and was learning to ride her bike; whenever she had to bike up a steep hill, her dad would always tell her, "Whatever goes up, always has to come down at some point," and he was always right.

Eventually the Cloves stopped because sky was darkening. Eve shimmied the bag off her shoulders and unzipped the compartment that held their food. She reached in and pulled out a sleeve of crackers and a water bottle. There were twelve crackers in total, meaning everyone got four and a bit of water. Emberly's stomach growled in hunger as she began nibbling on her first cracker. She knew this would not be enough to calm the hunger pains, but she forced it to make do with the portion she had. It would have to be enough for now.

"Before it gets dark, I'm going to go and find us something a little more filling to eat," she added as she grabbed the bow and arrow.

"And we can start a fire while we wait," Eve replied.

"Great idea," Emberly smiled.

She walked down the nearest slope, making sure to be quiet to not scare off any animals. She heard some rustling in a nearby bush and crouched down to listen. A squirrel jumped out from the bush. As quietly as possible, she positioned the arrow on her bow and drew the arrow back. She remained perfectly still as she tried to remember the things her dad had taught her. Pull the string tight to your lips. Deep breath in, aim, relax your fingers, then on an exhale, release.

The arrow sailed through the air, but made contact with the tree directly beside the squirrel, causing it to dart away. Emberly chased after it, but it was no use. The squirrel was too fast and Emberly was too tired. She went back to the tree to retrieve her arrow. She was so disappointed in her miss. She never missed. But she also hadn't shot an arrow in seven years, and her dad's bow was too big for her, so its balance was off. She needed more practice and to get used to its weight.

Emberly aimed at a particularly skinny tree about twenty feet in front of her, and shot the four arrows. The first one just missed the tree, almost scraping the bark as it shot by, but the others all made contact. Granted, they had hit in three different spots, and one was a little too high for her liking, but at least they had made contact. Emberly ran to retrieve the arrows then walked back to where she had originally knelt and took aim again.

Emberly didn't stop practicing until she was successfully able to hit the tree with all four arrows and have them land close enough to her intended target. Then she went back to hunting for food. The last thing she wanted was to go back to the twins empty-handed.

Before long, Emberly managed to hit and kill a rabbit. Although she felt a small pang of guilt, she knew it was the only way to survive.

Holding the rabbit in one hand, and the bow in the other, Emberly walked back to where the twins had started the fire. In the distance, she noticed something she hadn't noticed before. Emberly peered through a gap in the bushes and at the base the valley she saw a house, a large house. The setting sun made the house look like it was on fire.

It wasn't a modern house—more likely something you would have seen in the 1800s. However, it was magnificent. The house stood over three stories tall and had beautiful, lush green vines covering its exterior. The front door was guarded by a set of eagle statues that Emberly could only assume were coated in gold because of their reflection from the sun.

The lawn was equally as immaculate as the house. The grass was cut into a spiral-shaped pattern, and the perfectly trimmed hedges seemed to not have a single leaf out of place. And the garden was as big as the one she assumed to be at Buckingham Palace.

Emberly's eyes travelled around to the barn that sat across the yard. It was less extravagant than the house, but still well taken care of. Emberly looked to the two rows of windows that ran along the side of the barn, indicating it to have a loft. Then she noted that it was closer to the forest than it was to the house, and she got an idea.

She took off running in the direction of the twins. She reached them in no time, out of breath, placed the rabbit down and spoke excitedly.

"Okay, when I was coming back, I found a massive house," Emberly gasped out. "Our house could have fit in there thirty times over I bet. Anyways, their barn is close to the forest, and I think that if we wait until all the lights are out, we can sneak in there undetected and spend the night." Emberly could barely contain her excitement at the prospect of a warmer place to sleep.

"Em, we've ran from people two days in a row, I don't know if that's such a good idea," Eve pointed out and Zayne nodded in agreement.

"It will be fine. We'll sneak in after dark. Plus, I don't feel like sleeping in the open tonight. Do you?"

"We did yesterday," Zayne reminded her.

"Yes, but it was under a shelter and on a beach that we had been to before. That doesn't count. That's called camping. And since when are you not on my side, Zayne?"

Zayne looked at her and chuckled, "It would be nice to sleep in the barn...even for one night," he agreed. "I'm with Emberly on this one. Sorry, Eve." Eve gave him the stink eye and looked back at Emberly who smiled pleadingly at her. Knowing she was out numbered, Eve gave in.

"Fine," she sighed. "But expect an 'I told you so' if this turns into us running away from people again," she added. But Emberly and Zayne just cheered.

After gnawing on the cooked rabbit, they made their way to the forest line nearest the barn and stayed hidden in the bushes until it was dark enough to sneak in. Emberly could hear people inside the barn so they kept quiet. The animals made very little noise, which made Emberly much less concerned about them during the night.

Finally, the workers left and the barn was quiet. "I'll scope out the barn first," Emberly said. "You guys wait here until I tell you it's okay to come in."

The twins nodded

Emberly slowly crept alongside the wooden frame of the barn and looked at the door. The lock on it was pretty basic so would be easy enough to pick. Emberly looked around for a leaf with a sturdy stem. One of the kids in her class had once picked a lock to their classroom using only a leaf, so she knew it could be done. Emberly inserted the leaf's stem into the lock and maneuvered it around until she heard the lock pop open. She slowly pushed the door open, making sure to not make any noise and peered inside.

The barn was completely quiet; not even the animals made a noise. Emberly made her way through the barn, searching for any remaining workers. The light that shone through the windows provided her enough light to move around without knocking into anything. She finished her search and deemed it safe. She made her way back to the twins and ushered them inside. Emberly walked in first, with the twins following close behind. They managed to make their way through the barn and up the ladder to the loft without making a single noise.

They found a pile of hay in the very back corner of the loft and set their stuff down. They grabbed an old horse's blanket that was hanging on a rack near the stairs and placed it atop the hay. It wouldn't be the comfiest thing to lay on, but it would do for the night. The three of them snuggled up under the red blanket they got from Imani and Amilia to keep warm. Emberly kissed each of the twins on their forehead and looked up at the barn roof and thought to herself, *this might just actually work out.*

CHAPTER FOURTEEN

EMBERLY'S EYES SLOWLY OPENED and she stretched. She felt
more rested after a night of sleeping on hay than she had the
entire time they'd spent at the foster home. Emberly sat up and
allowed her eyes to adjust to the still-dark light. Based on the
colour of the sky, dawn was a couple hours away. She knew
she'd have to wake the twins soon so they could escape before
anyone found them, but they could have a few more minutes
of sleep at least.

Emberly rubbed her face in her hands and reached up to
tame the wisps of hair that had escaped her braids. But as she
turned her head to the side, she saw a figure—a boy—sitting in
the corner of the barn, watching her. Panic set in. She wasn't
sure how to react. Surely screaming for help wasn't the right
answer, nor was running. Instead she pressed a finger to her
lips to signal the boy to remain quiet then lifted herself off the
pile of hay, so she wouldn't disturb the twins.

The boy continued to sit on the barrel, completely unfazed
by their presence. He looked to be around her age, maybe a
little older. He calmly ran his fingers through his curly, dark
black hair that was so similar to her own, the gesture giving it a
slightly tousled look. She cautiously inched closer so she could
make out his features. His dark, hazelnut skin reminded here

so much of Imani; the thought bringing back a familiar ache of loss in her chest. The boy's confident manner and closed expression gave little in the way of what he was thinking.

She narrowed her eyes at the boy. He smiled in response.

So far, he seemed harmless enough, but she knew she needed to be careful.

His clothes were fancy and looked expensive. Perfectly fitted. Ironed and pressed to perfection. Not one visible wrinkle could be seen. Emberly resisted the urge to run her hands on her shirt to try to smooth out the long worn-in wrinkles. She would not be made nervous by this boy. She was Emberly. Her name meant fire. She had been through worse and faced enough in her time to not back down now. She lifted her chin high, stretched herself as tall as she'd go, and kept walking towards the boy.

He must live in the big house, she decided. He looked too clean and well-dressed to be one of the workers. As Emberly drew close, the boy stood up as well. He towered over her. He must have been close to six feet tall.

"I've never met you before. Are you kids of one of the workers?" he asked. His vibrant blue eyes kept contact with Emberly's.

Emberly wondered if she'd be able to lie her way out of this one. She'd hate to prove Eve right by having to run from people a third day in a row.

"Um, yes. We slept here the night because..." she tried to think of a logical lie, and said the first thing that popped into her mind, "mom's car broke down, so she walked home, but poor Lily and Jason were too tired," she said using fake names as she pointed to the twins. Just in case they did have to run, she didn't want to risk giving away their real names.

"Oh, is your mom Heather or Merida?"

This boy asked way too many questions.

"Merida," Emberly replied. But her confidence in getting away with the lie was shattered when the boy broke out in laughter. She looked over to the twins to make sure they were still asleep. Eve began to toss and turn, but Zayne remained still. She turned back to the boy and punched him in the arm. "Shut up. You'll wake the twins," she snapped.

"Oh, I don't want to wake the 'twins' now do I," he put the word twins in air quotes.

"What are you talking about?"

"There's no worker here named Merida, and I bet those aren't even your siblings," he continued to laugh. Emberly was not the least bit pleased.

"They are my siblings, and how dare you accuse me of lying," she quietly seethed. He just smiled and patted a spot in the hay beside him as he sat down. Emberly remained standing in front of him. Did he really expect her to fraternize with him after he just made her look like an idiot? "What do you want from me?"

"Nothing. Just an explanation."

"Of what? I have nothing to say," she crossed her arms and gave him a cold stare.

"Yes, you do. Because if you don't tell me why you're in my barn, I can very easily tell someone and you could get in some serious trouble. So, which one is it?" he smiled mischievously. Emberly rolled her tongue over her teeth, with her lips closed in disgust. He smiled, and she rolled her eyes. He was a menace.

"Fine," she spat. "We came from East Granby. We ran away from our foster home two days ago and needed a place to spend the night. So, if you don't mind, we will be on our way," she went over to where the twins were sleeping and woke them up. All the while fully aware of the boy's eyes on her.

While her back was turned, he picked up her bow and started to examine it. But when Emberly turned around and saw him holding it, she ran over to him and snatched it from his hands. "That's mine, don't touch it," she hissed through her teeth. He smiled once again, and she rolled her eyes.

"You know if you do that enough, your eyes will get stuck like that," he smiled.

"And did you know that if you don't stop smiling, your cheek will burst into flames," she snapped back.

"Don't tell on us please," Zayne begged in a small voice.

The boy smiled and bent down to be at Zayne's height, "I promise, little man." He had gotten much too close to her baby brother for Emberly's liking.

"Don't make a promise you can't keep it," Emberly warned the mysterious boy.

"What makes you think I can't keep it?"

"I don't trust anyone unless it's my family. You'll learn that some day. Everyone does." Emberly grabbed Eve and Zayne's hands and held tight. They all stared at the boy, and he stared back at them.

"Look, I promise I won't tell. But...can I come with you?" he asked breaking the uncomfortable silence. Emberly's eyes went wide in shock. This boy was crazy. She didn't know him—did he seriously expect her to let him travel with them?

"Um, no. I don't even know your name, and even so, I still wouldn't let you come. I know nothing about you," she turned to grab her backpack but was stopped by the boy's voice.

"Sam. My name is Sam Prime. There. Now we're one step closer," he continued to smile. His constant smiling and cheery attitude were starting to annoy Emberly. "I like to read, and I want to live in a castle when I'm older." Emberly rolled her eyes. He already did live in a castle. "And I live here, close to the town of Woodstock."

"Answer these two questions," she held two fingers up. "Why do you want to come? And what's in it for us?"

"Well, my dad is shipping me off to boarding school in Switzerland for starters. I don't want to go, but apparently, that's not an option—not when it's the 'finest school for young men and where he went when he was my age," he added in a sarcastic tone. "I'm supposed to leave today. The reason I came to the barn so early was that I wanted to say goodbye to my horse before I have to leave at five. And you're lucky it was me instead of someone else, because if it was any one else, you would be in an entirely different situation. One that most likely involved the police." Emberly tried to ignore Eve's elbow to her side.

"And number two," he continued, "I'm going to guess that you're trying to escape, most likely to Canada. Unless you are wanting to go visit Boston's Museum of Fine Art," he smirked and Emberly scuffed in annoyance. "You're trying to escape from here or wherever you came from to begin with. My cousin lives in Toronto, and unless you had a way to go about crossing, he could help us cross the border." Emberly just wanted to punch that smug look right off his face.

"I still don't trust you," Emberly shook her head. "Also, what happens when your parents find out you didn't make it boarding school?"

"Umm, I don't know. I didn't really think about that," Sam admitted.

"Of course, you didn't think about it," she scuffed and Eve tugged her away from Sam, to talk privately.

"We need him. You realize that, right?" Eve told her.

"No, we don't. We can figure out how to cross the border when we get there. I'm not asking some stranger for help, and I am definitely not bringing him along with us. Not to mention, based on his fancy clothes, there's a good chance he's never stepped foot in a forest, let alone lived in one."

"Em, he is literally surrounded by a forest."

"You know what I mean, Eve."

"Well, I don't care what you say. You're tired, hungry, and not thinking straight. We need him to help us or we might die."

Emberly pondered the decision. She still wasn't sure if she could trust him, but the faint neighing of a horse brought back the sudden memory of the dream she'd had at Ms. Margot's. The horses, the barn, the boy standing in the corner. It was almost exactly as it had been in her dream. Emberly looked back at Sam. She remembered trusting the boy in her dream. It was almost as if the dream had been a premonition of a future path she'd need to take.

She walked over to him and stuck out her hand. But as he went to reach for it, she pulled it away.

"Don't make me regret this. You so much as sneeze wrong, I will make you wish you had left for that boarding school, got it?" Emberly stretched out her hand again. Sam grabbed hold of it and shook. His ocean-blue gaze locked eyes with her and for a moment, everything stood still. Then he blinked, breaking the power of the moment.

Emberly pulled her hand away and grabbed her things. *Now is definitely not the time to be thinking of the colour of his eyes*, she chastised herself. She turned and saw that he was still watching her. She gave him the stink eye, "Are you just going to stand and watch, or are you going to do something useful?"

"Well, I was waiting for you to tell me what to do," he explained. Emberly knew that he was only trying to butter her up, which—and she wouldn't admit this to anyone—made her want to smile, but she wasn't going to give him the satisfaction.

"Well, at least you realize who's in charge here. That's step number one. Step two is getting a backpack and some clothes from your house. Nothing too fancy since most of our time will be spent outside. Some more food would also be great since we're beginning to run low. And anything else you can grab that would be helpful; matches, knives, and money if possible."

"I'm on it, Captain," Sam saluted her. She rolled her eyes. She was beginning to sense a trend. He laughed and left the barn. Emberly turned back around to face the twins.

"New rules, so listen up. We do not know this boy. Meaning, keep an eye on him at all times, and neither of you are to be left alone with him. You must stick together. Am I clear?"

The twins nodded firmly.

"Good. Now let's get ready to leave."

Sam returned a short while later and held up his bag, "I have everything. That is except the money. My father locks every dollar bill that ever enters the walls of our house up in the vault and only he knows the code." Emberly sighed but knew he was telling the truth. She noted that he'd also changed into a plain t-shirt and pair of shorts. They still looked nicer than anything Emberly had ever owned, but at least he wasn't wearing his fancy clothes any longer.

He opened the bag so Emberly could inspect what he had grabbed. She found nothing but what she'd asked him for. At least he had listened.

"Now what?" Sam asked.

Emberly went to open her mouth, but Eve cut her off wagging her finger at Sam, "Now, you go back to your house and say goodbye to your mom and dad." Emberly gave Eve a questioning look; that was nothing like what she was about to say. "We never got to give goodbyes to ours, so you have to," Eve continued.

Sam gave her a small smile, "I think I can manage that."

"I told you to stay quiet," Emberly hissed after Sam had left. "We should be long gone by now. We're wasting precious time."

"It doesn't matter. He may not see his mom and dad for a long time. I wish we could have hugged mom to say goodbye.

Sam needs to say goodbye." Emberly hated it when Eve was right.

Shortly after, Sam returned with a sad look on his face. Emberly truly felt sorry, but they had no time to stop and console him. They needed to go. They grabbed their gear then crept down the stairs and towards the barn door. Emberly poked her head out to check for people. The coast was clear. Sam inched the door open enough for them to squeeze out. They quickly rounded the barn and ran into the forest.

They spent the first part of the day walking, stopping only to briefly rest or to scarf down some food. Eve and Zayne were at the front of the pack, followed by Sam, and then Emberly. She still wanted to keep an eye on him.

As the day progressed, Emberly watched as animals came out to play. Squirrels scurried by, birds sang to them from their nests, and the odd deer cautiously questioned their presence from distant bushes as they passed.

The air was soft and calm, and the leaves covered the towering trees and created a leafy canopy for the four of them to walk under.

"Hey, thanks for letting me come," Sam later told Emberly as he slowed so he could walk beside her.

"Don't thank me. Eve made me." She kept her head straight and eyes focused.

"We both know that Eve doesn't control you. No one does. You decided to let me stay all by yourself," he looked at her with a friendly grin that Emberly returned with an annoyed sigh.

"What are you, my therapist? I don't need your free advice. The only reason you're here is that Eve said it was the nice thing to do, and I knew you could provide us with more food."

"No, *you* allowed me to come because there was a part of you that knew you could trust me."

"I already told you, I don't trust anyone who is not my family."

They walked in silence after that. His theory had soured her mood. The same pale blue sky and the animals flitting about the forest were no longer amusing to watch. Everything began to blend into an unchanging scene of nature.

That was, until Emberly heard the sound of rushing water nearby. The noise grew louder, as she quickened her pace. The others were not far behind when they reached a clearing and the source of the noise. It was more magnificent than anything she had ever seen. A waterfall, glistening in the summer sun, leaving them speechless.

The sun was still high enough in the sky that they had plenty of time left in the day to walk. It would be nice for the twins to enjoy the water, and Sam looked like he needed a break. Even she was amused by the idea of spending some time in the water.

"Come on," she said. "Let's take a break."

Sam laid down on a patch of grass, and the twins ran to the water. Emberly sat beside Sam and watched the twins splash and laugh in the sparkling water.

"I didn't think you were capable of laughter," Sam joked. She ignored his ignorant comment and kept her gaze fixated ahead, at the waterfall. It was beautiful. Emberly watched as the water cascaded over the ridge at the top and landed on the rocky surface before making its way down to the lake below, splashing up droplets of water as it made contact. Water sprayed the twins as they climbed the rocky walls of the waterfall. She smiled. She could sense Sam staring at her but she didn't care. He could stare all he wanted.

"What's wrong with you?" Sam asked. Emberly eyes widened.

"That was harsh," Emberly replied offendedly.

"Sorry, that came out wrong. What I meant to ask was why are you out here, on your own? You said you ran away from your foster home, but why?" Sam turned to face her.

Emberly let out a sigh and turned to him. Whether she liked it or not, they were going to be spending lots of time together, so it wasn't a bad idea to get to know each other a little.

"Well, we used to live in East Granby, until our mom died. We left the next day for a foster home just outside of Hampton. There were seven kids there. I was the oldest. The woman who ran the foster home was horrible to all of us. Some things happened, the other children were sent away, and now here we are."

"Did anybody tell you that you are a terrible storyteller?" Sam chuckled, and Emberly couldn't help but laugh. But his laughter soon morphed into a bright smile. Sam looked at Emberly closely and tilted his head. "And what caused this?" he went to touch her fresh scar that ran along the side of her face, but Emberly pulled away before he could reach it.

"It's nothing," she shook her head and focused straight ahead again.

"It's not nothing. Tell me what happened," he pestered.

"Get your nose out of my business, okay? It doesn't concern you." She was starting to get aggravated. "I've told you enough for one day."

"Fine. Fair enough. But my dad used to tell me that it is better to get it out rather than bottle it up."

It was not his place to tell Emberly what she should or shouldn't do. She turned to face him, a look of fury in her eyes, "I'm a private person. I don't need you or anyone else knowing the details of my past or what I've been through. We've been through hell! I don't tell people things because..." She clamped her mouth shut to stop the word vomit before she unintentionally shared too much.

Emberly turned towards the waterfall. She had just met this boy and yet she had come so close to telling him about her life. She was definitely crazy, hungry, or delusional.

She got up and took a deep breath before she reached for her bow.

"Get up. We're going hunting." she ordered Sam.

Sam stared in confusion. He realized he wasn't going to get anything else from her, so he better obey, "And here I thought that thing was just for show," Sam said, pointing at the bow in her hand.

"Yeah, because I brought a fake bow to the forest to impress the wildlife," she replied sarcastically, rolling her eyes again. This chemistry between them was real. Comfortable.

He gave her a short laugh and found his legs. Emberly called to the twins, telling them they would be back, and walked into the forest with Sam.

They walked deep into the woods, where the trees blocked out all wind and outside noises. Emberly held onto her bow, with the quiver draped over her shoulder. They got to a small clearing in the forest, and Emberly pulled Sam down to crouch behind a bush.

They waited motionless, until they heard a light rustling in the bushes. Emberly grabbed an arrow from her quiver and began to focus. A rabbit popped out of the bushes and wiggled its tiny nose. Sam watched her intently. Emberly notched her arrow and drew the bow string back. They continued to wait patiently. The rabbit timidly approached a patch of thicker grass and started nibbling.

Sam's gaze finally turned to the rabbit, and Emberly closed her eyes. She smelt the fresh air around her as she breathed deep, reopened her eyes and released the arrow. It went soaring through the air and hit the rabbit. The small animal lay motionless on the ground.

When they arrived back at the waterfall, the twins were sitting on the rocks, waiting impatiently. As Emberly was still relatively new to the whole "skinning animals" thing, Sam offered to take care of it. He said his grandpa used to take him hunting a lot and had shown him. Emberly was happy to not have to skin another furry creature.

They started a fire and placed the rabbit on the crackling flames. Emberly admitted that even she was impressed by Sam's ability to quickly skin and clean the rabbit.

Eve and Sam stayed by the fire to cook, giving Zayne and Emberly the chance to lay down on the rocks near the water to get a little rest from their days spent wandering the woods. The past three days had been long and tiresome, and filled with odd occurrences. Most of it still seemed like a weird dream to Emberly. She sat up and dangled her legs in the cool water as she watched the water fall over the rocky ledges.

The entire scene was mesmerizing. Tiny whirlpools formed at her feet as the water rushed from the waterfall. The reeds near the shore staggered in the breeze, while leaves fluttered down from the trees above. The wind was strong enough to blow some of her hair out of her braids, but not strong enough to wipe the smile from her face.

*Maybe this won't be too bad,* she told herself as she smiled up at the sky.

CHAPTER FIFTEEN

THEY HAD BEEN WALKING for days and were running out of food. They hadn't come across any more towns, and Emberly hadn't been able to kill anything for days. They were down to their last three protein bars.

Emberly's hunger pains were constant which made it difficult to sleep. After one particularly large growl, Emberly opened her eyes and realized she was laying on something soft. She looked up and saw Sam peering down at her. Her eyes went wide, and she shot up and slapped him in the face. He groaned and held his face.

"What are you doing?" Emberly screamed at him.

"You fell asleep in my lap after we switched night shifts. I didn't want to wake you," Sam replied, trying to defend his case. He continued to hold his face in his hand. "Why did you hit me?"

"Why were you watching me?"

"I already told you. You fell asleep, and I didn't want to move you."

"So? That doesn't mean you have to watch me!" she yelled at him, startling the twins awake.

"Okay, I hear you. I'm sorry for creeping you out," he took his hand off his face and stood up. "Let's get moving then."

It didn't take Sam long to realize he was never going to win an argument against Emberly.

It had been more than a week and Emberly still didn't know how she felt about Sam. Some days he was fine, like the day at the waterfall. But then there were days when he pulled stupid stunts like this. Stunts that caught her off guard.

They marched through the woods as the sun slowly rose above the tree line. Sticks cracked under their feet and bushes cut at their legs. But they were used to that at this point. The cuts and bruises didn't hurt anymore. Nothing did at that point. Not a wasp sting or a branch to the face. It was all a regular occurrence now.

They were nearing the colder part of September, so there were days where it was so windy you couldn't stand up straight. This was one of those days.

The trees blocked the wind slightly, but not enough. It pushed and pulled them in all directions and made it hard to stay on track. It took double the energy and they had little energy with no food in their stomachs. She never wanted the twins to be hungry, so any time they had food to eat, she would only eat half of her portion so the twins could have more food. Emberly was starving and getting weak. She couldn't handle it any longer. Without notice, she collapsed.

Sam gasped and tried to grab her before she hit the ground.

"Emberly!" Zayne cried.

"Emberly?" Sam asked frantically. "What happened? Are you okay?"

Emberly looked up at him with confusion in her eyes. She shook her head and tried to stand up, but could not.

"Don't try to stand up. Just rest for a bit," Sam told her.

"Don't tell me what to do," Emberly stubbornly mumbled back.

"Oh good. I thought you'd hit your head and it knocked the stubborn out. You scared me for a second," Sam replied sarcastically.

She rolled her eyes and stood up with the help of a nearby tree, "I'm fine. Let's just keep going. Okay?"

They shrugged their shoulders and walked on.

She knew she should probably stop for a longer break, but no amount of sitting would ease her hunger pains, and Emberly knew she wasn't the only one feeling them. So, despite feeling weak, the best thing she could do was to power through and hopefully get somewhere they could find some food. And so, she walked and tried to focus only on the steps she took, and not the gnawing in her stomach.

The walk felt like it went on forever. The hills became higher and the slopes steeper. Emberly struggled to get up them. She constantly fell but refused to let anyone help her up.

Sam kept looking back at Emberly to see if she was doing alright. They continued to walk but it just became too much. She collapsed to the ground again, unable to do more than twitch her fingers. She lied on the ground, helplessly.

"Do you need help now?" Sam asked, tilting his head in a way that made Emberly want to punch him again.

She continued to look at him but gave up trying to be mad, "Yes," she huffed.

Sam picked her up, carried her over to a nearby tree stump and set her down. Emberly took a few deep breaths but was still very light headed.

"Are you okay?" Sam asked, concern for Emberly etched across his face.

Emberly couldn't even muster the strength to nod her head. The twins were standing a few feet away from her, unsure what to do. Emberly didn't want them to worry. She was supposed to be the one worrying about things, not them worrying about her. She looked Sam in the eyes, nodded her head and gave him a weak smile.

He held her rough, dirt-covered hands as she tried to stand up, but just ended up toppling forward into his arms. Sam helped her sit back on the ground so she could rest against the tree stump, "I'm going to go see if there's anything up ahead. Somewhere we can find some food. You stay here. I'll be right back." Sam said as he sprinted away.

Eve and Zayne sat next to their sister. Zayne placed his head on Emberly's shoulder, and Eve held her sister's hand.

"Everything will be fine guys. I promise," Emberly told her siblings. They stayed like that until Sam came back.

"There's an abandoned house just up ahead. Maybe there's some food in there. If not, at least it can be a place to rest for a little bit," he said.

Emberly went to open her mouth, but Sam interrupted her, "And before you say 'we don't need a break', I'm going to remind you that you just collapsed two times and can hardly keep your eyes open. So yes, you do need a break," Sam gave her a grin.

Emberly raised one eyebrow, but even that action held no zap.

Sam walked over to her and bent down, but Emberly stuck her hand out to stop him, "What are you doing? I can walk. I'm fine."

Sam looked at her with his eyebrows raised up into his hair. He smiled in pure enjoyment and stepped aside. She stood up no problem and gave Sam an "I told you so" look before taking a step. And of course, fell to the ground again. The twins ran over to help their sister up.

Emberly hung her head low, a look of defeat on her face. She hated feeling weak. But Sam lifted her chin and gave her a look. It wasn't a look of passion nor pity. But a look of a friend that knew when another needed help. He turned to stand in front of her with his back to her and bent down. Then he helped her as she jumped on his back.

Emberly wrapped her arms around his neck. For that moment, she felt safe.

A short while later, they were at the old, abandoned house. "We're here," Sam announced.

The house was even more run-down than Ms. Margot's. Sam set Emberly down and went to test the door handle. "It's locked. I'll check in the little shed behind the house to see if I can find anything to pry the door open with."

He returned a few minutes later with a flat-head screwdriver.

Confused, since the hinges were on the inside of the doorframe, Emberly asked, "What's that going to do?"

"Just watch," he replied as he pushed the screwdriver into the lock. Sam gave it a couple of twists, and to Emberly's surprise, the lock magically opened.

Once they were in, they helped Emberly to the couch, ignoring her insistence that she could walk there herself. The three of them left Emberly alone on the couch to go search for anything that could be of help to them.

With nothing better to do, Emberly scoped out the room. The house—or small cabin which was a more apt description—wasn't as bad on the inside, despite its rundown appearance on the outside. It was relatively clean with a few pieces of furniture scattered about; the couch, a wooden rocking chair, and a coffee table. Emberly turned to the wall with the fireplace. The moose head mounted above the mantel and a few photos of guys holding up various dead animals sitting on top of it were the only decorations. *Must be used more as a hunting lodge,* she assessed.

There was no electricity, which made sense considering they were in the middle of the woods. The walls had no major gaps in them which kept the wind and chill out. Emberly supposed it would be quite cozy once you lit a fire. She mustered up the strength to push herself off the couch and walked over to the fireplace and mantel to take a closer look. She reached out and grabbed one of the frames to look at the picture of the hunter kneeling beside the carcass of a dead moose. She rolled her eyes and continued holding the frame as she knelt down to get a closer look at the fireplace. She reached out her hand to touch the log but instantly pulled her hand back.

Her heart stopped.

It was still warm. Which meant that the house wasn't abandoned and the owners could be home any second. And judging by their moose head and photos, they were not the type to be happy to find four random strangers looting their house.

Emberly's heart was racing as she jumped up from the ground, suddenly finding her strength. Sam heard her and came over asking what was wrong. All she did was point to the fireplace with fear in her eyes and he knew exactly what she meant.

They quietly called for the twins, who came rushing into the living room carrying armfuls of food. They quickly stuffed everything into Sam's bag, including the frame, but they weren't quick enough. The hair on the back of Emberly's neck rose when she heard multiple voices outside. They zipped up the bag and grabbed their stuff. She looked around for an escape path, and found something that could work.

Emberly dragged Sam and the twins to a nearby closet and just managed to close the doors as the men entered the house and asked why their door was unlocked.

They stood in the closet in complete silence. Emberly's heart was beating out of her chest. She didn't know what would happen if someone found them. They were obviously hunters, which meant they likely had guns and knives. Emberly held onto the twins with all her might, and Sam wrapped his arms around the three of them.

The closet was cramped, and something was digging into Emberly's back. She reached back to feel the cold metal of a gun barrel. She turned her head and saw what was hanging on the wall behind. This was where they kept their guns, and assuming they had gone out to hunt, any minute now those men would open this closet to put their guns away.

Emberly's heart rate elevated further when she heard a set of angry voices coming from just outside the closet door.

"Where did all of our food go?" one asked.

"I don't know, but it was all there when we left," another replied.

This was it. It wouldn't be much longer until they opened the closet door. Emberly whispered into the others' ears, "The second they open this door, we run."

They nodded, and waited.

And finally, their time came. The doorknob twisted and the closet door opened. The man on the other side stopped when he saw the kids standing inside. He turned his head to call for the others, but Emberly used that as her cue and pushed him as hard as she could, knocking him to the floor. They bolted out of the front door, just barely avoiding another man that tried to grab them.

Emberly turned her head and saw five middle-aged men chasing after them with guns in their hands.

They ran as fast as they could, but they could hear the men closing-in. At this point, it was only her adrenaline that kept her going.

The sounds of pursuit grew quiet, and Emberly thought perhaps that they had lost them. But without notice, a shot rang out and a bullet hit the tree to left of Sam's head.

"I suggest you stop running," one of the men shouted.

The four of them stopped and turned to face the men. All five of them.

"Well, well, well. Look what we have here. A couple of thieves," one of the men said.

Emberly swallowed hard. She went to hold onto the twin's hands, but only ended up finding one. She looked to Zayne's face and saw it flush with worry as he stared at a spot behind where the men were standing. Emberly followed his gaze and spotted a small figure hiding behind a tree. Emberly was relieved when she saw that it was her sister. Eve waved at them and gave her a thumbs up, telling them that she was okay.

"Do y'all know what we do to thieves?" another asked.

Emberly shook her head. The man held up his gun and smiled.

Out of the corner of her eye, Emberly watched in terror as Eve reached down and picked up a rock from the ground. Emberly wanted to call out to her sister to stop her, but she also didn't want to risk any of them getting shot if she said anything. So she watched with a racing heart as Eve threw the rock with all her might behind a nearby bush.

To Emberly's surprise, the rock didn't make a noise when it landed. What did make a noise was a large black bear that had been hiding behind the bush. Emberly realized that Eve hadn't planned to make a noise to distract the men. The bear, had been her intended target.

The bear sprang out of the bush and stood on its hind legs beside the men. Eve, ever so slowly, made a large circle behind the men and made her way over to Emberly. The men fumbled with their guns as they turned to face the black bear.

One of the first things that Emberly's dad had taught her, when they were hiking in the woods, was to never run away or to try to frighten a black bear. It was best to remain calm until the bear hopefully walked away. But these men, who were startled by its sudden appearance and nearness to them, had obviously forgotten that critical point and turned and ran. To no one's surprise, the bear chased after them. Once the bear was far enough away and distracted by the men, the four of them turned and ran.

They ignored the sounds of gunshots, the shouts of the men, and the roaring of the bear and ran as fast and hard as they could. Even against a bear, the five men still had better odds with their guns. It was only a matter of time before they stopped the bear and went back to chasing the kids.

Knowing they could only go so far, Emberly made a sharp beeline towards a massive beech tree. She motioned for Sam and the twins to follow.

"We need to climb this tree," she whispered. "We'll be able to see better from up there, and if we can get high enough, it's leafy branches will keep us hidden. We can stay up there until nightfall or when we know they're no longer chasing us."

Sam looked hesitantly at the tree, "I—I don't know how to," he replied.

Emberly looked at him, "How to what, climb a tree?" Sam nodded in response.

"What? But your house was surrounded by trees. How did you never learn?"

"Scared of heights," he replied simply. "Plus, my dad told me I was too clumsy to climb trees without falling out and breaking something in the process."

"Sure," she said, making a mental note to address this at a later time, when they weren't being chased by five maniacs with guns. "Well, I'll help you."

The twins went first to show Sam which branches to grab onto. Sam followed with Emberly pulling up the rear, making sure he was doing it right. They slowly scaled the tree until they reached as high as they could before the branches started to get flimsier. They each positioned themselves on different branches so it would be easier to hide, and to not put too much weight on one branch. They sat quietly as they surveyed the forest floor, keeping an eye out for the men.

Emberly looked at the twins. Both were calm. She looked over at Sam, who was clinging to the tree trunk with all his might. Emberly chuckled softly to herself. There was no way she was going to let this go without making fun of him for it.

They stayed in the tree for hours. Eventually, the sun started to go down and the air grew colder by the second, but still they stayed. Emberly could no longer hear the footsteps of the men underneath, but if she had to guess, they were still out there looking for them. Even if they weren't, Emberly still didn't want to risk the chance. Which meant they were staying the night in the tree.

Emberly tinkered with her bow while Eve and Zayne played Rock, Paper, Scissors. Sam stayed glued to the branch in front of her.

She chuckled again. He gingerly let go of the trunk with one hand to run it through his curly hair. Emberly could tell he was nervous.

"Psst. Sam," she whispered. He looked over at her and gave her a weak smile. "Are you okay?"

"What defines 'okay'?" he smiled.

Emberly rolled her eyes, but a little softer this time, smiled and looked up at the horizon. The weakness in her body had left as she ran for her life, but at that moment, sitting in the tree, it all caught up to her and her head started spinning. Emberly clung to the branch for support and focused on taking deep breaths.

"The better question is, are you okay?" Sam asked.

Emberly nodded, but Sam gave her a tight-lipped smile in return because he knew she was lying.

Eventually, the sun fell below the horizon, but Emberly's eyes stayed glued to the tree before her. She hadn't eaten all day and had slept terribly, just like every night prior. She desperately needed to rest—they all did—but it still wasn't safe to go down yet.

"Eve," Emberly whispered.

Eve looked over to her, "What's up, Em?"

"Take out the rope and cut it in two."

Eve's eyebrows pulled together in confusion, but she reached over to the backpack that Zayne had been carrying and untied the large rope from the outer straps it had been secured to. She carefully cut it in half using the knife Wyatt had Verity had found for them.

"Now what?" she asked.

Emberly motioned for Eve to throw her one of the pieces. She wrapped it twice around the trunk of the tree and her torso, then securely tied the ends together. Eve followed suit with her length of rope.

Emberly pulled hard at the rope, but its knot remained tight. Emberly smiled at her invention.

"Does that mean we're sleeping up here?" Sam asked anxiously.

Emberly shook her head in exasperation, "Yes, Sam. You and Zayne can stay awake first considering you're not going to let go of that branch any time soon," Emberly joked.

Sam scoffed, but they both knew she was right.

"Wake us in a few hours," she leaned her head against the tree trunk and closed her eyes.

That night, Emberly dreamt of a beautiful house. She walked through the monstrous front door, and her nose filled with the delightful smell of freshly baked bread as she followed its scent and entered the kitchen.

She found Eve and Zayne already sitting at a wooden table where a spread of food had been set up. Emberly joined them at the table and began to eat. All thoughts of worry that had been building up melted from Emberly's mind as they enjoyed eating like a family again.

That was, until Ms. Margot burst into the room and grabbed the twins, claiming it was their turn for a Correctional Day. As she watched them being dragged from the room, Emberly's heart pounded in her chest, and feelings of fear, worry, regret, and sorrow came flooding back with a vengeance.

Emberly could hear the cries of her siblings coming from the other room. But when she tried to get up to save them, she couldn't as she was strapped to the chair. Emberly struggled against her restraints. She flailed her body in all directions to try and break free but it was of no use.

Emberly's eyes popped open, and she looked around frantically. She calmed as she realized that it was only a dream. There was no Ms. Margot, no Correction Day for the twins, and the straps that had restrained her were only the piece of rope she had used to tie herself to the tree.

Emberly looked over at Eve who was still fast asleep. She watched as Eve's chest rose and fell, and she smiled knowing that Eve was alright. Then Emberly looked over at Zayne, who gave her a sleepy smile. She knew he needed rest, so she untied herself and threw the rope over to Sam who helped Zayne tie it to the tree.

The movements woke Eve, and once Emberly was sure that she was awake enough to not fall from the tree, Emberly untied her sister and tossed the rope to Sam.

She hadn't failed to notice that Sam's eyes were on her the entire time she was helping Eve, "Can't you look at something else?"

"Why would I?" he smiled.

Emberly made a fake gagging noise, "Go to sleep, Sam," she demanded.

He tied himself to the tree then looked at her once more and smiled before closing his eyes.

Emberly let out a huff. *He is so odd,* she thought. She refused to admit that the smile on her face had anything to do with him.

Eve carefully swung her legs over so she could face Emberly and grinned, "I like Sam."

Emberly chuckled, "I didn't even know you knew what liking someone was."

"Eww...no silly. I like Sam as a *person.* I don't like him, like him. *But,*" she said as she wiggled her eyebrows and looked over at Sam, "I think that you two should date."

Emberly rolled her eyes, "Girl, you're crazy."

"You didn't say 'no'," Eve said with a mischievous look on her face.

"No," Emberly replied with a chuckle. "Is that clear enough for you?"

Emberly chose to ignore Eve's responding laugh and instead turned her head to look at the sky.

She was rarely ever able to look at the stars in Greenville because of the city lights. But out here in the forest, the entire sky was lit up with stars. It was immaculate. Soon, Eve's gaze joined hers and they sat in silence and watched as the stars twinkled to the beat of nature's song. As though the soft chirping of the crickets and the whisper of the wind through the trees were the stars' own private melody.

They stayed like that, gazing at the stars as they moved and carried on their own journey across the night sky, until Emberly knew that dawn was only a couple hours away.

Emberly looked to the ground and found no signs of the men. They hadn't heard anything from them in hours. If they left now they could get a head start and get far enough away before the men started looking for them again.

Zayne, who was finally used to waking up early for chores, slowly began to wake on his own, but when Emberly looked over at Sam, she saw that he was still fast asleep.

"Sam," she whispered from her branch.

Sam's eyes opened, and he let out a sad breath of air, "I was hoping that this was just a nightmare," he whined.

Emberly rolled her eyes, "Welcome to my world, buddy. I've been wishing the same thing for the past three months, but I never wake up from this hellish dream. Best just come to terms with it now," she smiled devilishly.

Sam moaned as he untied his rope from the tree and threw it over to Emberly. She passed it to Eve who tied it back onto their bag.

"What's the plan?" Eve asked.

"I want to be long gone before the men start searching for us again, so we need to leave now—we can eat as we run. But first, I'll go check things out to make sure no one is around. Stay in the tree until I get back."

As quietly as she could, Emberly threw her bow and quiver over her shoulder and climbed down the tree. When she reached the lowest branch, she did a quick scan of her surroundings, looking for signs of anyone before she dropped to the ground.

Emberly stayed crouched and strained her ears to listen for sounds of the men. When she was met with silence, she nocked her arrow and started to walk the perimeter of the large tree. She'd made it almost a full circle when something large landed behind her.

Emberly whipped around and aimed her bow at the intruder.

"Woah, calm down," Sam said as he threw his hands up. "It's just me."

Emberly let out an exasperated sigh and lowered her bow, "What the hell are you doing?" she yelled at him. "I could have shot you. And what are you doing down here anyway? I told you to stay in the tree."

"I came to check on you," he replied innocently.

"Well, I don't need any help—not from you."

Sam just gave her a knowing smile.

Emberly rolled her eyes, "Let's just focus on getting the twins down and getting the hell out of here, alright?"

She motioned for the twins to come down. They reached the ground in record speed and ran over to Emberly and gave her a hug.

Sam shifted to move out of their way, but Eve reached out and grabbed onto his shirt with one hand then wrapped both of her little arms around his waist.

"What's up, Eve?" he asked, a little shocked at her gesture.

"You looked like you needed a hug," she said simply and hugged him tighter.

Zayne rushed over to and wrapped his arms around Sam as well, "That was scary, and you can't tell me that you weren't scared when the guys were chasing us."

"I think I was more scared climbing the tree," Sam joked.

Eve let go of Sam with one hand and opened her other as an invitation for Emberly to join. Then Zayne did the same; and finally, Sam's eyes met Emberly's, his gaze an invitation of his own.

Emberly took a deep breath and walked into their open arms. Her body was stiff as Sam wrapped an arm around her, but as his hold tightened, she could feel her heart opening itself up just a little wider.

Maybe she could grow to trust Sam.

Maybe her heart already had.

## CHAPTER SIXTEEN

IT HAD ONLY BEEN a week since they started their journey through the forest, but it felt like a year to Emberly. They had reached the boarder of Massachusetts only four days before and were making good progress. The wind was becoming harsher by the day, and some days the cold was unbearable. But they kept pressing on. The thought of one day having a house where they could live in peace was what kept Emberly's moving.

Luckily, Emberly had become pretty good with the bow and Sam proved quite useful with fishing, so they managed to find enough food to stave off the worst of their hunger pains. And they often came across rivers or streams which gave them access to fresh water to drink or bathe in. The worst now was the constant walking. Even with the cooler days, the nonstop pace was hard on their bodies.

It was on that day that the grueling pace seemed to finally catch up to them. Emberly started to notice Zayne's pace slowing. He had begun to shuffle his feet along the dirt floor, and his head hung low as he trudged along.

Emberly put a hand on his shoulder, "You okay, bud?"

Zayne looked at her with glazed eyes and nodded. He tried to move around her and keep walking, but she stopped him and knelt to get a better look at him.

His skin was ghostly pale and was covered in a light, waxy sheen of sweat. He looked sick and was most definitely not okay, "You're not fine. Sit down," she ushered him over to a large tree and sat him down beside it.

"Eve, bring me the backpack," she said.

Eve took the bag off her shoulders and walked it over to them. Emberly opened it up and grabbed one of the water bottles. There was only half a bottle left, but they could find more later. Right now, Zayne needed it. She handed it to Zayne, "Here, drink the rest."

Emberly dug back through the bag and managed to find one of the hard candies that the kids had packed for them at the foster home. She unwrapped the candy and handed it to him. Zayne looked confused as to why he was getting extra food, but he reluctantly took the piece of candy and ate it. He wasn't about to pass up candy.

When he didn't look better after drinking the water or eating the sugar, Emberly started to get worried. She looked around frantically for something, but she didn't know what. She was tired and hungry and couldn't think straight.

Zayne started to close his eyes and could barely hold his head up. Emberly's heart started beating faster.

"Emberly, what's wrong with Zayne?" Eve's asked with fear.

Sam, who had been assessing Zayne from the side, came to sit beside him. He tried getting Zayne to talk, but all Zayne could do was look at him with the same glassy expression.

"Zayne will be fine, Eve. I think he just needs some rest and a bit more food," Sam replied to her. But he looked at Emberly with a serious expression in his eyes. He jerked his head and motioned for her to move away from Zayne so they could talk.

"Eve, you stay here with Zayne. Sam and I are going to get some more water at the stream we just passed by. Make sure he doesn't go to sleep though. Tell him stories or jokes to keep him awake until we get back."

Eve nodded, and Emberly grabbed the two water bottles from the bag. Then her and Sam ran back in the direction they had seen the creek.

"Where is it?" she muttered aloud after ten minutes of running. She stopped and listened but heard nothing. Emberly huffed in frustration. She swore it hadn't been that long since they had passed it.

"We'll find it, don't worry," Sam reassured her as he reached for her hand.

She yanked her hand out of his grasp. It annoyed her how calm he was being, "Let's just keep moving. We can talk when we find the creek."

Sam held his hands up and took a step away, "Okay, fair enough."

They started running again, and thankfully, didn't have to go too much further. They finally came across the creek, and Emberly ran over to the water, with Sam trailing her. She knelt by the water and handed the other bottle to Sam before dunking her bottle into the clear, clean water. She filled it up then drank greedily from it before she dunked it back into the water and filled it up again. She wanted to make sure Zayne had as much water to drink as possible, so she didn't want to drink from the bottle later.

"You done?" she asked as she stood.

"Yes," Sam said as he finished twisting the lid onto his bottle. "But I think he's going to need more than just water, Emberly."

"Why don't we just worry about getting him the water for now, and we can figure out the rest later."

"Emberly, stop for a second and breathe," he said as he gripped both of her arms. "You're not thinking clearly right now. Zayne is probably severely dehydrated, malnourished, and in serious need of proper rest. Water will help, but it won't solve everything. We need to find a town so we can find him some medicine."

"Let go of me," she said as she tried to squirm out of his grasp. "He's my brother—not yours. Don't tell me what he needs."

"Why are you acting like this? I know that he's not my brother, but he is someone I care about."

"I said let go, Sam," she demanded, struggling further. Still, he held tight.

"No, not until you tell me what's really going on. You're worried about your brother, I get it. That's normal. But this is a whole new level. You're completely giving into your fears right now and not thinking with a level head. That's a dangerous thing to do in a situation like this."

"What would you know about dangerous situations," she spit back at him.

Sam looked deep into her eyes. He held her gaze then focused his eyes on her scar, "Zayne told me about your scar last night."

Emberly stilled, "What does that have to do with anything?"

"Look," he said, his tone gentler than before. She hated the look of pity in his eyes, "I know you still have a problem with fully trusting me or whatever, but it's been more than a week and I haven't done anything to you or your family. You can trust me. Just tell me what happened."

"I still don't see how this is relevant to how Zayne's doing. Besides, he already told you anyways. Why do you need me to say anything?"

"Because maybe if you talked about it—actually opened up to someone about it rather than holding it in—it will help you work through whatever emotions have you in such a state of panic and fear right now."

Emberly stayed silent and avoided his gaze.

Sam sighed, "Look, if for no other reason, then do it because it will help you calm yourself," he lifted her chin so her eyes met his. "You know you can't go back to Zayne and Eve in such a state. All you'll do is get them worried. Is that what you want?"

Emberly let go of the breath she had been holding. She knew he was right. One look at her and both the twins would panic.

Emberly took a deep breath, "One day—at the foster home—the seven of us kids actually had a day off and went to spend the day at a lake in the forest behind the house. We had a great time. Actually, it had been the most fun I've had in a long time. But when we got back, we found out that Ms. Margot's mom had died. She was actually pretty sick, and we hadn't even met her because she never left her room, so it was only a matter of time, but still..." Emberly looked Sam directly in the eye and saw that he was genuinely listening.

She took another deep breath and continued, "Well, for some stupid reason, Ms. Margot decided to take her anger out on us, and she started by hitting Eve. Me being me, I got mad and yelled at her. Then, she punched me in the stomach, and I fell to the floor and hit my head. If that wasn't bad enough, she kicked me until I passed out. And one of her kicks' graciously landed on the side of my face and split it wide open. Luckily for me, one of the girls there had experience in stitching up wounds and helped me."

She looked up at Sam, "And now I'm left with this scar as a permanent reminder of the place."

"Zayne only told me that it was the woman's fault. He never told me about the other stuff," Sam looked at Emberly with pity in his eyes. "I'm sorry that happened to you."

Emberly squirmed and broke eye contact with him, "Ya, well that's why I didn't want to talk about it. I know it sucks, okay? I don't need you telling me how sorry you are for me. I'm fine now, am I not?"

"That's not the point. That never should have happened to you."

"No, it shouldn't have, but I only had to deal with it for a little over two months. The other kids had been there for years, and now they're split up and living somewhere else. Who knows what's happening to them now."

Emberly felt a lump form at the back of her throat. She tried to swallow it down and desperately tried to blink back the tears that threatened to spill from her eyes. But one escaped and slid down her cheek. Sam noticed and brought his hand up slowly and wiped her tear away with his finger. She looked at Sam, and a small smile appeared across his lips.

She didn't stop the genuine one that spread across hers.

They returned and found Zayne in the same position as before, with Eve sitting beside him, one arm wrapped around his shoulders.

Emberly reached into the backpack and pulled out the tin of dried chamomile that Imani had packed for them. She opened the water bottle and added some of the flowers into it before handing it to Zayne, "Drink the whole thing, Zayne, okay?"

He nodded and started to drink. Eve stood up and grabbed both of their hands and pulled them away, "Zayne is getting worse, Em. I don't know what to do."

Emberly looked at Sam. He was right before, "I know, Eve. He needs medicine. There's got to be some sort of town close by."

"I thought I saw a road while we were walking," Sam said. "If we follow it, I'm positive it will lead us to a town."

Emberly nodded in agreement, "We'll all go to the outskirts of the town. Eve, you and Zayne will wait for Sam and I there while we go into town to find some medicine." To Sam she added, "Do you think you could carry Zayne, like you did for me the other day?"

If Sam was shocked at her willingness to ask for his help, he didn't show it, "Of course. Anything to help." He bent down and Eve and Emberly helped Zayne climb up on his back.

They found the road then started walking in the direction that Sam thought. Sure enough the dirt road eventually led them to a small town. Sam placed Zayne down on a rock behind a thick bunch of bushes. Eve sat beside him on the ground.

"Don't let him fall asleep, and don't let a single person see you guys. We'll be right back," Emberly told Eve.

"I'll be careful, I promise."

Emberly and Sam walked out of the forest and headed into town. They walked casually down the main road, as if they belonged there. The village was even smaller than Traiet. It had only two small streets.

It didn't take them long to find a store, considering this town only had one store. They walked into the general store. It was, Emberly noted, a lot similar to the one in Traiet. Emberly and Sam split up to look for medicine. It wasn't a big store, but they didn't need to waste any time.

Emberly walked down a few aisles until she found what she was looking for. Sam came around the aisle, and they looked until Emberly found a familiar plastic container. Any time Emberly had a sore stomach, felt sick, or had a headache, her mom would give her one of these pills. They never failed to help.

Emberly looked around, and even though she knew there was a woman at the counter that was watching them over the aisles, she pretended to put the medicine back on the shelf, but stuffed it into her bra. They tried to be as discreet as they could, but they didn't have time to wait for a better opportunity. They needed to get back to Zayne.

She and Sam turned and tried walking from the store as if they had changed their minds and no longer needed anything from the store, but were instantly stopped by a hand on her forearm.

"Hey! I saw you take that!" the woman yelled.

Emberly closed her eyes and took a deep breath. She knew there was no way of getting out of this without a scratch. She slowly turned to face the middle-aged woman.

"I'm sorry but I don't know what you're talking about," Emberly lied, her face a blank, expressionless, canvas. Sam stood still a couple feet behind Emberly and didn't say a word.

"Yes, you do!" the woman continued to yell. "I saw you stuff something down your shirt. If you filthy animals think you're going to get away with it, you thought wrong."

Then she looked Emberly and Sam up and down and rolled her eyes at their filthy clothes and dirt-stained skin in disapproval, "Plus, I don't sell to vagrants. Especially not the dirty ones," she snarled.

Emberly's blood started to boil and her lips twitched. She went to take a step towards the woman to tell her just what she thought about her "vagrants" comment, but Sam held her back and gave her a look that made her stay still.

So instead, she said, "You're mistaken. We didn't take anything, so we'll be going now." She turned to leave but the woman gripped her arm tighter and refused to let go.

Her nails dug deeper into Emberly's skin, and she let out a shriek, "You're not going anywhere."

"You're crazy! Let go of me!" Emberly screamed. But still, the woman wouldn't let go.

"The police are on their way," she snarled. "I called them the second you two walked into my store. I'll let go when they arrive."

Emberly's eyes went wide. She knew she was stuck, so she grabbed the medicine from her shirt and threw it to Sam who fumbled with it in his hands before clumsily dropping it on the floor. He picked it up quicker than he had dropped it and looked at Emberly, "Run! Give it to Zayne," Emberly told him.

Sam took it, the woman already lunging to grab him too.

"Now, Sam!" she pleaded. He took one final look at Emberly then ran from the store. Emberly knew he'd make it to the forest and that he'd take care of the twins.

The police had yet to arrive, so Emberly was hauled to the counter where the woman tied her arms with a scarf. It wasn't tight at all, and Emberly could have easily gotten out, but there was no use. The last thing she wanted was to lead the cops right back to Sam and the twins.

Not long after, a single police officer burst through the front door. A move that was completely unnecessary. He ran, huffing and wheezing, towards Emberly like she had just killed someone and quickly tried to handcuff her hands behind her back.

But Emberly refused to cooperate. She kept moving her hands out of reach of the officer, trying to buy Sam more time, but all that got her more trouble. The officer forcefully gripped onto Emberly's left wrist, making her wince, and yanked her arm back so he could properly handcuff her. He followed form with her other wrist.

With both wrists cuffed, he made her sit on the floor. He walked over to the owner and began to question her. That's when Emberly realized that this man most likely knew nothing about this job. She settled on the conclusion that he was probably just a volunteer, with no formal training and experience.

Once he finished questioning the woman, he led Emberly out of the store. But before they could fully get out the door, Emberly took the opportunity to flip the cashier off discreetly from where her hands were cuffed. She heard the woman scoff from behind her, and Emberly smiled.

"No cop car, hey?" Emberly asked when they got outside. Suddenly, his heavy breathing from before made sense. Emberly guessed that he had likely ran from whatever sorry excuse of a building he called the jail.

"No talking out of you until we get to the station," he replied.

The officer walked Emberly through the small town, as if he were taking her to be executed. His hand gripped tightly around her arm as the two continued through the streets. Emberly swore she saw him puff his chest out as people came out of their houses to see what all the commotion was about. She just rolled her eyes.

Within minutes they arrived at the police station—if you could even call it that. The place was barely bigger than the house she used to live in with her mom and the twins. Emberly looked around. The front room had only two desks, both just barely larger than a school desk. One of which had a police officer sitting at it with his legs resting on the desk, playing a computer game. *Real professional*, she thought. Behind the desks was a tiny room that she guessed was for interrogations. And beyond that was a skinny hallway that likely led to the jail cells. But based on the size of the building, Emberly didn't think there'd be many of those back there.

The police officer that was sitting at the desk when Emberly first walked in stood up and followed them to the small room.

The officers forced her into a chair then each took a seat across the table from her. Her escort from earlier grabbed a note pad and pen, "Ma'am, we'd like to ask you a few questions."

Emberly fought off the urge to roll her eyes. These guys clearly don't get enough action on the force.

Emberly clamped her mouth shut and looked down at the table.

The first man huffed in annoyance. Then the other one asked, "What is your name, ma'am?"

She didn't say anything.

"I said, what it your name?"

Again, she said nothing.

"I will give you one last chance. You tell me your name, or I will have to find it out myself."

Emberly knew he was bluffing. There was no way either of them would have the resources or the ability to figure that out. But he had begun to bother her so she replied, "Maya Roads," she lied convincingly.

"Maya" was the name of one of the girls from her kindergarten class. They had been friends until Maya moved away that summer. "Roads" seemed fitting considering her life had become one big journey the past while.

The man with the notepad wrote it down and nodded at the other to continue.

"What did you steal?" he asked.

"I didn't steal a thing," Emberly replied. Technically, it wasn't her that left the store with the medicine.

"Ms. Ruben told us that you grabbed something from the shelf and gave it to the black boy you were with, and that he ran from the store before she could catch him. Is that true?" Escort asked.

"First of all, you could just have said 'boy'. I'm not sure how the colour of his skin makes a difference in your story. And to be honest, I think Ms. Ruben isn't exactly all there, you know?"

The officer shook his head and stood up, obviously frustrated at the fact that Emberly wouldn't answer any of his questions. The other joined him and they walked into the front room, leaving her alone to her thoughts.

Emberly looked out the window towards the forest. She kept picturing how weak Zayne had looked sitting on that rock.

Emberly had to keep positive that Sam had made it back to the twins—to Zayne—with the medicine. She knew he would take care of them. It was the only thing that gave her a little relief from her current situation.

She continued to look out the window, lost in her thoughts, until the officers returned. Neither said a word. They just each grabbed her by her arms and led her down the hallway to the back corner of the building to where two little jail cells, each the size of a large closet, were located.

Shockingly, one of them was already occupied by a figure laying on the bed facing the wall, so they took her to the empty cell and pushed her in. She stumbled as she regained her balance and turned. They had already locked the door and were walking away, so she sat on the small cot that was on the far side of her cell and looked around. There was a small barred window high above on the back wall, along with a wooden crate in one corner of the cell, that she guessed was meant as a table, and an aluminum bucket in the other. Emberly could only imagine what the bucket was for.

Emberly buried her head in her hands and took a deep breath to calm herself down.

"What am I going to do?" she whispered to herself.

CHAPTER SEVENTEEN

EMBERLY PACED THE FLOOR of her cell, thinking of a plan to escape. She couldn't stay there. The twins needed her. Plus, Sam wouldn't survive a day alone in the forest—even with the help of the twins. She wracked her brain for a way to escape, but nothing came up. She couldn't even pick the lock because there was always someone watching her, and there was nothing for her to use anyways. She huffed and sat on the floor in frustration.

"Why" was the only word going through her mind.

*Why did I do that?*

*Why did I have to be so difficult?*

*Why didn't I just keep my mouth shut?*

*Why didn't I run with Sam?*

Emberly hung her head low as the questions continued to bounce around in her mind. Every bit of the situation felt surreal, but not in a good way.

A little whisper came from her left side, "Hey, girl."

Emberly looked to the other cell and found that her jail mate was now awake and sitting on her cot, wrapped up in a blanket.

Emberly moved closer so she stood right beside the bars that separated them. She looked closer, trying to see who was hidden under the shadows of the blanket and saw that it was a woman. She didn't look very old, maybe twenty-five, but her clothes were in disarray, her hair knotted and she had bags under her eyes. Yet her face was lit with enthusiasm and her green eyes filled with joy, making the other features only noticeable if you studied her face like Emberly had.

The woman flashed a toothy, joyful smile and stuck her hand through the bars, "Hi, there. My name is Arleta."

Emberly smiled timidly and clasped her hand in Arleta's, "Hello back. My name is—" she stopped herself before she said her real name, "Maya."

Arleta winked, "Maya, hey? Well, it's nice to meet you, Maya. What brings you over here to my side of town?" she chuckled.

"I guess I stole something...allegedly."

"Yeah, I heard. Noah there," she said, a little too loudly, as she pointed to Emberly's cop escort, "he abandoned everything when the store called. I've never seen him move so fast. Not even when there's a sale at the bakery in any of the neighbouring communities."

Emberly laughed. She heard the officer watching them grunt in embarrassment, which made her laugh more.

They sat there for a while before Arleta broke the silence and whispered, "So why did you 'allegedly' steal it?"

"Um, I needed to get some medicine for my grandpa who lives in a nearby town," Arleta frowned but didn't say a word. Emberly could tell she knew it was a false story but thankfully she didn't call her out on it. They sat in awkward silence after that until Emberly couldn't stand it anymore.

"Why are you here?" she blurted. Emberly didn't care if her question was inappropriate. She had to know. And, if she was being honest, it was nice getting to talk to someone else.

Arleta looked at her and smiled, then moved to sit closer to Emberly's cell.

"Shall I start from the beginning?"

Emberly eagerly moved closer as well and sat crossed-legged facing Arleta.

Arleta leaned in, "I've been here for just over two weeks now because people don't have brains in this town," she said the last part louder so the cops up front could hear her clearly.

Emberly chuckled, and Arleta continued, "I've lived in this town my entire life. The entire time, nothing's ever changed. People still act as though it were the 1800s. One day, I decided to come out and tell my parents that I was a lesbian. I was never really told anything about being gay or bisexual, or anything of those sorts, because no one here ever says a word about it. I never really knew much about it or what it really meant, only that I kept having feelings for other girls.

"Well, my parents, like most others in this town, were the type that thought that if the word 'gay' was never said aloud, then no one would be gay. So, it was no surprise that anytime I tried talking to them about my feelings, they would just dismiss them completely and tell me I was being ridiculous.

"Finally, one day, I decided to do my own research and figure out what all of it meant. When I knew more, there was no question about it, I was a lesbian. I tried telling my parents again, more confidently this time, and thought they'd have no choice but to listen to me. Unfortunately, instead of having a conversation with me about it, they tried to take me to the church to 'fix me'. Of course, I refused. I knew there was nothing wrong with me.

"But I could tell that they were scared and not ready to move out of living a life of ignorance, so I went along with it. I went to church and let them think they had fixed me, and never spoke of it to them—or anyone—for a long time afterwards.

"I lived that way, in fear of what people thought of me, for another eight years of my life, until I finally got fed up with living a lie. So, I made a plan to come out to the entire town, in a way that my parents and everyone else couldn't possibly ignore. I was nervous as hell. At a town meeting one day, I got up and told the entire town that I was a lesbian. Sure, I may have cussed a few times and yelled quite a bit while doing so, which they *claimed* is why I was brought to jail—disturbing the peace. But we all know why I was really brought here. They thought it was wrong to be a lesbian and were outraged at what I'd so freely admitted.

"Before I knew it, I was dragged out of the town hall meeting and brought here to 'think about my actions.' Which brings us to the present."

Emberly was in shock. She couldn't believe what had happened to this poor woman. Arleta never desired that. She was who she was, no holy water required.

"I am so sorry. That is the stupidest reason to put someone in jail. If it makes you feel any better, you at least have one person on your side in this town," Emberly winked.

Arleta smiled, "Thanks, Maya."

Emberly thought of a part of the story that didn't make sense to her, "Is it even legal to throw you in jail for that?"

Arleta chuckled, "Nope. They even tried to send me to a bigger jail, but when they contacted bigger cities, they said that a misdemeanor like disturbing the peace warranted nothing more than community service or a small fine—it wasn't anything worth being sent to a big prison for. Of course, they won't admit that it was really about the lesbian thing, so they keep pretending that my cussing and yelling was illegal and grounds for 'serious jail time'," Arleta scoffed.

"It does," the man on watch, Dale, interjected as he brought them some water.

"No, it does not," Arleta argued.

"I am a police officer, I would know."

"No, you're not," she shouted to his turned back as he walked away. "You are a volunteer police officer with no official training. You sit pretending you know what you're doing, when in actuality, the police department in Westborough, Massachusetts doesn't even know you exist."

Emberly snorted in an attempt to keep her laughter quiet, but it didn't work and Arleta started laughing as well.

They sat and talked for a while longer, both enjoying each others company. And despite the gravity of the situation, it was the first time in weeks that Emberly was able to just sit and somewhat relax.

Later in the evening, they ate warm, mushy— presumably canned—vegetables with a side of dry bread that the other guard, who Emberly now knew was named Kevin, had brought for them. He had slid the plates under their cell cages and backed off quickly like they were a couple of dangerous criminals. *These guys took this job way too seriously*, she thought.

It shouldn't have taken her long to finish the plate, but Emberly ate it slowly. It was nice getting to eat a warm meal—a full meal—in a clean place. She didn't miss having to eat while sitting on the forest floor or a fallen log, and it was nice being able to use cutlery again. And it was especially nice getting to feel full for a change.

But Emberly sighed. As nice as it was to have these small comforts, she couldn't enjoy them knowing that the others were somewhere out there in the forest—cold, thirsty, and likely hungry—and she had no idea when or if she would ever see them again. The reality of everything began to set in, and the food turned in her stomach.

She couldn't even focus enough to keep a conversation with Arleta, so she eventually grew quiet and just stopped responding.

She was sitting in jail and her family was stuck in a forest. Zayne could be dying or one of the others could have gotten sick for all she knew. Emberly stared at the bars that separated her from the outside world and just sat there. It could have been for only a few minutes, or it could have been hours, but she just stared until she eventually fell asleep.

Emberly's awoke to a particularly deep poke to her ribs. She was still sitting on the ground of the cold and dark cell. She looked and saw Arleta reaching through the bars that separated them.

"Ouch, what was that for?" Emberly whispered.

"I've been trying to wake you," Arleta explained in a whisper.

"Why?" Emberly questioned but Arleta just pointed to the guard and then held her finger to her lips. John's mouth was wide open, and drool was hanging from his chin. Emberly could even hear the faint snoring coming from his direction. Then Arleta poked her again, a little softer this time, and pointed to Emberly's window. Emberly squinted in confusion. Arleta shook her head.

"Grab that bucket in the corner of your cell and prop it onto that crate, in front of the window," Arleta pointed to the crate in the corner.

Emberly grabbed it and put the bucket on top.

"Now stand on top of that and look out the window. You have a visitor," Arleta said with a huge smile across her face.

Emberly climbed her way up the precarious step ladder she'd built, making sure to not make any noise while doing so. Once she was at the top, she grabbed onto the vertical bars of the window and peered through. She could see a small light flicker from the forest, and her heart began to race as Sam stepped out from the trees and shut the flashlight off. Her heart sped even faster as he approached.

When he got closer to her window, he stepped up onto something—most likely a crate—and was brought face-to-face with Emberly and smiled.

Emberly smiled in relief that he was okay, and she guessed that if he was smiling, it meant that the twins were okay as well. Hopefully.

"Are you okay in there?" he asked.

"Absolutely. Feels like just another day at the spa," Emberly chuckled.

Sam laughed, "It's nice to know you haven't lost your sarcastic sense of humour."

Emberly looked into his eyes. It was nice to see his face.

"Is Zayne okay?"

"He's doing fine. Turns out, he just needed a little break and some medicine," Sam reassured her.

Emberly sighed in relief.

"So, what's going on?" Sam asked.

Emberly wasn't sure how to answer that, "All I know, is that I'm here for one night, then in the morning a judge, with the opinion of someone from the 1800s, will decide my fate."

Emberly heard Arleta muffle a laugh from the other cell.

"Jail definitely hasn't changed you," Sam winked at her, but Emberly's face grew serious.

"I need to leave. We need to continue. But I have no idea how I could possibly escape from here, and it's dangerous for you guys to stay too long. It's too much of a risk of any of you getting caught, or not being able to find food, or—"

"We're not leaving without you," Sam cut her off. "I won't let that happen. So, if that was your plan, then you're completely insane."

"Then what's your brilliant idea," she challenged.

Sam looked down and was quiet for a few seconds as he thought. But then his head shot up, and a smile brightened on his face, "Okay hear me out. Our best chance for you to escape is after your hearing is finished. I'm guessing it will be held in the town hall just down the road," Emberly looked to Arleta who nodded her head in confirmation.

"Perfect! Our moment to run will be when you're led out of the town hall. Let's hope no one has you in handcuffs so it's easier to run. Since it's a small town, there will more than likely be a crowd around town hall, so I can hide among them. Look for me in the crowd when you get out; I'll try to move as close to you as I can, so we can run together the moment there's an opportunity for us. I'll think up some sort of distraction to give us that chance. Sound good?"

Emberly hated to admit it, but it was better than any plan she could have come up with, "Sounds good."

"Just make sure you don't do anything from now until then to cause them to put you in handcuffs," he joked.

Emberly laughed, "I'll do my best."

Sam reached up to the bars of the window and placed his hands on top of hers, "We're not leaving here without you. If we need to, we'll work on the fly tomorrow. But I promise we're getting you out."

He brought one of her hands up to his lips and gave it a gentle kiss, "I'll see you tomorrow."

Emberly could feel the heat rising in her cheeks as he hopped off the crate and hurried back into the forest; turning one final time to flash her a smile before he entered its shadowy depths.

She stared at that spot for a few moments; she could still feel his phantom kiss on the back of her hand. Then, when she was sure her cheeks were no longer flush, she stepped down from the window, put the crate and bucket back where she had found them, and sat on the floor.

She looked over at Arleta who was smiling mischievously. Emberly shook her head because she had dealt with enough teenage girls in school to know what Arleta was going to say next.

"I think he likes you," Arleta winked.

Emberly couldn't help but chuckle, "He can like me all he wants, but my focus is on my family. I need to concentrate on making sure they're safe."

Arleta pinched her brows in confusion, their movement a silent demand for Emberly to clarify. But Emberly just pointed to the front where Kevin was still sleeping. She didn't want to chance being overheard and risk him finding out about the others.

Emberly spent the rest of the night tossing on her lumpy cot, trying to fall asleep. But anytime she'd start to drift off, her brain would conjure up images of someone dying and startle her awake. The piercing screams of the repetitive dream followed her long into the night.

CHAPTER EIGHTEEN

THE NEXT DAY WAS dull. There was nothing to do, and while Arleta and Emberly talked, there wasn't much that Emberly could say without giving away anything about her past.

Their meals that day weren't any better than the night before. Dale had brought them cereal for breakfast and a cold chicken sandwich for lunch, but after a week on the run, Emberly was happy to have something more substantial than a few tiny crackers, so she ate it without complaint.

Emberly spent most of the afternoon sleeping. The nightmares the night prior had stolen any real chance for her to get proper rest, and she knew she'd need some for their escape later this afternoon.

Around mid-afternoon, Noah woke her up to let her know they'd be taking her to the town hall in an hour.

"Only one more hour," Arleta whispered eagerly after Noah turned to leave.

Emberly's pulse quickened as she recalled the details of Sam's plan. Only one more hour until she was taken out of here, and assuming Sam's plan worked, it wouldn't be much later until she'd be free.

"Arleta," Emberly whispered. "Grab that marker," she pointed to the marker that Noah had dropped outside Arleta's cell earlier in the day and had been too lazy to bend down and pick up.

"Write your phone number on my arm," she said as she pushed up her sleeve and stuck her arm through the bars. "Once I can get to somewhere safe, I'll call you and tell you everything. There are too many eyes and ears around for me to do it now."

Arleta grabbed Emberly's arm and began to write, "I'm going to miss you, hun."

Both officers came for Emberly shortly after. She stood up and shared a hug and whispered that she promised to stay in touch with Arleta through the bars, then she walked out of her open cell door.

They cuffed her hands behind her back and marched her out of the police station. Emberly stumbled over the uneven door frame but neither Noah or Kevin seemed to care. They just gripped her arms tighter and carried on through the streets.

Apparently, Emberly noted, the memo about her court case had gotten out, and as Sam predicted, a large crowd had already gathered outside of the town hall. They whispered to each other and pointed at Emberly like she was a dangerous criminal. They didn't bother her though. Right now, only one of the crowd of onlookers mattered to her.

Emberly's eyes scanned the crowd, and just as she was about to be pushed into the building, she spotted Sam standing slightly behind a group of people near the doors. Sam gave her a nod.

She turned to face the front. Their operation was a go.

Inside of the town hall, which turned out to be a multi-purpose space that looked to be used more often as a gym, Emberly saw that they had set up two folding tables and a couple of chairs.

Kevin removed her handcuffs and led her to one of the empty tables while Noah closed the doors, keeping everyone else—including Sam—out. *Apparently, it's going to be a closed hearing,* she thought.

Soon, a particularly tall man walked into the room and sat down at the table that sat opposite of hers.

"Miss Roads," the so-called judge announced, "Welcome. Let's get started."

"Now, a warning before we begin," he wagged a finger in her direction, "I want you to answer me truthfully, okay?"

Emberly nodded and leaned back in her chair.

"Did you or did you not steal something from Ms. Ruben's store?"

"I did not," she told the judge. Technically, she wasn't lying. Sure, she grabbed it from the shelf and had hidden it in her shirt, but she never actually left the store with it. She had handed it to Sam, who then ran from the store with it.

"Are you certain? Because we have proof that you and a friend stole a box of medicine."

Emberly's expression remained calm, "If me and a 'friend' stole something from the store, explain to me where this so-called friend went, because last time I checked people don't just vanish and neither do allegedly stolen items."

The judge squinted at her and wrote something on the notepad that was on the table in front of him. Emberly could hear the officers snickering behind her, but when she turned to face them, they instantly stopped. It made her feel like she was back at school.

The next five minutes continued in the same fashion. The judge would ask a question, and Emberly would try her best to dodge it. The judge would then sigh and write something else on the notepad.

"Let me go back to 'if there was a boy in the store with you'. Just to be clear, I have talked to someone who witnessed the boy running away from the store holding a plastic bottle. I appreciate you wanting to protect your friend, but there's no point in lying further."

Emberly pondered what he said then just gave in. There was no use keeping it a secret any longer. To be fair, it wasn't much of a secret anyways.

"Yes, there was a boy in the store with me," she admitted. "But he left, and I don't know where he is now." Technically, Sam *could* have since moved to stand somewhere else from where she saw him earlier.

The judge looked at her and finally seemed satisfied with an answer she'd given. But still, he made some notes.

Emberly relaxed in her chair. She didn't know what to expect. Hopefully, they would let her go without any charges, but there was a good chance that wasn't going to be the case.

Finally, after what felt like hours, the judge spoke, "I have concluded," Emberly's back straightened. "Miss Roads, that you will partake in community service for the next thirty days for stealing and resisting police authorities. You will stay in the jail during this period since you do not live here."

Emberly's heart sunk. Community service for a month? That wasn't a possibility. She'd have no choice but to make a run for the forest like Sam had planned.

"Now, Miss Roads, will you cause any further trouble for our officers while you're here?"

Emberly nodded her head.

"Good, then the cuffs can stay off so long as you behave. But," and he wagged his finger at her again, "one of the officers will escort you to and from your community service each day, and if you cause any issues for them, your days of service will be increased. Understood?"

"Understood, sir," Emberly nodded.

"Then case closed. We'll meet again after the thirty days to discuss your release. Have a good day, Miss Roads."

Emberly stood from her chair and took a deep breath to brace herself for what would come next. Kevin opened the front doors and Noah grabbed onto her one arm and escorted her out of the room and into the crowd gathered on the street out front.

Emberly looked around and found Sam in an instant. He gave her a cheeky wink and mischievous smile, and she couldn't wait to see what he had planned.

Luckily, Noah was stopped by a group of people asking about what the judge had decided. His grip on her arm loosened while he and Kevin tried to clear a path through the onlookers.

While they were moving people out of the way, Emberly watched from the corner of her eye as Sam shoved a large man who'd had his back turned to Sam. As he did, he also tapped the shoulder of a small, stockier man standing beside him. The smaller man turned and came face-to-face with the larger angry man who shoved him backwards, thinking he had been the one to push him. Sam ducked out of the way, narrowly avoiding a fist thrown by the smaller man.

Soon, fists were flying everywhere, and more people became involved in the fight. Including both officers that had run over to try to stop it—completely forgetting about Emberly.

In two strides, Sam was standing at her side, "Time to go."

It was now or never. Emberly's legs sprang into action. She pumped her legs faster when she heard people begin to yell at them once they realized what had happened. Emberly looked back and saw both officers, and a few of the townspeople, running after her, their faces red with anger.

But it just added fuel to the fire, and Emberly ran faster. "See ya later!" she called to them as Sam pulled her into the forest.

They ran through the bushes and trees, trying their best to dodge any sticks or branches that could poke their eyes out. After what had to have been a mile and a half of running, they stopped at a large tree.

"Climb," Sam commanded.

"But, what about Zayne and—"

"Just, climb," he repeated urgently.

And so she did. Emberly scaled as fast as she could with Sam, surprisingly, right behind her. She was greeted at the top by a familiar pair of smiling faces, "Eve, Zayne, you're here!"

"Emberly!" they cried as they leaned over to hug her, careful to not fall out of the tree. "We missed you!"

Her worries washed away as she held them both.

"Zayne, are you okay?" she asked, remembering that his sickness was the reason this all happened

"Yes, I'm doing much better. Sam and Eve took real good care of me!"

Emberly looked over to Sam and mouthed the words "thank you" then went back to hugging the twins.

He smiled in response, but then his eyes cast downward and his smile dropped.

"What happened to your arm?" he asked in concern. He reached for Emberly's elbow and he grabbed it gently. She looked down and noticed that she had a long, shallow cut on her elbow. She hadn't even realized it had been there. She must have gotten it when they were running through the woods.

She tried to pull her arm back, but Sam's grip was too strong and he held on.

"Sam, it's fine. Don't worry about it," Emberly tried reassuring him, but he wouldn't listen.

He started rummaging through his backpack until he pulled out a water bottle and one of Zayne's shirts that had gotten torn one day climbing a tree and was now useless.

He poured the water over her cut and was gentle as he used the shirt to blot it dry.

Emberly tilted her head to the side and smiled, "You worry too much," she chuckled.

"I'm just glad you're back," was all he said.

Emberly leaned over and gave him a kiss on the cheek, "I'm glad to be back," she whispered.

CHAPTER NINETEEN

EMBERLY COULDN'T SETTLE THAT night. Her adrenaline was still pumping through her veins. She was so sick of running, yet she was unable to stop. She never took the time to process her decisions—to choose the right one.

Which is why they found themselves, for the second time on their short journey, spending the night in a tree avoiding the enemies. Knowing she wouldn't be able to sleep a wink, Emberly offered to keep watch that night so the others could rest.

With nothing to distract itself, Emberly's mind raced through everything that had happened over the past short while. They had run from an abusive foster lady, the woman from the post office in Traiet, then five men with guns, and now, she had run from the cops and some angry townspeople.

She needed a distraction. She had to stop thinking about everything that had happened before her anxiety went into over drive. As if drawn by a magnet, Emberly's eyes were pulled to Sam's sleeping form.

She watched Sam as he slept. His face was calm and his body relaxed. It was the complete opposite to how he normally looked when he was awake and sitting on a tree branch. Emberly sighed.

Then as if he knew he had caught her attention, he blinked his eyes opened and he met her gaze. The corners of his lips tipped up in a smile. She studied the way his dimples deepened when his smile widened at her. Unable to stop the nervous tick, Emberly reached to her chest and grabbed onto the arrow pendant of her mother's necklace.

Sam's eyes followed the movement of her hand, but his look intensified as he brought his ocean-blue eyes back to hers. The way he looked at her with his steady gaze made her breath catch. Butterflies flew in her stomach. She averted her gaze, and focused instead on the rising sun, embarrassed for letting her feelings overpower her.

But even as she forced herself to look at the sun, Emberly could not stop thinking that nothing in all the galaxies could possibly shine brighter than how his eye's shone in the light of that morning sun.

When the twins woke up a few hours later, they all decided to stay in the tree until nightfall when they could guarantee that no one from the town would be looking for them. Plus, a break from walking would be a nice change. In the next couple days, they would be crossing the border into New Hampshire where they would be more than halfway to Canada. They could afford to rest.

The twins entertained themselves by playing games, and when they grew bored, they'd beg Sam to tell them a story.

Of course, he always indulged them with a made up story of monsters and dragons and far-away lands. Through it all, Emberly stayed silent. She wasn't in the mood for conversation, so she just leaned against the trunk and watched the birds fly by and the clouds change form.

Sam swung his legs over one side of the branch so he could look directly at Emberly. "Tell me the truth. Are you okay?" Sam asked.

She kept her gaze on the clouds, "You asked the weirdest questions at the oddest times. You realize that right?"

"Answer the question."

"No. I don't need to answer the question," finally she looked over at him.

He raised his eyebrows at her, "Emberly, answer the question. Please," he added.

"Fine. It was scary. Are you happy?" she huffed. She didn't know why she was so mad or why she was taking everything out on him, but anger just seemed like the right emotion to feel right now.

"I was just asking a question. There's no need to be defensive," he jokingly punched her in the arm.

Emberly shoved him back. He lost his balance and began to fall from his branch, but Emberly lunged forward and threw her arm out and grabbed hold of his flailing hand and helped pull him back up.

She let out a stiff laugh, but her face fell to stone, "I'm still scared," the admittance was barely a whisper from her lips.

"What did you say?"

"It's nothing. It's fine," Emberly sighed, changing her mind. She didn't want to go there.

"You're lying to me," he accused. "How many times have we had this conversation, Emberly? I know you don't like being vulnerable, but does it look like I'm going to judge you? I know you had a twisted childhood, and I understand that, but it doesn't mean you can't let someone in—that you can't let me in."

He seemed genuinely mad. She cocked her head sideways, and tried to figure him out; to figure out this feeling she had about him. But instead of admitting anything—aloud or to herself—she leaned forward and pressed her lips against Sam's.

His lips were frozen in shock at first, but softened as he began to kiss her back. Emberly had never kissed anyone before, so she hadn't known what to expect. But, she concluded, that it felt like a proper kiss should. Not awkward or weird, but natural.

After a few moments, she pulled back. Sam opened his mouth to speak, but no words came out. He just stared at her in shock.

"Was that vulnerable enough for you?" she asked.

"I am never going to understand you, Emberly," he said.

"That was the point," she said, both recognizing it for the lie that it was.

Sam chuckled and reached out to grab her hand. They sat like that, holding hands, for a little while longer. Not saying a word. Just listening. To the birds. To the silence.

Sam finally broke the silence, "What was it that you had said before?"

"It was nothing."

"I don't believes it was nothing. I want to know."

When she looked at him, he added, "I promise I won't judge. You can trust me. You don't have to do this alone."

There was that word again. Trust. A word that meant many different things depending on who said it. But, hadn't he proven he was worthy of her trust? He'd been there for them every step of the journey so far. He helped her find food and water for the twins. He helped carry her after she'd fainted. He helped when the hunters were chasing them. He even took care of Zayne then helped her get out of jail.

Yes, she supposed, Sam seemed worthy of her trust.

"I'm fourteen, okay? I didn't sign up for this. Do you think I know what I'm doing? Because if you do, then I should be in a movie. Do you think I wanted to be told to deal with life at the age of seven? To deal with my baby twins who needed their mom, but ended up having to settle for only me? I can't deal with supporting a family. I can't deal with finding a job. I can't deal with the weight of not knowing if I'm doing the right thing. But I am. I have to. Because I have no choice. I can't let them down," she looked at Sam and wiped away the straggling tear that had fallen from her eye.

He looked at her with pain in his eyes, almost as if he too would shed a tear.

Sam carefully moved from his branch to Emberly's, reached over and wrapped his arms around her, as if to protect her from anything that could cause her further harm. "You're no longer doing this on your own. I've got you."

Those last three words were the only ones she had ever wanted to hear. Those words told her that she was finally safe, and that was the only thing she had ever wanted to feel. And with those words, she instantly broke down. Streams of tears fell from her cheeks and onto Sam's arms. "I've got you," he repeated into her ear.

Sam kept his strong arms wrapped around Emberly until her sobs stopped and her breathing calmed. Emberly took a shaky breath and twisted to face Sam. He gently wiped away the tears from her cheeks.

"Thanks."

"Any time," he smiled as he pulled her back to lean against his chest.

She didn't know how long they stayed like that, with her leaning against him, both staring out at the sky and the forest. But at one point, a strong breeze blew some of her long, wavy hair into her face. Sam grabbed the strands with his hand and started to twirl it around his fingers.

"Cut it," Emberly said in a moment of spontaneity.

"What?" Sam asked confused.

She used to adore her long hair, would pride herself on its length. But its length had since become out of control long. It was forever getting caught on nearby branches as they walked and was a constant hassle to deal with, forever getting tangled and knotted. And when she really thought about it, the thing Emberly had really liked about her hair was how it helped her hide while she was at school. It was almost as if her hair had been a way for her to become invisible.

"Cut it," she repeated. She didn't need her safety blanket any longer.

Sam still looked confused. "Why? I thought you liked your hair."

"I do. I did. I just—just cut it. Please," she smiled. She dug around in her backpack and pulled out the knife. "It doesn't need to be perfect. It just needs to be done."

Sam hesitantly took the knife from her hand. Emberly closed her eyes as he grabbed a chunk of her hair, took an audible exhale, and began to cut.

With every slice of hair, Emberly could literally feel her safety blanket falling away. It made her nervous, but she kept her breathing steady through it. She reminded herself that it needed to happen. That the time for her to hold onto things was over.

Finally, Sam grabbed the last chunk and without a second thought, sliced it clean off. He checked the edges and made sure they were halfway straight before he handed Emberly the knife—and her hair. She held the knife in front of her face and positioned it so she could see herself in its reflection. Her mouth fell open as she touched her hair.

It now fell just above her shoulders. Her waves and new found curls, bounced outwards, giving her hair more volume. She felt like a different person.

And different, she decided, was exactly what she needed.

She turned to Sam and smiled, "Thanks."

She held the hair in her hands. For a second, she longed for it to be back, protecting her. But then she reminded herself that she no longer needed its protection. She, Emberly Clove, was already the protector of her new family and herself.

She stuffed her hair into an old box that used to contain crackers and put it in her backpack. She'd burn it the next time they built a fire. And with that, Emberly sat up taller. She felt immensely lighter, as if the hair had weighed a thousand tonnes. She smiled proudly at herself. At her new life.

At the new Emberly.

After the twins woke up amazed at how well Emberly looked with her new hairdo. They spent the rest of the evening playing games, sharing stories, and truly getting to know Sam, which wasn't as bad as Emberly had pictured it would be. If she had to admit it, she found everything she learned about him to be rather...pleasant.

The sun started to set, and the beautiful red and burnt orange colours of the sun filled the sky. Birds sang their night-time lullabies, and the fireflies began their nightly dance.

It all looked like a romantic scene from a movie. It was breathtaking.

They all sat there, Emberly and Sam still sharing the same branch, and watched as the gorgeous night progressed. But soon, Emberly's eyelids started to droop and her body grew heavy.

Sam looked down at her and smiled, "Are you tired yet?"

She went to roll her eyes but ended up just closing them instead.

"Maybe," she admitted as the twins laughed.

Eve tossed them a rope, and Emberly tied the two of them onto the large branch then looked back at Sam. He held his arms open, and she nestled against him.

She fell asleep immediately.

Arleta and the townspeople filled her head with nightmares that night. Pitchforks lit their angry faces as they cornered Emberly and Arleta. The thick blanket of the night sky added an extra level of eeriness to an already terrifying situation.

Emberly spun in circles trying to find a way to escape. But there was no way out; no gap, no person to help cause a distraction. They were trapped. The people kept advancing. Their circle growing smaller and smaller, suffocating the freedom of the two girls.

Emberly's breath grew frantic, and her heartbeat was rapidly rising in her chest. She tried to focus her breathing, but her mind didn't cooperate.

The mob drew closer, the tips of their pitchforks so close that Emberly could reach out and slice her finger on one of their pointy ends. Then Arleta pointed to a newly formed gap in the ring of people. They ran for it.

As she dove for freedom, Arleta disappeared and two men grabbed Emberly's arms and lifted her from the ground. She squirmed and tried to escape their grasp, but the men refused to let go. They forced her to kneel and turned her around to face a person standing in the middle of a circle with a gun to their back.

Emberly tried to scream at the person, to warn them of the gun, but they couldn't hear her. She screamed and screamed at the person to run, until her voice grew hoarse from her cries. Still the person remained, frozen in place.

So instead, Emberly tried to open her mouth to tell them that it was going to be okay, but her lips would no longer open—her mouth was being sewn shut with a needle and thread. The needle slowly wove in and out, drawing blood each time it pierced through Emberly's skin. The blood trickled down her chin and stained her shirt as Eve and Zayne yelled in the background for it to stop.

The townspeople returned, led by Ms. Margot. They all cheered while the needle finished its last stitch and the string was tied off. But as the needle began to drop to the floor, a shot rang out and everything went dark.

Emberly's eyes shot open, and she bolted up into a seating position. She ran her fingers across her mouth and frantically looked around. She swore she could still feel the pain of the stitches that had been sewn into it in her dream.

"Hey," Sam whispered, "you okay?"

"Ya, I'm fine. Just had a bad dream."

"Want to talk about it?"

Emberly thought back to her dream—the nightmare. She remembered the townspeople with their pitchforks, the man with the gun, and the stitches in her lip, and she shuddered. No, she did not want to talk about it.

She shook her head.

Sam hugged her tight, "Okay, but I'm here if you do."

Emberly nodded, and Sam yawned.

"Now it's your turn to sleep," she said. "I'll stay watch."

Sam didn't hesitate. He leaned against the trunk of the tree and fell asleep almost immediately.

Emberly looked up at the moon which had now made its way to the center of the sky, to the blanket of stars that kept it warm and safe.

She stayed like that, with her head craned towards the sky, until a hand grabbed onto her shoulder and gently lowered her down. She looked up at Sam.

"What? You looked uncomfortable," he smiled groggily.

She smiled and watched as Sam fell asleep with Emberly held tight in his arms.

CHAPTER TWENTY

EMBERLY STAYED AWAKE THROUGH the remainder of the night. She wasn't sure she could go back to sleep after her dream anyways.

When she eventually felt Sam's leg twitch as he woke, she turned to face him. She looked Sam in the eyes.

"You feeling better?" he asked.

"I'm fi—I am better." She corrected herself.

Sam chuckled and shook his head in laughter, "Good. How's your elbow?"

"It was just a scratch. You need to stop worrying about me. I can take care of myself."

"So you've said," he winked at her. "I was just making sure... because I care," he replied, his eyes taking on a serious look as he said the last part.

She'd never really had someone that cared about her as much as he did. Sure, she knew her mom loved her and that she did—in her own way—love Emberly. But her mom had turned into a different person after Emberly's dad had died. She spent most of the time in her room, and had become consumed with her own worries and issues, not really noticing or aware when Emberly, or the twins, needed something from her. She wasn't truly there for them the way that kids needed a parent to be.

So, Emberly taught herself how to fill her own needs and how to soothe her own emotions or troubles. And she took those learnings and taught herself how to do that for the twins so they never felt uncared for or unnoticed. She was aware of the emotional damage that had been caused to her throughout her childhood and the last thing she wanted was the twins to feel that way. She protected them from the pain of the world like a shield from a flame. And even if the twins couldn't protect her the same way, they cared for her and they were the only ones who ever did.

But he cared. A boy she didn't know less than a month ago cared. And knowing in her gut that he truly meant it, brought a smile to her face. A real smile.

"I know," she smiled, hoping it conveyed what she couldn't say—*I care about you too.*

"Alright," she said, turning her face to hide the blush she knew had started to rise on her cheeks, "you wake the twins, and I'll go down and check to make sure the coast is clear."

"Emberly, you are not going down there. You're the one they're looking for. It's too risky for you to go," Sam reminded her. "I'll go."

Emberly lifted an eyebrow, "If they see you, they'll put you in jail too. I wasn't the only one stealing."

"So, who will go then?" Sam asked.

"Me. I'll go." Zayne piped in.

Emberly looked over at him. He was rubbing the palms of his hands against his eyes as he tried to fully wake. She opened her mouth, about to tell him that it was too dangerous for him to go, especially when he had just been so sick. But then she reminded herself that it was okay to let others help too. And really, it was the best option. So, she took a deep breath, and nodded, even though it terrified her, "Fine, but if anyone sees you and asks what you're doing, you lie. I don't care what you say, just lie."

Zayne nodded and carefully climbed down the tree.

It wasn't until Zayne nodded that everything was "all clear" that she released the breath she had been holding. She wasn't sure why she was so nervous. It's not like the townspeople were dangerous; but she hated putting either of the twins at risk. Her job was to protect them.

The three of them scampered down the tree to join Zayne. At the bottom, Sam handed Emberly her the bow and arrows. She snatched them out of his hands, but paused and added a thank you, before she flung both over her shoulders.

Even though they were pretty sure no one from town was anywhere near, or even still bothering to look for them, they decided to head in the opposite direction from town. Emberly took the lead and ran north, or as close to north as she could tell—the odd set of bushes or body of water derailing them slightly at points.

After sometime, they stopped at a small lake where they could fill up their water and take the opportunity to hopefully catch something to eat and clean their clothes and themselves.

Eve put down the backpack she'd been carrying and unzipped it. Emberly took out the empty water bottles and filled them up while Zayne grabbed some firewood and helped Sam make a fire.

The fire crackled and popped, and sparks flew at them as they sat near it, trying to warm up. The air was getting colder as the days pressed on. Even at the beginning of October, it was already cold enough that a fire during the day was needed. Soon they would have to make a fire every day just so that they could keep themselves warm from the harsh winter air.

They let the fire wilt away until there was hardly any flame left, then Emberly grabbed some water from the lake and tossed it onto its embers to completely put it out.

They collected their supplies and continued.

They set off down the length of the lake and continued to walk north. Emberly hung back and allowed Eve, Zayne, and Sam to walk in front.

Of course, it didn't take long for Sam to notice and fall back to join her. "Why are you walking by yourself?" he asked.

"Just wanted to think," she let a hint of a smile touch her lips but continued to look forward.

"Well, something has been on my mind as well," he said.

"And what may that be?"

"That I don't really know much about you. We've been together for what, three weeks, and I really only know that your name is Emberly and a little about your time at the foster home. Oh, and that you're extremely stubborn," he laughed.

Emberly chuckled and elbowed him in the ribs, "Okay, well, my full name is Emberly Blaze Clove. There, is that enough information for you?"

Sam shook his head, "Did I forget to add that you're very private."

Emberly smiled at that, "Fine but I ask the questions first. What's your full name?"

"Sam James Prime. Next."

"How old are you?"

"I had turned sixteen a week before you took me with you guys."

Emberly stopped in her tracks, for two reasons, "We didn't take you, you invited yourself—let's make that clear right off the bat. Also, you're sixteen?"

"Yeah," Sam answered as if it were obvious. "I'm in grade eleven. Why are you so surprised?"

He could be driving. Wait—he should be driving. But they didn't have a car for him to drive anyways, so nothing that could be done there. Sixteen, she thought. Emberly wasn't sure why it was such a big shock for her.

When she didn't immediately respond, he nervously asked, "How old are you?"

"Fourteen. I turn fifteen in December."

Sam bobbed his head up and down, "Oh okay. Ask me something else."

"Favourite colour?"

"Yellow. Yours?"

"Red. My mom used to tell me that both my grandmas liked the colour red, and I never got to know them very well, so it makes me feel closer to them. Also, it reminds me to stay tough and brave at all times."

Sam knowingly looked at her, "I don't think you need the colour red for that."

Once again, Sam was right. Emberly knew that she was fierce and brave. She didn't need a colour to prove that. She smiled.

They walked in silence for a few moments while Emberly tried to work up the courage to ask the question that had been on her mind for a while.

"Why did you come, Sam?"

He raised his eyebrows and shrugged his shoulders, "I thought I told you. I didn't want to go to boarding school."

"No, why did you *really* come?" Eve asked. "People don't just up and leave their families like that."

"No, that's the truth. My mom was always nice to me, but my dad was always too agitated and rude towards me and my mom. He would get mad over every little thing, so the night before you guys slept over in the barn, the two of us got into another argument about school. He got really mad, as did I, so the decision to leave was actually really easy."

"I suppose that makes sense..." she replied. Emberly looked at Sam, but his expression told her immediately that there was something else he hadn't yet told her.

"What else, Sam?" she asked.

He looked sheepishly at the ground, then pulled her over to a patch of grass to sit, "Okay, and don't hate me after I tell you this next part."

Emberly already knew she wasn't going to like what was going to come out of Sam's mouth.

"I wasn't actually planning on staying with you guys the entire trip to Canada. I just wanted someone to tag along with for a bit. I was going to leave that very day anyways—that's really why I was in the barn that morning. But when I saw you guys, I thought it would be a good opportunity to have some company for a bit. So, I planned to just walk with you for a couple of days then split off in my own direction."

Emberly's blood pressure started to boil.

Sam looked at her face, "It was stupid and thoughtless of me. I know that now. I honestly thought it'd be easier for us to part ways after a couple of days. For us to each go our own way. But then I got to know you guys and decided that I didn't want to part from any of you—especially from you. I just...I wanted to tell you. To be honest about it," he looked her directly in the eyes. "Don't be mad, please."

"Oh, I'm not mad. I'm furious," she shot straight up from the log and looked down at him. "I knew I should never have trusted you. You were a stranger, and I put my family at risk and I went to jail because of you! Because I thought you were a good person. How could I not be mad?"

Sam stood up slowly with his hands raised, as if to calm the beast that had awoken within her, "Emberly, I know it was stupid, and I there's not a single part of me that could ever leave you anymore. Not now that I know you guys. I swear."

"Oh, you swear?" Emberly replied in a fake sympathetic tone. "That makes it all better."

She shot him a cold look and walked over to her siblings who had been watching the interaction between the two of them—

unsure of what to do or how to calm it, "We have been through so much shit and have survived on our own for years now. I didn't need you then. And I don't need you now. You were just an accessory that happened to come our way."

"Emberly, what else do you want me to say. I screwed up and made a mistake. I am so sorry."

"And to think that for a second, I allowed myself to have feelings for you. To trust you. How dare you!"

"Emberly, I—"

"Just leave, Sam."

She grabbed their items from his backpack and divided up the remainder of the food they had stolen from the cabin and shoved his backpack at his chest.

Sam looked bewilderedly at the twins, then back to Emberly, "Where am I supposed to go?"

"You can go wherever the hell you want. You had planned to leave us before, well here's your chance. Find another path to walk on."

"Emberly," he begged, "I told you I was sorry. I've been with you for how many weeks. I helped you when you got weak. I helped Zayne when he was sick. I even helped you get out of prison. You *know* me."

"Do I, Sam?" she challenged.

"Yes, you do. You know that I'd never do anything to hurt any of you. I messed up; I can admit that. I know I hurt you, but I'll never do it again. What else do you want me to do to? Let me stay," Sam pleaded, "I'll do anything. Just give me a second chance."

"Giving someone a second chance is like giving them another bullet because they didn't hit you the first time," Emberly said coldly.

"You can't just leave me out here," he said, getting progressively angrier as he switched the path of the conversation. "I can't change what I had thought, and I didn't actually do it. So drop it."

"No, you don't get to be mad at me. You screwed up. I warned you that if you messed up, even once, you were done. Don't think for one second that the rule had been taken off the table. Now, leave."

Sam looked at her, prepared to say more. To argue more. But he knew she wouldn't be backing down. So, he looked at the twins, smiled kindly at them, then turned back to Emberly.

"Bye," was all he said before he walked into the thick of the forest with his backpack slung over his shoulder and his head hung low.

Emberly watched him until he disappeared from view. Then she collapsed to the ground beside the twins and tried desperately to hold back her tears.

"Emberly, we can't just let him leave," Eve told her.

"Yeah. He's going to get lost." Zayne added.

Emberly looked at them, "We don't need him. We'll be fine, and so will he," she added.

They twins knew there was no way they could convince their sister otherwise; not when she was angry like this. So, they nodded in defeat and kept quiet.

Emberly couldn't believe that she had ever trusted him. That she had...it didn't matter now. What's done was done.

Wanting to distract her thoughts, Emberly decided to go into the forest and hunt for something for them to eat.

She trudged through the bushes and found a great open space to spot a rabbit or small woodland creature. She tucked herself behind a bush and the waiting game began.

Unfortunately, hunting was not as distracting as she had hoped. Instead of giving her mind something to focus on, she found herself completely alone with her thoughts; which at that point, was an awful idea.

Emberly wanted to get Sam out of her head, but she couldn't seem to shake him free. She needed to focus on her own family, but she couldn't. Her mind kept drifting back to Sam, which only brought up feelings of anger, and if she was being really honest with herself—hurt.

Emberly shook her head and tried to refocus on the task at hand, but it just shifted gears towards their newest predicament—she had to come up with a new plan to get into Canada.

If they couldn't sneak over the border, she'd somehow need to find someone that could give them fake citizenship papers so they could get in. At the very least, they'd need those papers before they could start working. But how would she manage that?

Luckily, something moved in the bushes, distracting her from herself. Two small squirrels ran into the clearing as Emberly prepped her arrow. She would need to do this fast if she wanted both squirrels before they ran away. Emberly aimed further ahead and shot the first squirrel. The other one stopped in its tracks and watched his friend. But that just made it easier to hit.

She returned to the twins with two squirrels and a happy expression on her face. They cooked the squirrels, a decent meal at that point, and Emberly suggested they share stories of their past to help get their minds off everything.

"Remember how Mom would always hide candy that she would steal from work around the house on Christmas?" Eve recalled.

"Ya, and we weren't allowed to eat any of it until it was all found," Zayne started laughing.

That had been the only Christmas tradition they'd ever had at their house. And Emberly wouldn't even call it a tradition. It was a way to distract the twins from realizing that they never had a tree or presents. It wasn't even their mom who hid the candy. It was Emberly. Their mom just took the credit while she sat in her room. If they ever did get presents, it usually was something their mom so luckily found at work or was given by a friend.

*This is nice,* Emberly tried to convince herself. She had missed spending time with the twins, so maybe losing Sam wasn't so bad.

She chose to ignore the little voice in her head that kept calling her a liar.

Eventually, they grew tired of the stories, so cuddled up under the red blanket, in front of the fire, and Emberly sang.

But something was not quite right. There was one person missing. A person she longed to have sitting beside her.

The sun started to set, while the moon appeared from the other part of the world.

Zayne fell asleep, but Eve stayed awake, "We had a plan, Emberly. What do we do now?"

Her eight-year-old sister was always the one to think first—or worry first, which made the most sense in the situation.

"We'll figure it out when we get there, baby. I told you, nothing is going to happen to us. We were on our way to Canada before we met Sam, and that plan hasn't changed. We just run into a bump in the road. It's all good, I promise."

Eve smiled up at her sister, "Yeah, I know we'll be fine, but I miss Sam. He was so nice. He said sorry. Why did you tell him to go?"

Emberly wouldn't have admitted it out loud, but there was a kernel of truth to what Eve was saying. Sam did apologize, but after that, how could Emberly ever trust him again.

Yet, Emberly knew that Sam was an exception. She sighed, "You're correct, Eve. Sam is a good guy."

"And," Eve added, "A good guy *for you.*"

Emberly looked at her sister in utter confusion.

Eve shrugged and explained, "I heard you tell him that you liked him. I think you guys would make a nice couple."

Emberly's cheeks turned bright red as a blushing flame licked up the sides her face, "Past tense, Eve. I *liked* Sam."

But Eve gave her a look that meant Emberly would not get away with the lie, "Not the way you just blushed. You still like him."

"Maybe I like hanging out with him, but I don't trust him."

"You don't trust anyone...except for me and Zayne. You never have. You like him, and you won't admit it."

Emberly hated when Eve was right.

"I agree with Eve," Zayne piped in. "We saw you guys kiss in the tree."

*Okay...so apparently, they weren't sleeping.* Emberly told herself slightly embarrassed.

"Alright, I think you guys are too tired. Let's go to—"

A bloodshot scream rang from the forest.

Emberly shot up and looked around. She grabbed her bow and quiver and told the twins to follow close by with a flashlight so she could see both in front of her and make sure the twins were still okay.

They ran in the direction of the deafening screeches and stayed low so they would be undetected. For a brief moment, the screaming stopped and they followed suit. But when the noise rose again, it was louder and more frantic. They stayed low behind a bush and listened to the crunching of leaves and sticks under the feet of the person who was running. The movement stopped and all was eerily quiet.

Emberly grabbed the flashlight from Zayne, and pointed it towards the noise. There stood Sam, stiff as a statue and pinned against a tree in sheer terror.

She then pointed her flashlight to what Sam's wide eyes were directed at and saw a bobcat staring him down.

Emberly had never seen a wild bobcat before, but she had gone into a cage with some twice a day while at the foster home, which meant she knew how to handle them. Or at least, she hoped she did. But this one was wild and looked scared, and therefore, potentially erratic.

With the flashlight in one hand and her other hand free, Emberly carefully proceeded to get closer to the bobcat.

She kept her eyes on the bobcat, but from her side, she could hear Sam telling her something. She tried to tune him out and keep her focus on the bobcat. She needed to save Sam. Yet again. She reached out to the bobcat to calm it, but it was too scared.

Emberly's heart was racing but she needed to stay calm. And she needed to get Sam to stop screaming and talking.

She slowly turned her head, keeping her eyes on the bobcat, so she could tell him to be quiet.

But seeing her head turn toward his, Sam started talking again, "Emberly, I'm so sorry. I really didn't mean to hurt you or the twins. You guys are the best family I've ever had. I don't want to die knowing you'll be mad at me. Please forgive me. I'm so sorry."

"Shut up. You're not going to die, but you need to stay quiet while I do this."

She could see Sam nod his head, "Now slowly walk over to Eve and Zayne, but keep your hands up as to not frighten it."

She turned to fully face the bobcat again, and a smile crept across her face. She recognized this bobcat. She noticed its clipped ear, scarred eye and the branded number seven on its side. Features that were hard to miss. This bobcat was one that had escaped from Ms. Margot's during the tornado. It looked happier than before. Well-nourished and lively. Emberly had a soft spot for this particular bobcat. It was the first one to come to Emberly during her first day at the home.

She held her hand out. The bobcat timidly sniffed it before it recognized her and leaned into her touch, allowing Emberly to pet it. Emberly was relieved the bobcat still knew her.

They were unbelievably lucky. She couldn't believe that it had ventured this far away from home. Though, as Emberly supposed, she and the other kids probably weren't the only ones that refused to view that place as "home" and wanted to get as far away from it as possible.

"Thank you, girl, for not hurting my friend. We're going to leave now. Enjoy your new life," she gave the bobcat one last pet goodbye and returned to the twins and Sam.

The bobcat left shortly after, and Emberly's heart slowly went back to a respectable pace.

Sam's mouth hung open. Emberly looked at him with a smug expression and walked back to the twins.

"You're welcome, by the way," Emberly stood there and watched Sam.

He looked over at her and closed his mouth, "Thank you," he replied, still in shock. "How—how..." He couldn't seem to get the words out.

"An old friend," was all Emberly decided to say. She was still trying to decide if she should take him back with them or leave.

"Well, goodbye," she said, taking the cowardly decision. She turned to leave, not missing Sam's soft sigh from behind her.

"Wait," Eve stopped her, "We can't just leave him here. He was on his own for half a day and would have died if it weren't for you."

Emberly turned around to face her sister and Sam.

"Yeah, he needs us. Plus, you know we need the help crossing the border," Zayne reminded her.

Emberly pondered the thought for a while. The past couple weeks had been the most "relaxed" she had felt in months... no years. And even though it physically pained her to admit it, she knew it was because of Sam. Not only was it how his cousin was able to help them or that he provided obvious strength and endurance. It was because he held her together. Like Imani had. Even if she had been beyond angry at him, she knew when she looked into his eyes at that moment, he was truly sorry and Emberly believed him.

"Fine but if he tries to pull something stupid—"

"I'll push myself off the cliff for you, deal?" he interjected.

Emberly refused to let a smile cross her lips. She wasn't going to let him have that privilege.

"You're damn right you will," she gave him a smug look and turned around to leave.

Emberly took the lead, walking back to camp. The twins and Sam followed, but soon Sam made his way to the front to walk beside Emberly.

"Thanks for letting me stay with you," he paused, "and the twins," he added.

"Well, it was either that or apparently let you get killed, so... don't mention it," Emberly kept her eyes on the road ahead. She refused to acknowledge the small part of her that was happy to have him back in their group.

But, as if he still heard what she didn't say, Sam chuckled. Then he titled his head and looked at her as it he'd suddenly remembered something.

"Before I left," he started, "you said you had feelings for me."

Emberly sighed under her breath. She was hoping he would have forgotten.

"So?"

"So, is it true?"

"Does it matter?" her tone was sharp as she responded. "Let's just get back to camp and go to bed," she added, making it clear that there'd be no further discussion of it.

Thankfully, Sam dropped it.

CHAPTER TWENTY-ONE

DAY AFTER DAY THEY continued walking. It had almost been a week and a half since the incident with Sam and nothing changed. They tried to avoid towns and cities and made sure they stayed as camouflaged as possible. They occasionally would find an information building in some smaller towns and would check to make sure they were going the right way. They had entered Maine four days earlier, which was their last state to travel through and by far the easiest considering it was mostly covered in trees.

Sam hadn't pulled—or admitted to pulling—anything else stupid, which gave Emberly lots of time to think about the situation. What he had thought of doing was wrong. Sam knew it. She had trusted him and had let him into her family. Even though he didn't actually run away—had chosen not to after getting to know them—it didn't make it any better. It broke her trust. And she didn't give that away easily.

Emberly tried to look at the positives. Even if he was going to leave them, he did help them the days he was with them. He even carried her when she couldn't walk, despite her protests that she could do it herself. He also risked his safety to get her back to the twins when she was at the police station. She knew Sam was sorry, mostly because he kept repeating it. And yes, it had been a stupid idea on his part to ditch them, but at least he hadn't actually left. She supposed that had to count for something.

Emberly was still quite cautious around Sam. So, when they walked, she'd try her best to keep her distance, and when it came time to keep watch, she made sure Sam was never left alone at night. She still didn't fully trust he wouldn't still sneak away.

When Emberly was on watch one night, Sam began to wake up even though it was still pitch dark out. She watched him stretch his long arms out.

"Will you ever stop watching me like I'm going to run away?"

"That depends on what you do," Emberly warned.

Sam sat up and looked at Emberly, "Emberly, we need to talk. You've been weird around me ever since I came back. I know you're still mad at what I had admitted, and I don't disagree with you that it was wrong of me to have planned that, but I think this is about something more."

Emberly scrunched her eyebrows up and looked at Sam, "What are you, my therapist or something? There's nothing more. I just don't need you running away on us. We need you to get us into Canada, and that's all. After that, you can go live whatever damn life you want," Emberly spat in frustration.

"Yes, but you were finally warming up to me, and now I feel like you're further away."

"Well, that happens when someone breaks another's trust."

"So that's it then?"

Emberly looked at Sam and huffed in frustration, "Sam, why does it matter? It happened, it's over now."

"Why does it matter?" he repeated. "Well, I thought that we were becoming pretty good friends."

Emberly looked over at him, "Your point?"

"My point is that I was hoping you could start trusting me again. That we could go back to the way things were," Sam replied.

"Look, I'm not saying I couldn't ever trust you again, because I do think you're a good guy who made a very stupid, decision. I just don't know if that's a door I want to re-open," Emberly said honestly.

"I know, and words can't express how sorry I am for breaking your trust and making you doubt my intentions," he replied. "It was a stupid idea that I thought I could get away with when we were strangers. But then I got to know you," he paused. "Sort of. And I knew that I wouldn't be able to live with myself if I left. It was a selfish thought that I regretted immediately, and I wouldn't blame you if you never trusted me again. But, just please promise me you'll think about it. Trusting me, that is."

Emberly didn't respond. She didn't know what to say. Instead, she studied Sam out of the corner of her eye. She looked up at his dark black hair which was a curly mess and the dirt that outlined his jaw like contour. It had been a while since they had found a lake big enough to wash themselves properly. But somehow Sam was still remarkably beautiful. His little dimples even showed as he smiled, when he realized Emberly was staring at him. He quietly laughed and Emberly looked back up at the stars, embarrassed to have been caught.

Sam moved to sit beside Emberly, then reached over and placed his arm around her shoulder. At first, Emberly stiffened at the gesture and tried to move away, but Sam just put his hands up as a sign that he wasn't going to do anything, then slowly lowered his arm back around her shoulders. That time, Emberly didn't move for whatever reason. She just straightened her spine in defence, not knowing how else to act. She felt calm under the protection of his arm. It felt odd. She looked at him. He was watching the stars in a way that made him look older and wiser, but still a child at heart. Emberly didn't know what to make of him some days.

Sam made her feel as though she was the most special thing in the world. This made Emberly feel like the constant void of darkness that had eaten away at her since she was seven, was instead overfilled with light. He made her feel as though the void never existed in the first place. Every smile, every look her way made her heart happy.

Sam kept her grounded. He always made sure she was feeling okay. Sam made her want to break down the walls she had built around herself, and the twins, and build new ones. Ones that he was allowed into as well.

Emberly's spine loosened just a fraction as she settled.

Out of the corner of her eye, she saw Sam look at her. Then, he leaned closer and whispered in her ear, "You can relax. I promise I'll never hurt you again. You can trust me."

Emberly looked at him with a kinder eye. She so desperately wanted to believe him—to be able to finally let go and relax. To not always feel so alone.

She took a deep breath and smiled warmly at Sam, "Sam I'm sorry I snapped at you. You were just telling me the truth. I let my insecurities and fears control my reaction."

"Don't be sorry. Even if I didn't ditch you, it still wasn't right of me to have planned it. You have every right to be mad. I got lucky when you showed up in the barn that day, and I almost threw that out the window. You changed my life, Emberly. The person I found in the barn that day wasn't only courageous, powerful, and witty, she was also one of the kindest people I've ever met...even if she tries her best to hide it," Sam smiled.

His smile deepened and he gently lowered her head with his hand to rest on his shoulder. Emberly wanted to freeze this moment in time. She had felt so alone for so long, that she had convinced herself that there would never be someone that would be there for her, to help take care of her for a change. And then she met Sam. With that acknowledgement, she let go and fell into his hold.

They stayed that way for sometime. Neither wanting the moment to pass. But, when the sun finished its climb into the sky and there was no longer anything to watch, Sam began to gently rub his hand along Emberly's arm.

"Are you asleep?" Sam whispered.

"No," she replied. She hadn't fallen asleep, though she probably should have. But she hadn't wanted to move. Sitting there, wrapped in Sam's arm had felt so comfortable. So safe.

Reluctantly, knowing they had to start their day, they got up to stretch and woke the twins.

Emberly looked in the backpack and grabbed out her last semi-usable shirt. The shirt she had on now stunk and needed to come off. But the one she held in her hands wasn't much better. They hadn't had enough room in their backpack to grab the proper amount of clothes for the journey and every day new rips or tears appeared.

Emberly pulled her shirt off and quickly put the other one on before the cold air touched her skin. She kept her same pants on though since they were the only ones she had brought and she didn't particularly want to freeze her legs. She straightened out her shirt, then walked over to everyone else after they had changed.

"How much farther until Canada?" Eve asked. It was a tough question to answer because of how far they had to travel in general. Emberly had never been good with time. She knew they were headed in the right direction and that they had already been traveling for almost two months but the "how much longer" question was one she could not answer honestly. Luckily Sam pipped up.

"Well, in the last town we visited, four days ago, we were just entering Maine. Meaning we have about two to three days left of walking."

The twins jumped for joy. Even Emberly couldn't stop her excitement from bubbling over. The thought of soon being able to live in a house and sleep in a bed put a smile on her face.

"We should probably figure out what we will do in Canada once we get there," Emberly asked everyone. The joy stopped and turned to concentration.

"I'm positive that Jaylon won't mind if we stay with him in Toronto. Once we get to a town close enough to the border, I can call him and get him to help us," Sam replied.

Emberly nodded and everyone came to agreement. Eve reached into the backpack and pulled out a dishevelled box of crackers they had found on a hiking trail a couple of days back. They would have to ration it for a while.

As they ate, Emberly looked around. She would miss the forest. Even if it was almost winter, there were still bright colors everywhere. The sky seemed like an endless pool of water, bright with sun light. Although their whole adventure felt as though the trees would never end, Emberly would miss the forest.

After they ate and packed up, they started their day of walking. The twins walked with a little more pep in their step, knowing it was almost over. Even the birds above sang with a little more force than usual. As if they could sense the excitement floating up to them from below.

Emberly couldn't stop smiling as she watched the twins and thought about the new life they'd all soon have.

"Is there a reason you're smiling so big?" Sam asked.

Emberly's eyes stayed glued to the twins as she answered the question, "We get to start over," was all she said. It was all she needed to say. Sam understood.

They continued down through the red and yellow forest. The trees had just started to change and showcase their beautiful fall colours. Even the sun seemed to rise higher and shine brighter.

Finally, they reached a little field of grass with a small pond nearby and decided to set up camp for the day. There were no houses to be seen for miles, which meant they wouldn't have to hide in the trees and could swim and wash themselves. They could even take the opportunity to hunt for some more food.

Emberly decided to lay down in the field near the pond and sighed a breath of relief. But having too much energy to rest, Eve laughed and jumped on top of her, and Zayne quickly followed suit. Emberly couldn't help but laugh. Sam laughed at the sight of the three of them piled on the ground. Then, in Emberly's honour, he announced that he'd have to tickle them as punishment.

The twins shrieked and took off with Sam, and Emberly, in pursuit. The four of them ran around the field like school children during recess.

Eventually, they made their way over to the small pond to refill their water bottles and wash their clothes. Emberly grabbed her bow and quiver and flung them over her back.

"I'm going to get us something for dinner. Any requests?" she asked the group.

"Yes, can you teach me to hunt?" Eve asked with a tone of hope in her voice.

Emberly smiled and nodded her head. Eve would never have gotten the chance to learn how to hunt from their father but that didn't mean Emberly couldn't pass on the knowledge.

"Zayne, do you want to go, too?" Emberly asked.

Zayne shook his head, "No, someone's got to stay here and take care of Sam."

"Fine," Emberly laughed, at the same time Sam called out a "Hey!"

"Come on, Eve," Emberly said. "Let's go see what we can find to eat."

They made their way to a small clearing, where Emberly stopped near a set of thicker trees and handed Eve her bow, "Okay, are you ready?" Emberly asked.

Eve enthusiastically nodded her head.

Emberly positioned Eve's body so she was in the proper stance. She then placed her hands on top of Eve's and pulled back the empty bowstring so it was right against Eve's cheek. Emberly carefully let go and instructed Eve to remain in position, "Okay, now let go of the string."

"Almost perfect," she said when Eve let go, marvelling at how steady her sister had held the bow, despite its size. "Let's try again."

Eve practiced until she was able to properly pull back and release the string without any help. When Emberly was confident enough that Eve could handle the bow, she reached into her quiver and pulled out an arrow and placed it on the string.

Eve looked up at her, and Emberly could tell she was a little hesitant, despite how well she did during practice.

"Take a deep breath to clear your head," Emberly instructed as she placed her hands on Eve's and helped Eve aim the arrow at the tree across from them.

"Now, release," Emberly told her after she let go of Eve's hands.

Eve focused on the tree and took another deep breath before she released her arrow.

Eve jumped up and down in excitement when it flew straight into the tree. Granted they were only six feet away from the tree, but still, it was impressive she had hit it.

After a few more attempts, Eve no longer needed Emberly's help. It was getting close to dinner time, so Emberly took the bow and arrow back to hunt. They walked back so they were closer to the pond and sat down behind a bush as they waited for some animals to show up.

"Thanks for teaching me, Em. This is fun," Eve whispered.

"Good," Emberly smiled. "We should do this more often."

Eve nodded, and she leaned into her big sister and embraced her in a hug.

Emberly returned the hug but felt Eve suddenly stiffen at her side just before her body erupted in a shudder.

"Eve? What's wrong?" she asked as Eve's arms fell from her side.

"I have that weird feeling again, Emberly," Eve whispered. "The same one I got just before we found out that Mom had died," she clarified. "I've had it almost all day."

Emberly's heart stopped beating, "What are you talking about?"

"I don't know. I just feel like something's going to happen. Something bad," Eve paused to look at Emberly.

Emberly strained to keep her face void of expression, even though panic set in—the last thing she wanted was to worry Eve further, "How long have you had this feeling?"

"Well, the feeling got really bad just now—but, lately, every time I try to imagine living in Canada, I can't. It's almost as if we'll never get there."

Emberly inner panic rose even higher as she asked, "Then what do you think will happen?" Emberly asked.

But before Eve had time to speak, a deep voice from behind them answered for her, "It probably has something to do with us."

Emberly recognized the voice immediately, and her heart started beating faster than a hummingbird's. She shot straight up onto her feet, taking Eve by her arm and pushing her behind herself to protect Eve as three men appeared from behind the bush.

Despite there being only three men instead of five, Emberly knew exactly who they were. The hunters from the so-called abandoned house they had stolen food from, and they looked even angrier than before.

CHAPTER TWENTY-TWO

"Well look what we have here," one of the men said. He had a giant beard and an evil smile that crossed from ear to ear. He reminded Emberly of a bad-Santa.

Emberly tucked Eve further behind her back and grabbed one of her small hands. Emberly could feel Eve's hand shaking in fear. Or maybe that was just her own.

"W-what do you want?" Emberly stuttered. "How did you find us?"

"We've been following you and waiting for an opportunity for when you were by yourself," he gestured to Emberly, "because you seemed like you were the boss,. But now we have both of you so I guess this will have to do," another man stated simply. He was tall and quite large which made it very difficult for Emberly to believe they followed them on foot the whole journey. They towered over her. These men were giants, much taller than Sam. Sam!

At the thought of him, something clicked in her head. The boys needed to get out of there as fast as they could and leave her and her sister behind. But before Emberly could do anything, or even think of anything, Eve let out an ear bursting scream. Instantly, all guns were cocked and pointed at the both of them.

"I'd stop hollering if I were you," one of the men warned.

Emberly's hands shot straight up, as did Eve's. Yelling for help might not have been the smartest move, but she had no choice.

The same man walked over and shoved Emberly to the ground. He then grabbed Eve and threw her beside Emberly and warned them both to stay kneeling and stay quiet.

The girls stayed frozen in place. All three of the men's guns were pointed directly at them. Emberly didn't even want to breath for fear they would shoot her.

After a long while of waiting, Emberly began to believe the boys had indeed hid. That was until Emberly heard the blood curdling cry from a small boy in the bushes. *Zayne!*

Emberly's heart leaped from her chest and she scrambled across the ground. She'd hardly even moved before one of the men brutally stomped on her leg, and held her in place. She let out her own anguished cry in response to the pain.

"We told you to stay kneeling," the man said as he grabbed Emberly by the collar of her shirt and dragged her over to Eve.

Emberly's leg throbbed, but the knowledge that it likely wasn't broken helped calm her down a little.

Not long after, a fourth man stepped out of the bush holding both Zayne and Sam by the back of their necks.

The man standing behind Emberly went over and grabbed hold of the backpack that was on Zayne's back, and used it to throw him to the ground beside Eve. The other forced Sam to kneel beside Emberly, then kicked his back so he fell into a heap on the ground.

Sam got up with a grunt and knelt beside her. The four men just laughed at the display.

"What do you want?" Emberly asked, turning towards the man who seemed to be in charge.

Two of the men repositioned themselves so they were standing behind the kneeling children, while the other two stayed in front with their guns still pointed at them. There was no where to go.

Emberly's panic set in. They were surrounded by four men with shotguns. Emberly knew there was no chance of them escaping unharmed. Nothing was scarier.

"Give us your bags and your weapon," the one said, pointing at Emberly's bow.

The boys threw their backpacks into a pile and all eyes turned to Emberly. She took a deep breath, gripped her bow tight in the palm of her hand, and threw it into the pile as well along with her quiver.

"Good. Now where's our stuff?" the tall bearded guy asked.

The four kids furrowed their brows, "The food?" Emberly asked.

"No. Our cocaine," he explained with an exasperated huff.

Emberly eyebrows scrunched together, "What?!" Emberly scoffed, "We don't have your cocaine. We don't even know what cocaine looks like. We stole food from you—not drugs."

The men started laughing hysterically. Then the bearded man snapped his fingers, and one of the men who was standing behind the group grabbed Eve.

"Eve!" Emberly screamed. She tried to grab hold of her sister as she was dragged away, but there was no use. She felt a gun barrel push hard into her skull.

Eve was led in front of Emberly and shoved to her knees.

Emberly wanted to scream. She wanted to run to her sister and hold her close. But she couldn't. The man had kept his gun pressed to Emberly's head, and she knew she couldn't run away from this one.

"Tell us the truth, or she dies," the man from earlier repeated.

Emberly didn't know what to say. They didn't have any drugs with them, but she knew that they would shoot Eve if she said that they didn't.

Out of the corner of her eye, she saw Sam crawl on the ground toward his backpack. She wanted to reach for him to stop, but she felt the end of the gun press harder against her head.

"Don't worry about me," Sam said, pausing to look back at her. "I'm just going to check to see if we have it."

Two of the men pointed their guns at Sam as he searched through his backpack. Though time seemed to stand still, Emberly felt her heart race as Sam searched through the bag. Then finally, Sam stopped looking through his bag and handed the man the back pack.

"Like we said, there is nothing in here," Sam explained. The man rolled his eyes and tossed the bag to his partner beside him. and watched as the fourth guy grabbed Sam by the collar of his shirt and threw him to kneel next to Emberly. The man with the backpack rummaged through it until he found the frame Emberly had grabbed from their house. He took it apart and sure enough a bag of cocaine had been placed between the glass and the frame. Emberly's eyes went wide as the guy in charge snatched the clear plastic baggy. He moved the bag from side to side until he had sectioned off enough for the four of them to see the computer chip at the bottom.

"This was another reason we found you. You see this right here," he moved the cocaine around in the bag until they were able to see a small computer chip at the bottom of the bag. "We track all our drugs for this exact reason. So we can hunt you down and deal with you." He gave them a smug look as Emberly tried to stay calm and collected but it didn't work and she snapped.

"You got what you wanted, now give our sister back," Emberly demanded.

The man laughed. It was so loud that it seemed to rattle the earth around him.

Then his piercing eyes narrowed onto her face, and Emberly's breath grew heavier. He moved closer to her and bent down so they were face to face. There was still a man behind her holding a gun to her head, so Emberly refrained from doing anything stupid.

"Or what?" he reached down and fondled one of her breasts, giving it a tight squeeze. He held it in his hand, and Emberly's face grew red. Not just from anger, but from embarrassment as well. She tried shoving him away, but he was so massive that he hardly even moved. All he did was laugh and finally release her.

Who did he think he was? She was fourteen years old, and he was grabbing her—after threatening to kill her sister—and the rest of the men were holding them at gunpoint.

Emberly couldn't speak. For the first time, she truly didn't know what to do to escape this situation. She was helpless.

But if she couldn't speak, that didn't mean Sam couldn't. "Are you kidding me?" Sam seethed looking up at the man, rage in his eyes.

"How could you do that to her? How could you even *think* about doing that? It's disgusting, and total bullshit! You got what you wanted, but instead of leaving, you harass her because she wanted her sister back—who, for the record you still have kneeling in the dirt with a gun to her back. Just because she's a woman doesn't give you the right to do that to her. To any of them!"

Emberly had never seen Sam so furious. He was always so kind and never quick to anger. Everyone had their limit, she guessed.

The man walked up to Sam, who stretched his back to seem taller than he was as he knelt. Even though he only came up to the man's waist. The man wound up his arm and punched Sam in the face.

Sam fell to the floor in a heap and laid there, holding his cheek. Emberly watched him squirm on the ground, trying to gain the power and will to get back up again. It infuriated her. His nose was bleeding and Emberly was almost sure it wasn't the only thing bleeding considering the pool of blood that formed around him.

"Just stop!" she yelled finally. "You got what you came for, so just leave!"

The men all looked at her but only one spoke.

"We're not done here," replied the other man who had the gun to Emberly's head. Emberly was confused at what else they could possibly want. They had nothing left to give unless the men wanted the shirts off their backs. But to be fair, there was hardly much left of those either.

"If you'll remember," the man said, "There were five of us. Until your little sister here pulled that stunt with the bear. We managed to kill the bear, but not before he killed our friend. So, we thought it only fair, that we return the favour."

The men looked at each other and smiled. The man who had his gun pointed at Eve walked around to face her front.

All Emberly could hear was the sound of a gun firing. Her eyes went wide as the bullet pierced Eve's chest.

Eve cried out in pain and her body fell limply to the ground. Time stilled, and Emberly went numb.

The men watched with smug smiles on their faces as blood leaked from Eve's body. Emberly could see the red puddle forming on the ground. She jumped up and ran for her bow, snatching it off the ground before taking a run at the men. She didn't care if she died in the process. The men had already killed a piece of her when they shot her sister. So many pieces of herself had been killed.

The death of her father killed a piece of her.

The death of her mom killed a piece of her.

The many beatings killed numerous pieces of her.

The death of her sister killed almost all of her.

Would it make a difference if every piece of her died? She would hurt so much less. She wouldn't have to deal with those missing pieces if she was one of them. She would no longer hurt the way others had hurt her and she would go limp beside her sister, who's pieces wilted away by the second.

But Sam stepped in front of Emberly and wrapped his arms around her and pinned her in place so she couldn't move closer to the men.

"Let go of me!" she screamed, but Sam refused let her go.

The men backed away from Eve's body, allowing Zayne to rush over to her side. Rivers of tears ran down his face.

Emberly squirmed. She tried to break free of Sam's hold, but he held tight. She tried desperately to break free, so she could run over and protect Zayne as well. She was terrified they'd try to kill him as well. She couldn't lose him too.

But the men just stood there, watching the scene play out with smiles still on their faces.

"You're all monsters!" she yelled at them, tears streaming down her cheeks. Her chest heaved up and down from exhaustion.

Zayne had flipped Eve onto her back and was trying desperately to staunch the flow of blood, "Eve," he cried out. "Eve, please stay with me. Don't leave."

Emberly's heart broke as she watched her little brother try to stop Eve from bleeding out. She couldn't tear her eyes away from Eve's lifeless body.

"How could you?" she spat. "You're all monsters!"

The men laughed, and the man in charged bowed, "It was our pleasure."

Then they ran into the forest.

Finally, Emberly broke free from Sam's grip and she ran over to her sister, "We need to get help. Check the map. Where's the nearest town?"

But instead of looking for the map, Sam gently placed his hand on Emberly's arm and looked at her with pity in his eyes, "There's no use. The closest town is hours away. There has been nothing around here for days. She has minutes at best."

Emberly looked Sam in the eye. *No. No, she refused to accept that. There was no way this was happening, that this was real.*

"You're wrong!" she yelled. She grabbed one of the bags and shoved it into Sam's arms, as a way of trying to tell him they had to leave that second.

But all he did was drop it at his feet, "I wish I was."

Her eyes, so full of anger and hurt, softened as she realized he was right. She fell to the ground, kneeling again—but in her sister's blood this time. Tears soaking Emberly's face as she picked up Eve's hand.

Eve's body that had been writhing so aggressively in pain before had now fallen so eerily still. Her heaving breaths were barely a whisper of air, and her cries of anguish were barely more than the tiniest of whimpers.

Emberly let her head fall to Eve's chest as she wailed. Her little sister, the happiest person Emberly ever knew, was dying.

All for nothing.

Emberly looked at Eve's face. A face that grew less lively by the second. A face that wouldn't live to see morning.

She would never again see Eve's bright smile. Streams of tears-stained Eve's cheeks, and her skin was paler than that of a ghost.

*It should have been me*, Emberly thought. Not Eve. It was her who had convinced the twins to run. It was her who had put her siblings in danger when she had decided they should run from the foster home. All of this was Emberly's fault.

Emberly gently lifted Eve's head and shoulders and propped her up against her lap. She wanted to provide as much comfort to Eve as she could in her final moments.

"Emberly," Eve softly whispered. "Thank you—for every-thing," she gasped.

Emberly tried to control her tears, but it was no use. The tears rolled down her cheeks and landed onto Eve's chest as it rose and fell—each time weaker than the last.

Emberly desperately hoped that it would be like in a movie where the main character's tears would fall onto the injured person's body and bring them back to life. But no matter how much she wished, she knew that no amount of tears could ever heal the wound. No amount of tears would wipe away the pain.

Eve tried to speak again, but the words were halted as she choked on the blood that had started to run out of her mouth.

Emberly carefully lifted Eve's head higher from her lap so she could cough out the blood in her throat. Eve turned her head even more and began throwing up chunks of blood onto the dirt floor. Her back heaved from the motion and she howled in pain. Emberly laid her back down on her lap and Eve let the blood leak from the side of her mouth. No longer caring to spit it out.

Emberly wanted to look away but she wouldn't. She wouldn't let herself look away. She didn't want Eve to suffer alone.

Eve's eyes fluttered open and she beckoned for Emberly to bend lower so Eve could talk to her. She did as Eve asked and placed her ear right up to Eve's mouth, "Get to Canada. Live the—" a raspy breath rattled in her lungs. "the life we wanted," she whispered. "Just don't forget me."

"How could I ever forget you?" Emberly smiled. "You're my little sister—the heart of our family—always and forever."

She forced her smile to grow larger, wanting Eve to know she truly meant it.

But who would remember their inside jokes when they both died? Who would remember the mischief they got into; the stories they had made up together? That was the thing about death. The people closest to you always remember you, but what happens in one hundred years when they are all gone? Who would remember?

Emberly reached down and hugged Eve.

Zayne wrapped his arms around the two of them, and Sam wrapped his long arms around everyone.

They sat there until Eve mustered the strength to speak again, "Can you do two more things for me?"

"Anything you want, Eve," Zayne told her, choking on his tears.

"While I die, I want to watch the sunset. Can you prop me up against a tree?" they all nodded with tears in their eyes and stood up. Emberly held Eve in her arms as she walked over and propped her body against a tree. Sam followed behind, carrying Zayne's weeping body in his arms.

Blood, mixed with dirt and tears, stained their clothes, but none of them cared. In that moment, nothing else mattered besides Eve.

Emberly sat next to her sister, while Zayne sat on the other side of his twin. They each rested their head on her shoulders as the three watched their final sunset together. Sam picked up one of Eve's hands and held it firmly in his own, which made her relax a little bit.

They watched as all the colours changed in the sky around them. Emberly looked up at Eve's face, and it could have been just Emberly's mind trying to make things better, but she could have sworn that Eve's face was lit up by every colour in the sky, even if the colour from her face drained by the second.

"What was the other thing you wanted Eve?" Sam asked, re-membering she had asked for two things.

"Oh yes. Em, can you sing to me? One last time," Eve smiled weakly at Emberly, her energy fading faster. Emberly nodded. Tears blurred her eyes, and her throat stung from screaming, but she began.

Don't fear. Stay near.

You'll be alright.

Sleep tight my baby, until night—

Emberly began to choke on her words. Her sobs grew deeper and tears streamed down her cheeks. But she pushed on. For Eve, she needed to finish.

Close your eyes. Listen closely.

You'll always be safe, so long as

You're with me.

Emberly choked through the last words of the song, knowing it was the last time her sister would ever hear them.

"We love you so much, Eve," Emberly reassured her. She took a deep breath and kissed Eve on her forehead. Zayne held his twin in his arms and sobbed, knowing that it would be the last time. Agony ruled his emotions as he wept over his dying sister. His twin, with who he shared a womb, was dying and there was nothing he could do.

"I love you guys more," she whispered with her final full breath.

Emberly felt Eve's soul leave her body. Her last spark, her last shed of innocence—of life—was gone. Emberly looked at her sister, whose unseeing eyes still stared up at the sunset. Emberly lifted a hand and closed Eve's eyes. Then her bottom lip started to shake and she couldn't bear it any longer. She draped her arms around her sister and gave into her tears. She had never cried so much in her life. The twins had always meant more to her than anything or anyone in her life.

And now Eve was gone. She had been through so much pain and torture, and she would never get the chance to live a normal life. It wasn't fair.

Emberly cried until her eyes were dry. Her face pressed into her sister's neck. Eve's body felt frail, as if the very essence of her—her soul, her light—was what had given weight to her body. Eve was truly gone.

After a long while of wishing everything had just been another horrible nightmare, Emberly stood up slowly. She watched as Zayne remained tight to their sister's side, his eyes red from crying.

Emberly took a deep breath in an attempt to control her emotions. Sam walked over to her and lifted her chin with his hand. She looked up at him, and he looked down at her. The corners of his lips pulled into a soft smile, and he nodded slightly. At that moment, her body went limp.

Luckily, Sam caught her just before she hit the ground. He gently lowered Emberly the remainder of the way and placed her in his lap, cradling her in his arms, making her feel safe.

She wept into his shoulder while he gently stroked her hair. She could feel the tears that fell down Sam's cheeks and onto her hair. Emberly stayed with Sam. Zayne needed time to be alone with Eve, and Emberly needed to cry. But most of all, she needed someone to hold her as she cried. She took a deep breath to calm herself and pulled her head from Sam's shoulder.

"How are you feeling?" Sam asked her.

Emberly thought back to the last two hours. She was held at gunpoint and sexually assaulted. Then spent the last hour crying because her baby sister had been shot in the back and died. *How was she feeling?* "Numb," she responded.

"How's your face?" she asked, motioning to the bruises already forming by Sam's eye.

"Decent. How are you feeling about the whole...situation?" Emberly knew he wasn't talking about the Eve situation.

"It was the most helpless I've ever felt," was all she said. It was all she could say.

Emberly looked behind her to find Zayne asleep beside his sister, his head rested against her shoulder and his back against the tree. Their hands were interlocked. Emberly smiled wistfully at the sight. She got up and walked over to her brother, wanting to be beside him. She kissed him on the head and whispered "I love you" in his ear, before going to the opposite side and curling up next to her sister.

Emberly looked up to the sky. She hadn't realized how dark it had gotten outside until she saw the beautiful stars littered across the sky. They reminded her of Eve. *Maybe she was already one of them. Watching out for them from above.* The thought gave Emberly a tiny bit of comfort.

Before falling asleep, she spotted Sam standing against a tree, looking out at the forest in front of him. She watched him for a while before he noticed she was staring at him. He smiled kindly at her, and she motioned for him to come over. He hesitated for a moment before nodding and walking over.

Emberly rolled to her side so her back was pressed against Eve, and Sam laid down so they were facing one another.

"Why were you standing over there?" she whispered.

Sam shrugged his shoulders, "I thought someone should stand watch, and you guys looked tired. Also, I didn't want to intrude."

Emberly shook her head. "Don't be ridiculous," she said. "It's not intruding when it's family," she smiled, hoping he'd grasp her meaning.

His answering smile proved that he did.

She heard a rustling noise behind her and turned her head to investigate. She found Zayne pulling the red blanket out of one of the backpacks.

He walked back over to them and Emberly shifted closer to Sam and held her other arm out to Zayne, indicating for him to curl between her and Eve. She knew there was no way he'd leave Eve's side tonight.

Zayne laid down and curled between his two sisters, and Emberly covered Zayne, Sam, and her with the blanket.

But just as she closed her eyes, she saw Zayne move. He grabbed the corner of the blanket and covered Eve with it.

"I don't want her to be cold tonight," he explained.

"That's a great idea, Zayne," she smiled.

## CHAPTER TWENTY-THREE

MORNING SLOWLY ARRIVED, AND Emberly looked up at Sam, her eyes still blinded by the harshness of the morning light. At one point during the night, she had sat up and placed her head on his lap since the ground was getting terribly cold at night.

He smiled down at her and stroked her hair, "Go back to sleep," he whispered softly. "It's still really early."

"I can't now that I'm already up. Besides, it's our last long day of walking and I want to get a head start to clear my mind."

Sam shook his head in amusement, "Whatever you want."

Emberly smiled softly and shook Zayne awake. He rubbed his eyes and hugged Emberly before looking over at Eve.

"Are we leaving soon?" Zayne asked glancing at Eve.

"We'll eat first, then hit the road for the last time."

Zayne smiled at the knowledge that they would be in Canada soon, but his smile turned mournful as he looked back to Eve.

Emberly knew what he was thinking, it wouldn't be the same without Eve.

In order to preserve the last of their food, they came to the decision to put off eating for a while. Not to mention none of them were particularly hungry as a result of the night prior.

Instead, they all stood up and crowded around Eve, deciding what they should to do with her.

"We sure as hell can't leave her like this," Emberly pointed out. She looked at Zayne and turned to Sam to whisper in his ear. "An animal will eat her." Sam nodded and Emberly looked back at her sister.

"We could bury her," Zayne offered as a solution.

"Yes, but we don't have anything to dig a hole with," Emberly contradicts.

"We could try to dig a hole with tree branches," Sam suggested. It was by far not their best option, but it was still something. So, Emberly agreed and they went to search for some branches that could be used to dig and started to dig a hole right in front of a tree.

They began to dig and started off strong. However, with no shovels, it was going to take them a long time. The only way they would be able to retract enough dirt to make a hole, was if they scraped it all away instead of digging. So that was what they did.

They worked at it for hours, sweat beading down their faces even though the wind was chilly.

By noon the hole was no more than a foot deep. The sun began to set but that didn't stop them. They continued to dig. They stopped occasionally for water breaks throughout the day but other than that they worked. They were going to finish.

The sun had fully set over the horizon, and they were using their flashlight to see. They sat down, exhausted, and pulled out the last of their food and rationed it off. They ate a little extra that day knowing they had maybe only a couple days left and still had three- quarters of the box of crackers left to eat.

"We should wrap Eve in the blanket when we bury her," Zayne suggested.

Emberly turned to him and smiled, "Great idea Zayne."

Emberly helped Zayne carefully wrap their sister up in the blanket. As she was doing it, Emberly saw Sam grab the knife from the bag. She raised a brow at him when he caught her staring at him in confusion.

"I was thinking I could carve out Eve's name in the tree if that's okay?" Sam asked.

"That would be perfect Sam. Thank you."

While Sam carved Eve's name into the tree, Emberly looked around and wondered into the forest until she found a small patch of wild flowers. She pulled three flowers from the ground and walked back to where the boys were standing, and handed each of them a flower to place on Eve.

"We'll miss you, sis," Zayne said as he took a deep breath to stop himself from crying.

Emberly wrapped her arms around Zayne and held him as he cried silently in her arms. Emberly didn't shed a tear at that moment. She just watched her baby sister laying there, wrapped in a blanket, and eternally watching the sky without a beating heart.

The only thing keeping Emberly together was knowing her sister was forever safe in the afterlife.

Emberly broke free from the embrace after several minutes and walked over to Eve. She needed to say goodbye one last time. She laid on her stomach, placed her flower in the hole, and moved her short hair behind her ear.

"If you can hear me, Eve, I want you to know that I love you so much. Always and forever. And I promise to never forget you," Emberly whispered as she fought back the tears. The flower in Emberly's hand drifted softly and landed on Eve's body. This would be the last time she would see her sister, but she knew that some day they would be together again.

Emberly's legs seemed to have developed a way of walking on their own since her brain was foggy that morning. Eve was the only thing running through her mind. She tried not to focus on the idea of never being able to see or talk to Eve again, so she thought about everything they had done together.

She thought about their time together with Zayne when their mom was at work. About the countless times Eve and Zayne tried to play pranks on Emberly, and the many times their pranks would fail. She thought of how whenever Eve would get nightmares, Emberly was the first person she went to. She would crawl into Emberly's bed in the middle of the night, and Emberly would hold her as she fell asleep.

So many great memories raced through Emberly's mind as she walked through the forest. No one talked. There were too many things to think about. But they never stopped, because they knew that the next day would lead to their future. It wouldn't involve Eve, but Emberly knew she was still there with them.

The sun shone down brighter than ever, as if Mother Nature was creating a mockery of the prior day's tragedy. The leaves on the ground crunched under their shoes as their feet stomped down like elephants after many days without rest.

"Wait," Zayne called out suddenly. "I need a break." Emberly and Sam turned to find Zayne leaning against a tree.

"How much longer?" Zayne panted.

Sam rummaged through the bag and pulled out the map, "Well, if I'm reading this right, we should be able to make it to a little town called Grand Isle, Maine by sunset. Then I can call my cousin to see if he can get us the citizenship papers."

"That all sounds good except for the part where you said 'if he can get us the citizenship papers'. So, there's a chance he can't?" Emberly asked.

Sam's expression turned sheepish, "Well, here's the thing. I haven't talked to my cousin in four years, so I'm not sure if he still can or not."

Emberly's eyes grew wide, and she began pacing the forest floor, "What happens if we can't get them? Do we just stay here in Maine or find somewhere else in the US to live? Where will Zayne go to school? Will we be able to get jobs? We are only fifteen, how will we survive? We've come this far, I don't—"

"Emberly, calm down," Sam interrupted her. He grabbed her shoulders and turned her to face him. "It's going to be fine. Yes, I haven't talked to my cousin in a few years, but I can almost guarantee that he can still get them for us. You have nothing to worry about, I promise."

Emberly opened her mouth to speak, but Sam cut her off. "I know, 'don't make a promise you can't keep'," he smiled, "but I swear I will keep this one." Emberly knew he shouldn't promise something he very well had no idea if he could keep or not but she didn't have the energy to argue with him over it at that moment.

"Okay," Emberly nodded as she started to cool off, "I believe you."

A small cough reminded them that Zayne was still there.

"You like each other. You guys would make such a cute couple. Eve and I both said it," Zayne said.

Emberly and Sam exchanged glances, but they both broke into nervous laughter.

"Why are you laughing?" Zayne told them. "It wasn't a joke. You both like each other. It's obvious."

Emberly had no idea Zayne even knew about "liking someone" but apparently, she was mistaken. Emberly kept her head down, as did Sam. Neither knew what to say.

Emberly didn't know how to feel about Sam. Well, maybe she had a bit of an idea. They had been together for a while, and they had become quite good friends. But she knew that they *had* become more than just friends by now. She liked the way he laughed when she rolled her eyes at him. She liked the way he didn't care if Emberly was in a mood. How he'd still help her through whatever she was going through even though she insisted he didn't need to. And, she liked the way she could be normal around him in a way she never could with any other person in her life besides the twins.

Emberly was mixed with emotions as she stood there, staring at the ground. Finally, she got the courage to look up and take a deep breath. She looked at Sam. Yes, she was pretty sure she knew how she felt about him. And if his answering stare was any indication, she was pretty sure she knew how he felt about her.

Zayne just rolled his eyes and gave them both an "I told you so" look, breaking the tension and causing both Emberly and Sam to chuckle.

The walked over to where Zayne was standing, and reached into the backpack he'd been carrying. They pulled out the last of their food, which was yet another reminder to Emberly that they needed to get to Canada before they starved.

As Emberly nibbled on a cracker, she imagined what it would be like to sleep on a bed again or to be able to eat food that hadn't come from a forgotten box of crackers in the woods. She could change into clean clothes and not have to worry about where they would stay. She could take a shower, rather than bathe in another icy creek. Not to mention the most important thing of all. They could stop running in fear.

She could finally feel safe. That is—providing Sam's cousin was able to pull through for them.

Emberly shook herself and grabbed the empty food bag and stuffed it into Zayne's backpack. She hoped that it would be the last time they'd ever have to eat on the floor again.

Emberly was done with walking through the forest. Her body was covered in scars, blisters and bruises. Her hair was a tangled mess, despite being shorter. Even brushing couldn't get all the knots out of it at this point.

Sam and Zayne didn't look any better.

But soon, as Emberly kept reminding herself, the long torturous hours of walking and running would be over. They were so close.

"We're almost there guys," Emberly smiled. Based on where the sun was and how long Sam figured it'd take to get to the town, Emberly estimated they had a little over an hour left.

Zayne whooped for joy and started running.

Emberly laughed but soon found herself and Sam running after him. Knowing they had such little time left gave them all a surge of energy, and they refused to just walk.

Adrenaline rushed through her body and kept Emberly going. Her body no longer felt sore, and her legs were no longer tired. Even her bow and quiver that kept jabbing her in her back as it swung back and forth couldn't stop Emberly from running.

She ran, with Sam and Zayne in tow, until they finally reached a large town sign. The village of Grand Isle.

"So, what now?" Zayne asked. Emberly looked at Sam.

"Well, I guess I have to go and call my cousin. We'll need to find a phone," Sam responded.

Emberly nodded but then remembered something. The three of them were filthy. They would draw a lot of attention if they were to walk into a store like that.

"We need to wash up first. I think I saw a creek somewhere around here while we were running," Emberly suggested.

The boys nodded.

She led the way through the forest to the creek. They took off their clothes and washed themselves in the creek.

They had grown somewhat comfortable with the fact of only being in their undergarments around each other when they bathed, but not completely. Emberly still stood on one end of the creek while Sam and Zayne washed themselves on the other side.

Emberly dunked herself in the water, making sure not to slip on the rocks she planted her feet on. She rung her hair out and grabbed one of their old shirts to dry her shivering body off as best as she could. She used the shirt to then scrub the dirt from everyone's clothes.

Soon Sam and Zayne returned, and Emberly handed each of them their 'clean' clothes.

Once they were as clean as they could possibly get, they made their way back towards town to find a phone.

Luckily, they didn't need to look very far because there was a general store right on the edge of town. Emberly placed her bow and quiver against the store to limit the suspicion about why she had it and they made their way inside.

The little bell that hung from the door frame, rang in Emberly's ears as they pushed the heavy door open. For a moment, Emberly had flashbacks to the last time her and Sam had walked into a general store. *This time would be different*, she promised herself.

Still, Emberly cautiously looked around until a young woman peeked her head out from a back room and smiled brightly at them. She walked over to the kids, not caring what they looked like, and her smile widened. She kind of reminded Emberly of Eve.

"How may I help you?" she asked in a cheery voice.

Emberly couldn't help but smile back at her.

"We were wondering if we could please use your phone," Emberly replied.

"Of course, right this way."

She led them behind the front counter where she pointed at a shiny black phone on its surface.

Emberly looked over to Sam, and he walked up to the phone and started dialling a number. Emberly crossed her fingers in hopes that someone would pick up. It rang once, then again and again. All hope Emberly had dwindled away with every ring of the phone. But when she finally heard someone's voice on the other side, Emberly's heart leaped for joy.

"Hey, Jaylon. It's Sam."

From the corner of her eye, Emberly noticed that the woman was watching them from behind a shelf, so she stood on her tippy toes and whispered into Sam's ear, "Is there any way you could talk quieter? That lady is listening."

Sam nodded and started speaking again, "Jaylon, est qu'on peut parler on français? C'est important et je ne peux pas faire entendre à personne ce que je m'apprête à te dire."

*He was speaking in French! Brilliant.* Emberly turned her head slightly and saw that the lady had turned to leave. She probably couldn't understand a word. Sam glanced over at her, and she gave him two thumbs up to continue.

There was a muffled response from the other end that Emberly couldn't make out, but Sam nodded in response.

*At least he understands*, she thought. She didn't really know any French, so for all she knew Sam could have been ordering food rather than asking about citizenship papers.

But as their conversation on the phone continued, Emberly trusted that Sam would say the right thing.

"Tu ne peux pas dire ce que je viens de te dire à personne. Comprends-tu?" Sam said before finishing the phone call and hanging up.

He faced Emberly, but kept his facial expression neutral. Emberly wasn't sure if that was bad or not. He walked past Emberly, thanked the woman for the use of her phone, and walked out of the store.

Emberly and Zayne followed suit, nervous that Sam's lack of expression meant that something bad had happened.

Once the cool air hit her face, she grabbed Sam's arm and turned him to face her. She was eager to know what his cousin had said.

At Sam's silence, her heart rate quickened, and it beat faster the longer Sam took to answer.

"Well," Zayne finally asked, breaking the unbearable silence. "What did he say?"

"It's not good news..." Sam trailed off.

Emberly's heart dropped. She knew it. His cousin couldn't help them. It was the news she had been dreading to hear. Now what would they—

"He can't come with the citizenships papers until tomorrow."

"Wait, what?" Emberly had to stop and think about what Sam had just said.

Then it clicked, "Does that mean he's coming?" Zayne asked, a speck of hopeful joy returning to his face.

Sam lifted his head and a smirk appeared on his face. He nodded, "He's coming tomorrow with the papers and taking us to live with him!"

Zayne jumped in the air in excitement, but instead of joining in, Emberly punched Sam in the arm, "Don't joke about that! Jeez. You scared me."

She wanted to be mad at him for pulling that prank and scaring her like that, but how could she...knowing they would soon be in Canada.

She wrapped her arms around them and pulled them into a tight hug. People must have thought they were crazy; three dirty-looking kids standing outside of the general store and hugging, but Emberly didn't care. She knew they were dirty and that their clothes were torn. She knew they had backpacks over their shoulders and Emberly bow and quiver leaning up against the store where she had left it. She knew, and still she was too happy to care.

She let go and took hold of the situation. She looked at Sam, "Okay, so we need to stay somewhere overnight, right? What time did your cousin say he was going to be coming, and where will he be?"

"He said he would meet us in the back alley of the general store at five in the morning so no one will see us."

"Good. That means we need to get some sleep because we'll have another long day ahead of us, and we don't want to be late." The sun had started setting sooner and rising later, which meant that it would be hard for her to tell exactly what time it was. They would just have to guess

"We should probably just go back to the forest and go to sleep now," Emberly suggested.

The boys agreed, and they set out to sleep in the forest for hopefully the last time.

Zayne yawned, so Emberly sat on the ground beside him and ruffled his hair, "Zayne, you can go to bed now. I'll stay up tonight so you and Sam can both get the rest you need."

"You need sleep too," Sam told her. "I'll watch first, then I'll wake you up so you can be in charge of waking everyone up. Deal?"

Sam was finally understanding how Emberly worked. She nodded happily. Zayne laid down beside Emberly and fell asleep instantly.

Emberly knew she needed to sleep, but she wasn't quite ready to. Instead, she turned her head to look at Sam.

"How do you know French?" she questioned him.

Sam chuckled.

"Jaylon's parents and mine thought it'd be a useful skill to have. It didn't matter if *we* wanted to learn or not. Their ruling was always 'if it was important to them, it had to be important to us'. So, they got us a tutor."

"Since Jaylon and his family lived in the town close to our house, they'd come over every Sunday where we'd be taught for hours in my dining room.

"For years we had to take those weekly lessons. We were never allowed to miss a class, even if we were super sick and were hurling into the toilet. And our tutors were mean. They'd hit us on our hands with rulers if we slacked off or got an answer wrong. It just made me want to do the work less."

"Then when Jaylon graduated four years ago, I was stuck doing it on my own, which made it even more unbearable. And when I told my parents I wanted to stop, they signed me up to go to a French boarding school. Of course, I begged and pleaded for them not to send me there. But my dad would just claim it would be good for me. In reality though, I knew it was because he just wanted me out of the house."

Emberly grabbed Sam's hand and squeezed it. In a way, she was lucky that her mom hadn't ever really cared about her school work. She was always too busy, so she never signed up for parent teacher conferences and never bothered to look at Emberly's or the twins' report cards. It was up to her to keep her own grades up since there was no one there to push her to do so. But she liked it that way.

"Some days," she said, wanting to break the tension, "I wish I spoke another language...but not the way you had to be taught," she winked.

Sam chuckled.

"Goodnight, Sam," she whispered.

"Goodnight, Emberly," he replied. Then he leaned over and kissed her on the forehead. "Sleep tight."

Emberly's cheeks felt as though they were on fire, and butterflies swam in her stomach. She laid down and put her head in Sam's lap, and he draped an arm over her to help keep her warm as she drifted off to asleep.

CHAPTER TWENTY-FOUR

"You ready to go?" Emberly asked the next morning as they packed up their gear.

"I am *very* ready," Zayne almost yelled.

Emberly and Sam chuckled at Zayne. He was a complete ball of excited energy. He'd even woken up on his own this morning, well before it was time to go.

"Then I guess we better get moving," Emberly laughed as she slipped her bow and quiver over her shoulder. She took a deep breath and smiled. What they were about to do was dangerous and illegal but at that point, she didn't care. Not as long as they made it. Plus, what was one more illegal thing to add to their list at this point.

The three of them left the protection of the forest and crept through the sleeping town. Emberly grew more nervous with every step she took, and she didn't think she took a full breath until they had safely made it behind the store.

They didn't have to wait long before Emberly spotted a set of lights from a car driving their way. It came to a screeching stop beside them, which made Emberly nervous that someone had heard the noise and would come out to inspect. What made her even more nervous though, was the thought of it not being Jaylon in the car.

Emberly held onto Zayne's hand and watched as the driver's window rolled down.

"Need a ride?" the man—Jaylon, Emberly assumed—jokingly asked.

A huge smile was plastered on Sam's face as he walked over to the car, "Thank you so much, Jay. I owe you."

"Yes, you do," Jaylon laughed.

Relieved that it was indeed Sam's cousin, Emberly walked over to the car. When she got close, she realized that he looked nothing like Sam. Even while sitting, she could tell he had a taller, more muscular frame. His emerald green eyes were a stark contrast to Sam's ocean blue ones. His straight, blond hair was tied up in a bun on the top of his head and tattoos covered his arms like sleeves.

Jaylon's eyes shifted to behind Sam, "So, this must be the family you were talking about," he looked at Emberly and gave her a warm smile.

She nodded affirmatively.

"Well get in then. Before someone sees us."

Emberly grabbed Zayne's hand and got in the backseat as Sam climbed in the front. Jaylon started the car and they sped off. The tires kicked up dust and small rocks as the car rolled down the gravel roads.

"I need to know how this is going to work," Emberly said as they left Grand Isle. She refused to do anything unless she knew what the plan was. Jaylon just chuckled.

"I like her already," he spoke in Sam's direction. "So this is how it's going to play out," he told her, turning his attention to the rear view mirror so she could see he was talking to her. "My job is secret. Something not many people know about. But what you do need to know about it is that I know what I'm doing. I've done this a million times and for cases twenty times bigger than yours and haven't been caught once." Emberly could tell he wasn't lying, and at that point she really didn't care to know the specifics of his job because she had a feeling she wouldn't like to know the details.

"So, do we get to see the passports?" Emberly asked.

Jaylon reached into the glove box and pulled out a bag and handed it to Emberly. She grabbed it and found a bunch of different passports inside. She pulled them all out and read them to herself.

They all had the same last name except for the passports that were for a sixteen-year-old boy. Emberly appreciated that Jaylon had let her and Zayne keep the same last name as each other. She also noticed that while each passport had a different first name on it, presumably for them to choose from, each middle name on the passports were their own, which made it easier for Emberly to let go of her name while still holding onto a part of who she was.

She separated the passports into the different piles, passing Zayne and Sam their piles and kept her own. She noticed that none of them had pictures and was about to ask when Jaylon spoke, "I wasn't able to get pictures on such short notice—not ones that would have matched your features. These will work well enough for now, and once we get to Toronto I'll get photos taken of you guys, and get a set of social security cards, proper passports, and birth certificates done up for each of you, along with a new license for Sam."

Emberly looked at the fake passports she held in her hand, and the thought of changing her name weighed heavy on her heart. She loved her name and never wanted to change it, but did she have a choice anymore? She took a deep breath and flipped through the names.

*Nance? That didn't suit her. Kathryn? No way. Amara? Absolutely not.* She continued to look at cards as she ate from a bag of chips Jaylon had brought along with him. Never in her life had she tried BBQ chips until that moment, and they instantly became her favorite, which could have also had something to do with the fact that they weren't stale crackers. Emberly was about to give up when she noticed that there were two cards stuck together. She peeled them apart and read it. Aidan Emberly Fortier. It was perfect. She knew that Aidan meant fierce because her mom used to tell her the most random names and their meanings to help Emberly go to sleep when she was younger. She smiled to herself knowing it was the perfect name for her.

She looked over at Zayne and showed him the passport she chose. He gave her a big hug and told her he still needed more time to decide.

She turned to the front to where Jaylon and Sam were deep in conversation. She tapped Sam on the shoulder, "Say hello to Aidan Emberly Fortier."

Sam's smiled when he heard the name, "It's perfect," he told her.

Emberly knew it was a great fit for her and was happy that Zayne and Sam liked it as well.

"I still need to look through mine," he said as he started to sort through the passports Emberly had given him earlier.

"So, I heard you don't like Sam," Jaylon said as he looked at her through his rear-view mirror. Her head jolted to the mirror to look at Jaylon.

"Jaylon," Sam hissed.

Apparently, Emberly wasn't supposed to have heard that. She shook her head and smiled, "Well, you're not completely wrong."

Sam turned around and looked at her.

"Of course, I didn't like him when he first joined us on our journey, but now, I guess I've realized that he's not that bad," Emberly smiled, and Sam playfully rolled his eyes and turned back to face the front.

"So, do you just tolerate him, or do you think he's okay?" Jaylon asked.

"It depends on the day. He can be a real pain in the butt some days. But more often than not, I think he's okay," she chuckled.

Emberly saw Jaylon look over at Sam and smile.

"I think he thinks the same of you. If his smile gets any bigger, he's going to stretch his face."

While they drove, they talked and listened to music. Emberly hadn't felt so carefree in forever, and it was a major improvement from the constant walking that they'd been doing.

"So Sam, what name did you pick?" Zayne asked. Zayne had already decided on the name Tayton Zayne Fortier for himself and was happy about it. As was Emberly.

Sam turned around and looked at Zayne, "Sean Sam Belton. I kind of like it," Sam smiled.

"Well, I really like it," Zayne reassured him.

Emberly chuckled and smiled at Sam. She couldn't agree more.

He turned back around and just in time because they had arrived at the border. Emberly's heart started to race. This was the moment of truth. *After all that time, were they going to make it to Canada?* The car fell silent but Jaylon spoke up as they pulled into one of the security lanes.

"Okay, so this is how it's going to work. I have ... friends we'll call them, that work in this lane specifically. They know we're coming and are going to let us in. They still need your pictures and everything. If we went to any other booth, they would send us back and we could even to jail." That bit of information scared Emberly even more than anything. There was a high chance this wouldn't work, but they had come too far to not try. "Any and all searches that come through this lane are done by my guys so you don't have to worry about them finding anything." Emberly nodded her head but didn't say a word.

They reached the front of the line and pulled up to the booth Jaylon's friend was working at. Jaylon and his friend talked for a little bit as the friend looked at the passports. He smiled and handed the passports back. He said goodbye and Jaylon drove away from the booth and into Canada.

Emberly could breath again. "It worked!" was all she could get out.

"Yes, it did. Ladies and gentlemen, welcome to Canada!" Jaylon came up to a bridge and started to drive across it. Emberly looked behind her and smiled. They were in Canada! Their plan had worked.

She grabbed onto Zayne and hugged him with all her might. A tear rolled down his face, and she held him tighter. The hardest part was now over. Their lives could truly begin.

Emberly flung her arms around the seat and hugged Sam by the chest. She hugged him so tight she felt like she was suffocating him but he didn't move nor push her away.

"I've never seen you so happy," Sam said looking at Emberly. She released her grip and sat back in her seat. She couldn't stop smiling.

"That's because she hasn't been," Zayne told him.

They all burst out into laughter as Jaylon continued to drive down the road to New Brunswick towards their new life.

"So, what's exactly happening now? Are you leaving us to fend for ourselves or what?" Emberly asked. She had to know.

"No, I'm not going to leave you by yourselves. You'll come stay with me in Toronto until you're able to settle elsewhere. Right now, we're driving to a town called Campbellton where I have to drop off this car since it isn't mine. I had to borrow it for work. Can't exactly take fugitives across the border in my own car, now, can I?" he chuckled. "From there we'll get on a train to Toronto. Sound good?"

"Yup," Emberly smiled.

Finally, Jaylon drove past the Campbellton town sign. He drove through the city at a slower pace than before, and pulled into a parking lot in the back alley of a large building. Emberly grabbed her bow and quiver and was about to get out of the car, but Jaylon stopped her.

"You guys can't go out looking like that. It will draw too much attention"

He opened his trunk then gave them all a pair of pants, shirt, clean underwear, a box of baby wipes, and a brush.

"Emberly, look out the window while Sam and Zayne change, then we'll get out to let you change. Those baby wipes are to clean the dirt from your face and the brush...well that's self-explanatory."

Emberly nodded and turned to look at the beautiful graffiti on the concrete walls. She grabbed the new hair brush and began to brush through her knotted hair. She had to section it off into small sections to be able to run the brush through, even with it being much shorter.

Soon the two boys finished and they all got out of the car to let Emberly change. She undressed and used the wipes to clean her body, then slipped on her new clothes. They fit perfectly and Emberly was beyond excited to get to wear something that was clean and didn't have any holes. She grabbed another wipe from the container and scrubbed her face clean.

When she finished, she looked in the rear-view mirror and did a double take. She hadn't seen her reflection in months and was shocked at the difference she saw. There was a maturity and seriousness to her eyes that was even more pronounced than before. Her tan had deepened from all the time they had spent outdoors, and now highlighted the green in her eyes and matched the richness of her raven black hair. And her hair, with its much shorter length, now showed off her long neck and strong jawline, not to mention the scar that ran along the side of her face.

Emberly lifted her hair to get a full look at the scar. Unfortunately, it looked like it hadn't healed properly as it was still quite noticeable. She knew it would lessen with time, but for now, she'd just have to get used to her new look. *At least,* she rationalized, *it would forever be a reminder of how strong she was, inside and out. And that,* she smiled, *wasn't so bad.*

Emberly stepped out of the car and flung her bow and quiver over her shoulder.

"Oh yeah, I forgot you had those," Jaylon looked at the weapon slung over Emberly's shoulder. "If anyone asks, you're going to a competition in Toronto. No one should question you on the train." Emberly nodded.

Jaylon popped open the hood of the car, and with two swift looks to either side, he hid the keys inside. It looked like it was almost natural for him to do it. It made Emberly even more curious about what his job entailed, but she could just ask Sam later. She wasn't about to bombard Jaylon with her questions. He closed the hood gently and led everyone through the back alley until they reached a main road, leaving the car behind for someone to eventually pick up.

They walked down one more street before arriving at what seemed to be an old train station. Jaylon walked up to the ticket booth and purchased tickets for each of them, then they walked into the station as they waited the arrival of their train.

A loud voice over the intercom announced that all passengers of train sixteen were to board immediately. They boarded the train and found a booth that would fit all four of them and piled in. Emberly sat on one bench with Zayne, and Jaylon and Sam sat facing opposite to them.

Emberly looked out the window and watched as the train slowly pulled out of the station, then moved swiftly down the tracks.

Emberly laid her head back and closed her eyes. Why was she so nervous? They were finally in Canada and on the train to their final destination. She should be happy—elated, relieved even. But she couldn't settle her nerves. She tried to take a deep breath to calm herself, but that did not help. So, she just looked out the window as the buildings of Campbellton wilted away.

After a couple minutes of listening to Jaylon and Sam talk and watching Zayne slowly fall a sleep to her right, Sam got up and went to sit between Emberly and the train car wall, leaving Jaylon by himself on the bench in front.

"Nervous?" she heard Sam ask her.

"No. Why would you ask me if I'm scared?" she scolded.

He smiled, "I didn't ask you if you were scared. I asked if you were nervous. You think I don't know you, but I know you better than you think."

Emberly looked away and crossed her arms, "No, you don't."

But Sam grabbed one of her hands and held it. She looked down at their interlocked hands. And she couldn't help but smile a little.

"The least you can do is tell me the truth, Emberly."

She looked him in the eyes and knew there was no way of getting out of it. "I don't know what's going to happen to us in Toronto. Yes, I know we're staying with Jaylon for now, but we can't stay with him forever, right?

"And, Zayne has to go to school. My new citizenship says that I'm seventeen which means I either go into grade twelve knowing nothing or just not attend school. If I decide the latter, I know I can go back to school eventually, but I'll need to get a job now to make money for Zayne and I to live."

She took a deep breath and continued, "Your citizenship says you're eighteen on it, and you won't want to live with us after this since your end of the deal pulled through. And then Zayne and I will be by ourselves and I'll have to get a second job just to take care of the two of us and will eventually turn into my mom and never be home to take care of him or spend any time with him. And—"

"Emberly, it's going to be fine," Sam rubbed a hand on her lower back until her breath returned to its normal pace.

She opened her mouth to continue speaking, but Sam decided it was his turn to talk and held up a hand to stop her, "Now, let's get one thing straight. I'm not going to leave you. I promise. And I don't make promises I can't keep," he smiled knowingly. "I would never do that to you. I have had more fun in the past two months with you guys than I have ever had in my entire life." He winked at Emberly.

"Also, I know you have been through hell these past few months. I can't even begin to imagine what you must be going through over the loss of your mother and Eve. But even if it stays like this for awhile, I'm still going to be here and I'm pretty sure Zayne's not going anywhere either."

Emberly had lots to worry about, but if all the worry was spread between three people, it didn't seem as bad.

"Thanks," she whispered into Sam's ear as she hugged him.

Feeling less nervous, Emberly rested her head against the back of the booth. Though she was tired, Emberly still couldn't fall asleep, so she laid there with her eyes closed and listened to the rhythmic noise of the train as it slid along the tracks.

"So, is she always stubborn like that?" Emberly heard Jaylon ask Sam when they thought she was asleep.

"Oh, that's the best she's ever been," Sam joked.

Emberly was just about to open her eyes and give him her two cents when Sam continued, "But, I think that's what I like about her most. It shows her passion. To me, she's perfect. Yes, she's sarcastic and stubborn and can be very bossy. But I love all of that about her. Even when I feel like she's being a little over the top, I can't wait for her to get that cute little smile on her face afterwards when she feels she's put me in my place. That smile is what makes all of it worth it. I'm telling you, Jaylon, I don't know where I'd be if I hadn't found her and her family. I'm happier than I've ever been, and I'm so thankful I went to the barn that morning."

Emberly's heart melted. He really did like her. Loved her even. She didn't want to smile because then Sam would know she was listening, but her heart did the smiling for her. And the funny thing was, she thought he too was perfect.

*Yes*, Emberly finally admitted to herself, *she did like Sam.* And not only as a friend.

Emberly and the others woke to a voice booming through the corridor, yelling "Next stop, Toronto!"

She couldn't believe how close they finally were. At this point, it was excitement, not nerves, that kept her from falling back asleep. Apparently, it was the same for Zayne who had cuddled up beside her and was staring out the train window.

Trees and broken fences flew by as they counted the minutes to when they'd reach Toronto. Emberly told Zayne stories to help pass the time. She knew how much he loved them. No matter if it was a known fairy tale or a story she'd made up on the fly, Zayne was forever enthralled by them.

As Emberly was in the midst of telling Zayne one of her stories, she looked out the window to find large, white, snowflakes falling from the fluffy clouds above. She pressed her hands against the window and peered out. As if she were a little kid looking through a candy store window, waiting for the salesperson to unlock the front doors so she could come barreling in.

The flakes fell thicker from the starlit sky as they approached the city of Toronto. Emberly stared in awe at the glistening lights of the city's tall towers and the soft blanket of snow that had already covered the ground. It looked just like a scene from a Christmas movie.

The train pulled into the station, and Emberly was so excited to get off that she almost forgot her most prized possession. She raced back to her seat and grabbed her bow and quiver and threw them over a shoulder as Zayne grabbed her hand and dragged her back down the train's corridor. They reached the doors, and Emberly jumped off the steps and landed in a pile of the fluffy white snow.

Emberly looked around and smiled. The snow continued to fall to the ground around her, and she stuck her tongue out to catch the large flakes. Zayne grabbed her hands and they laughed and danced in the snow.

Snow had always seemed to make her happy, but there was something so beautiful about this moment. The snow, the lights, the thought that they were finally free to start their own life...Emberly had never felt so magnificent.

The two of them threw themselves onto the ground and began to flap their arms back and forth, each creating a lovely snow angel beneath them. Sam and Jaylon stood in the crowd and laughed at them. People stopped to watch them as if they were crazy, and the truth was, they were crazy. Because crazy was the only way their plan could have worked.

And it had. They were in Canada. They were free.

CHAPTER TWENTY-FIVE

EVEN THOUGH SHE HAD slept almost the entire train ride
to Toronto, Emberly couldn't resist the temptation of the
comfortable bed. It had been a long time since she had felt the
blissful caress of cool cotton sheets as she slept. She had to share
the bed with Zayne, but she didn't care because she didn't have
to sleep on the ground or on an old mattress covered in stains.
She was finally comfortable, and even better, warm.

Emberly and Zayne had to share Jaylon's small guest room.
It was quite small, with space for only a double bed pushed
against the wall and a nightstand beside it, but—and maybe
it was because it was the first safe place they'd slept in a long
while—it felt more luxurious than any room they'd ever slept
in.

She slept soundlessly that night after she had taken a shower. She was woken suddenly when she felt a small finger poke
her shoulder. She faced Zayne and reached to stroke his hair.

"Morning, buddy. What's up?"

"I was just wondering what we're doing today."

That was a question Emberly had been pondering herself.

Just then, she heard footsteps outside their door and Sam
popped his head into their room. Last night, Sam had been
kind and volunteered to take the couch when he saw the size

of the guest bed. Emberly insisted he didn't have to, but he wouldn't listen to her. She knew it would have been cramped having the three of them on the bed, but still, she had missed having him sleep next to her.

"Morning," he said. "I heard you guys talking and came to check on you."

Emberly moved over in the bed to make room for him. Sam sat down, even closer than necessary, she noted with a smile, "So, what's the plan, Em?" he asked.

"I've been thinking, Zayne should go to school. The first of November is tomorrow, and that means that there are still two months of school until Christmas break. There's no point in keeping him here if he can't do anything else. What do you think, Zayne?"

"I think it's a great idea," he replied excitedly, shocking Emberly a little. Normally, Zayne wasn't the type to get excited to go to school. He typically kept pretty quiet at school, which usually resulted in the other kids making fun of him for it. Emberly was proud of him.

"While that is a good idea," Sam added, "we don't have any school records that have Zayne's new name. How do you propose we do that without looking suspicious?

As everyone thought about it, Jaylon poked his head through the semi-closed door, "Sorry, but I couldn't help but overhear. I have a person who works with me and one of the largest school boards in Toronto who can help with that. I can talk to her today to confirm, but I'm pretty sure she could put your new names into the system. It would be completely illegal, but you wouldn't have to worry about school records or anything because she would make something up. Would that work?"

Emberly looked at him, her eyes wide.

"So, you're saying that this girl could put our new names into the school system, make up a fake past, and no one would know?"

Jaylon smiled and nodded.

"Well then, yes," Emberly laughed, "I think that would work."

It was certainly better than anything she could have come up with, and there was no way they could just call their old school and have Zayne's records sent up to them here, especially since they'd have his old name.

Jaylon left to make breakfast and Emberly turned back to Zayne, "Zayne, are you sure you're okay going back to school? I know you missed a lot of school, but you're a smart kid and I can always help you."

"I am, I promise. I was hoping I could go back to school."

Emberly could tell that Zayne was truly excited about the idea of going to school, and she was excited for him, "Well alright then. As soon as Jaylon's friend can get everything sorted, you'll start school."

"Thanks Em," he hugged her.

"Why don't you head to the kitchen and get some breakfast? Sam and I will be there soon."

After Zayne left the room, Sam turned to Emberly, "So, what's our game plan, coach?" Sam chuckled at his joke, but Emberly just shook her head.

"Well, I don't know about you, but we can't stay with Jaylon forever. So, as much as I'd like to go back to school, the best thing to do right now would be to get a job so we can save up some cash. Then, at a later point, we can start doing some online courses on our own. I know it's not ideal, but it's the only way," Emberly stopped talking and looked at Sam who was staring at her.

"What?" she asked in confusion.

"Nothing. You are just really cute when you're serious."

Emberly tried to stop her cheeks from turning red. But when the effort proved no use, she turned her head to hide the blush and continued, "So, do you agree?"

"Yes. But we'll need to make up resumes to bring with us, then we can start looking for jobs later today. We can register Zayne in school when we get the information, and he can start either next week or the week after."

"Perfect," Emberly nodded efficiently. "Now that that's settled, let's go eat." Her stomach rumbled as she spoke the last words, as if to help emphasize the idea.

They walked into the kitchen and found Zayne and Jaylon chatting at the table. Emberly grabbed a plate and piled a bunch of fruit on it. They had eaten berries almost every day in the forest but nothing tasted better than store bought fruit. She sat down and popped a piece of watermelon in her mouth. It tasted like pure bliss on her tongue, and her taste buds tingled as she sampled everything else on her place.

As they ate, Jaylon helped them write up their resumes and find a list of suitable jobs. Emberly was amazed at how fast he was and was relieved to have his help. Before they even finished cleaning up the dishes, Jaylon had printed off their resumes and had written out a list of all the companies and their addresses for Sam and Emberly to go to. Happy to have that task done, Emberly went to take a shower.

Emberly walked into the shower and the warm water instantly relaxed her body. Even if she had showered the night before, the memories of the warm water made her long to take another. The water cascaded down her back like a waterfall. Its pressure massaged her sore muscles and gave her a sense of peace.

Emberly got out of the shower and put on some clothes that Jaylon had gone out to get that morning before they woke up. She took in her reflection in the mirror. She was finally clean, her hair was free of knots, and she was dressed in clothes that were not torn and tattered. She felt new. Emberly smiled at herself, and left the room so Sam could take a shower.

Their afternoon was spent job hunting. Jaylon had stayed back at home with Zayne while Sam and Emberly bundled up in warm clothes and headed into the snow covered city to find jobs.

After having the occasional door shut in his face, Sam was lucky to get a job at a small local boutique.

"Your turn," he said after she finished congratulating him.

"Actually, I was thinking—why don't we just go home and try again tomorrow," she replied. "We've hit almost every place that's hiring in this neighbourhood, and I'm pretty exhausted."

But Sam saw right through her nervous lie and pulled her towards a new street they hadn't yet been down, "Not a chance. If you can have your face stitched up, hunt for food, walk for days on end through a forest, and run from hunters, you can find a job."

She tried to grumble, but her heart wasn't in it. Not when she knew he was right. Despite being excited for this new life of theirs, she was nervous. Nervous to find a job, nervous to be solely responsible for Zayne, nervous to fail. Before, there was always a backup plan. Even when they lived with their mom, she was always able to scrounge up leftovers from the restaurant for them to eat. Ms. Margot's house was the same. Sure, they got the occasional beating, ate terrible food, and had horribly uncomfortable beds to sleep on; but they still had a place to sleep and food in their bellies. Even while on the run to Canada, there was always the idea that they would eventually get here and everything would finally get better—would be perfect.

And that is where the pressure came from. Now that they were finally here, there was nothing left to do but sink or swim. And Emberly could admit to herself that the idea of sinking was terrifying.

"Emberly," Sam whispered as he tilted her chin up with his hand, "you can do this."

Emberly smiled. Yes, she told herself, *she would do this.*

Emberly grabbed hold of Sam's hand and began to walk down the street. They made it past all of four buildings when something in Emberly made her stop. She turned her head to her right and saw a sign in the window of a coffee shop that read, "We're hiring!". Emberly almost burst out in excitement when she read it. Something about this place felt so right.

She held tight to her resume, stood tall, and entered the store. She walked past a line of customers and went over to a woman that was bringing out a box of cups from the back room, "Hi. I read the sign out front, and I'd like to apply."

"That's perfect! As you can see," she said as she pointed to the long line of customers and only two employees running around desperately trying to fill orders, "We're in desperate need. Just give me one minute, and I'll be right with you."

Emberly nodded and went to sit at the table the woman had indicated for her to wait at. Luckily, despite the line being long, the customers flowed through at a rapid pace, so Emberly didn't have to wait too long.

The woman from earlier walked over to Emberly with a smile on her face, "Hi, I'm Tatiana. I'm the manager here."

"Hello, my name is Aidan," Emberly introduced as she stood to shake Tatiana's hand.

"Nice to meet you, Aidan," she motioned for them to sit down. "I'll be frank. We're very short-staffed right now. We just hired one person the other day, but as you could see, we need another. Have you ever made a cup of coffee?"

Emberly laughed and answered with a confident yes.

"Well then, you're hired!" Tatiana exclaimed. "Would you be able to come in at seven tomorrow morning for training?"

Emberly wanted to jump for joy, but she figured that wasn't exactly professional, so she nodded enthusiastically instead.

"Great! We can go over the details of the job then. See you tomorrow," Tatiana said as she got up.

"Thank you so much. I'll see you tomorrow," Emberly declared as she rushed out the door.

She ran into Sam's arms, and he caught her and spun her around, "I knew you could do it, Em!"

She laughed as he set her down,

"You sure did," she smiled. "Thanks for believing in me."

"Always," he responded.

They rode the bus back to Jaylon's house and crowded into the kitchen to eat. Emberly's mouth watered at the scent of the tacos Jaylon had made for them. She hadn't eaten since breakfast and was hungry. Not starving, because she knew from experience what starving truly felt like, but still, she couldn't wait to eat. Jaylon set the food on the table and they sat around and shared stories as they ate. Just like one big family. It was the perfect ending to a stressful and tiring day.

After dinner, Emberly walked to her room to get ready for bed. She still wasn't used to having a full stomach—the feeling was almost foreign to her. She looked around the room with a huge smile on her face.

When they had left their home, they hadn't been able to pack much to take. Then, when they had left the foster home, they had taken even less. But now, with her old family photos hanging on the walls of her new room and a closet full of clothes for her and Zayne, she felt like she'd amassed a wealth of treasures.

As she flipped through her clothes in the closet, she was startled by a knocking noise. Emberly turned her head and saw Sam leaning against the open doorframe. He was wearing one of Jaylon's button-up shirts and black pants. They were the same clothes he had worn when they had gone out to search for jobs, but his shirt was no longer fully buttoned up, which left his chest exposed. Emberly didn't know where to look first.

After countless hours of walking and carrying backpacks, his shoulders had become wider and his abs more prominent, and Emberly couldn't help but stare. He smiled when he saw that Emberly was looking at him, but then his smile grew more serious as he went to go sit on her bed. He motioned for her to join him.

"Are you okay?" she asked nervously as she sat down. But he stayed silent and wouldn't make eye contact with her. "Sam, what's going on? You're kind of scaring me."

"Sorry," he shook his head vigorously, as if he were trying to detach himself from his thoughts, "I just have a lot on my mind."

"Want to talk about it?" she asked.

Sam looked at her and gave her a half-hearted smile. Emberly hadn't seen him this nervous before, and it was a little unnerving

"I really like you, Emberly, but not only as a friend," was all he said.

Emberly's heart stopped for a few seconds. At first, she didn't say anything. She just looked at him, their eyes fixed on one another.

Sam had hinted at his feelings a few times in the forest and Emberly had heard him say a version of those words to Jaylon on the train when he thought she was asleep. But this time, his words were directed to her and couldn't be clearer.

They sat in awkward silence while Sam waited for her to respond. She didn't know what to say or how to act. No one had ever liked her before. But that was likely because she never really let anyone get close enough to her for them to get the chance. But with Sam, it was different.

Emberly knew how she felt about him. So now, it was just a matter of having the courage to say it.

"Me too," she whispered.

"What did you say?" he asked, knowing full well what she had said.

"I said. Me. Too."

"What do you mean?"

Of course, he just had to push her buttons. But Emberly looked at his cute face and couldn't resist, "I like you too, Sam."

The admittance had taken all the energy in her body to say, but she actually felt pretty good after finally saying it out loud.

"But," she added, "I don't want to ruin our friendship, because I honestly don't know what I would do if I lost you."

"That's not going to happen," he reassured her.

"Well, it's an ongoing theme in my life, so who knows."

"Emberly, I'm not going anywhere. I promise. But I get it. Our friendship means a lot to me too, so I'm okay taking it slow."

Emberly wrapped her arms around Sam and hugged him tightly. They held onto one another for a while.

Finally, Emberly let go, "Thanks for coming to talk to me, Sam."

Sam got up from the bed. He looked much less nervous, "You know I always will."

Just as he was about to walk through the doorway Emberly spoke up again, "Sam, I heard what you said to Jaylon on the train about me," she admitted.

He stopped and turned, "And?"

"Did you mean it?"

"Every word," he smiled.

"Good," she smiled back. Then he left the room.

Emberly woke the next morning with the brightest smile on her face. She quietly shimmied herself out of bed so she wouldn't wake Zayne and changed into the best outfit she could put together for her first day of work.

She found Sam waiting for her at the kitchen table. They were going to take the bus to work together because the two stores were close. They ate fast, cleaned their plates, then tiptoed to the front door and threw on their coats and toques before rushing out of the house to catch the bus.

Emberly grew nervous as the bus approached their stop, "What if they don't like me?" she asked, more of a thought than an actual question.

"You're going to do great," Sam reassured her. He gave her hand a squeeze as the bus pulled up to their stop. They hopped off the bus and started to walk towards the boutique Sam was working at.

Before opening the front door, he turned to look at her and gave another encouraging squeeze of his hand, "You got this."

"I know," she smiled deviously. "Good luck to you, too."

The two parted ways and Emberly turned the corner and walked down the street to the coffee shop.

She swung open the door and was greeted instantly with the smell of coffee. She walked to the counter, and Tatiana recognized her immediately. She told her to go around the side and into the backroom to find her apron.

In the middle of struggling to tie an apron around her back, another girl showed up for her shift.

"Here let me help you," the girl offered.

"Oh, thank you so much. I probably would have been here for hours if you hadn't come."

The girl laughed in response and something about the familiar joyfulness of her laughter made Emberly slowly turn around.

Her jaw dropped when she saw a face that she had missed so dearly over these past few months, "Imani?"

CHAPTER TWENTY-SIX

"IMANI, IS THAT YOU?" Emberly stood in shock as she took in the face she feared she'd never see again.

An equally shocked Imani stood opposite her. The two girls stayed there, neither moving as if scared to break the illusion of the other standing in front of them.

Then Imani smiled and broke the trance. She threw her arms around Emberly "I never thought I would see you again, Em. I can't believe you're here. You cut your hair! It looks amazing!"

Emberly chuckled at Imani's burst of excitement. Yes, it was definitely her friend. She couldn't believe it. The sheer chance of them finding each other like this, after all this time and after so many miles. It was unbelievable, and yet, here they stood.

But common sense quickly sunk through Emberly's wondered daze, and she grabbed onto Imani's shoulders. She needed to quickly explain some things to Imani before anyone else came into the room. Their stories needed to match up.

"It's Aidan now," Emberly said with a wink.

It took Imani all of two seconds to grasp what Emberly had meant, "Got it," she smiled. "If anyone asks, we can say we were friends when we were toddlers."

Emberly smiled at Imani's quick mind. She knew she could count on her. "We can talk after work? There are some things

I want to fill you in on, but it'd take too long to explain and I don't want anyone to hearing us."

"Good idea."

"How are you though?" Emberly said as she sat down on one of the benches in the staff room. "What happened to you after we left? I've been so worried."

"We went to New Brunswick before we came here. All four of us actually. Amilia and I got fostered out to a family, and Wyatt and Verity were put in a group home. The people looking after us weren't very kind. Nothing like Ms. Margot, but it was still pretty bad. And the group home that Wyatt and Verity were at was terrible as well. We had been given the address of the group home so we mailed them a letter and exchanged phone numbers and made a plan to run away together. We hopped on a train and rode out here. We now live at Verity's uncle's place, and it's pretty great."

"Wait, why wasn't Verity staying there in the first place? Why was he sent to Ms. Margot's?" Emberly interrupted. She couldn't imagine having to go to a foster home when there was family that she could have stayed with instead.

"Well, his uncle was a lot younger than Verity's dad and couldn't legally look after Verity until he had turned eighteen. And by the time he came of age, he wasn't able to find where Verity had been sent. Apparently, Ms. Margot liked to keep the list of kids she had at her place private. Likely due to the slave labour she forced on us. And she didn't exactly allow for us to write any letters to loved ones either. So, he was never able to figure out where Verity had been sent.

"But when we came out here, Verity looked up his old address and luckily found him still living there. He and his wife let us stay there and haven't said a word about us to anyone. They can't have kids, so they're going to try to permanently adopt the four of us," she finished with a big smile on her face.

"That's a terrible start, but what a great ending," Emberly smiled. "If you've got a place to stay, why did you get a job? Aren't you going to school?"

"Well, it's not easy taking care of four children, and I wanted to help out, so I got this part-time job. Plus, Tatiana is his sister and she's great with my situation," she chuckled. "I wouldn't advise telling her about you though. Even my story was hard to comprehend for her. Yours would be much worse."

At that moment, Tatiana walked through the door and found them laughing together, "Do you guys know each other, or are you just that friendly?"

"Well, those are both correct answers," Emberly teased and winked at Imani. "But we knew each other when we were little."

"Then that's one less thing to worry about. We should start up now though. It's going to start getting pretty busy soon."

Tatiana gave them a tour around the shop then took them behind the counter to train them on the machines. The two girls picked it up fast and were soon making a few simple drinks.

The rest of the day felt as though they were working together again at Ms. Margot's house, but this time it was fun. They had fallen back into the same seamless rhythm with one another.

Emberly still couldn't believe that they had found each other. It must be true that best friends will forever be connected, no matter how far away they are.

At three, Tatiana let them know that it was time to go home, so Emberly and Imani headed to the back to remove their aprons and grab their things.

"So, where are the others?" Emberly asked as Imani helped undo her apron, "Are they at school today?"

"No, they're going to school next week, and so am I. But I'll take shifts after school and on weekends. What about you guys? What are the twins up to?"

Emberly's body stiffened. She hadn't yet told Imani about Eve. She walked over to the tiny bench that rested in the corner of the staff room and sat down to tie a shoe that didn't need to be tied, "Eve, umm. Didn't make it out of the forest," Emberly muttered.

Imani's face turned to confusion, and Emberly waited, continuing to fiddle with her shoe until Imani figured it out. Finally, it dawned on Imani. She dropped her apron on the floor as she covered her mouth with both hands, "How?" she asked, a mixture of shock and sorrow appearing on her face.

Emberly tossed her apron into the laundry bin then got up and casually walked over to the locker Tatianna had given her and grabbed her coat, "It's a long story, and I don't want anyone to hear."

Imani ran over to Emberly and gave her a big hug, "Of course, we can talk about it later. But oh, Em, I am so sorry. Truly I am. Is there something I can do?"

"No, but you're a sweet friend for asking," Emberly smiled. Then she looked at the clock on the staff room wall. "We should probably get going. Sam's off work and is probably already waiting for me out front."

"Okay, let's go," Imani replied. "But wait, who's Sam?"

"Umm, well, he's a new friend that we met on the way," Emberly fought to control her blush. She seriously needed to work on that. "You can meet him if you'd like."

Imani eagerly grabbed her stuff out of her own locker and practically dragged Emberly out the door as they waved bye to Tatiana.

When they got outside, there was what could only be described as a small crowd waiting for the two of them. On one side stood Zayne and Jaylon who had apparently taken the bus to come greet them after their first day of work. Beside them was Sam, who had indeed been waiting for her as she had expected. And on the other side Amilia, Verity, and Wyatt stood alongside a man and a woman that Emberly could only assume to be Verity's uncle and aunty.

The kids ran to Emberly and almost knocked her over as they barreled into her for a hug. Verity clung to Emberly arm and wouldn't let go. Emberly laughed and bent down to hug each of the kids.

"I missed you guys so much," she said, squeezing each of them. "I've been so worried about you."

They stood back and, unsurprisingly, Amilia spoke first, "Zayne told us about Eve. We're all so sorry," Amilia said sincerely.

Emberly smiled. Amilia reminded her so much of Eve, that it put a smile on her face.

"Thanks, guys," she hugged them again, then straightened. She was about to go over and introduce herself to Verity's uncle and aunty, but just before she could, Imani dragged her over to stand in front of Sam and Jaylon instead. "So, which of the two of you is the so-called Sam that joined them on their little adventure?" Imani demanded.

Emberly almost started rolling on the ground in laughter as she took in Imani's serious expression. Imani was acting like the most protective best friend, and Emberly loved her even more for it.

Sam chuckled, and raised his hand, "That'd be me. But, just like how Emberly is now Aidan, I'm now Sean."

Imani looked Sam up and down as if she were scanning him for a virus or something, "And do you have anything to say about my best friend?"

Imani laid into Sam thick, and Emberly absolutely loved this side of her.

"Well, she's very bossy and has insane trust issues."

Imani scoffed, "I already knew that. Tell me something else."

"Hey!" Emberly cried out in defence.

But Sam just looked at Emberly and smiled, "Well, I also kind of like her."

Emberly didn't even try to control this blush. There was no point.

"Awe. That's so sweet. Alright, I have no further questions."

Emberly laughed at her friend.

"Although, I do remember coming up with the idea for you guys to run away. So, if it weren't for me, none of this would have happened," she said, motioning to the two of them. "Some thanks are in order I presume."

"Yes. Thank you very much Imani. What would we have done without you?" Emberly said sarcastically.

"I truly don't know," Imani responded. And this time, all three of them laughed.

Soon the sun began to set and they had to part ways and go back home. Emberly gave each of the kids a hug, saving Imani for last, "I'll see you tomorrow. Don't be late. I'll need help with my apron again."

Imani chuckled and nodded her head.

Back at the house, Emberly flopped down on the couch in utter exhaustion. Even though she had walked through a forest for months with hardly ever a break, working was harder than she thought it would be. Not only had she spent most of her time on her feet, hustling around, but she'd had to memorize many different recipes and processes for everything. Emberly hadn't put that much information in her brain at once in a very long time.

Emberly could vaguely hear the voices of Sam, Zayne, and Jaylon talking about her from across the room, but she didn't bother opening her eyes. At that point, she honestly didn't even think she could.

"What do we do with her?" Jaylon asked.

"She's had a long day. Let's just leave her there. We'll put a plate of food for her in the fridge for when she wakes," Sam suggested.

They murmured more words back and forth that Emberly wasn't able to decipher, so she quit trying and gave in to sleep instead.

Emberly woke in the middle of the night and walked sleepily to the kitchen. She looked at the clock on the wall and it read three in the morning. That meant that she had slept for over ten hours. No wonder her body felt as though she could run ten miles. Her stomach growled, which was fine because there was no way she'd be able to fall back asleep any time soon. She opened the fridge and found a plate of chicken and rice for her inside. She didn't want to wake anyone by using the microwave, so she decided to eat it cold.

Emberly also didn't want to turn on a light and risk waking anyone, so she took the plate back to the couch where she could eat it under the light of the moon.

The darkness of the room made Emberly feel almost as though she were back in the forest keeping watch over everyone. And, for some odd reason, it made her sit back more comfortably on the couch as she stared into the abyss.

She was in the middle of eating and staring at the dark wall across from her when she heard a familiar cadence of footsteps coming from the hall.

"What are you doing up?" she whispered as Sam rounded the corner.

"I couldn't sleep and heard you moving around, so I came to see how you were doing."

Emberly took a big bite of her chicken and spoke between the mouthful. "I'm good. Why can't you sleep?"

Emberly took another large mouthful of food. They had been eating the bare minimum for months now and she had lost so much weight that the thought of eating seemed almost foreign to her. That was, until food was placed directly in front of her. Then she had no trouble eating.

"Bad dream," he explained.

Emberly set her now-empty plate onto the coffee table and laid her head down in Sam's lap, "Tell me about it," she said looking up at him.

"My brain was playing the last few months on repeat, and it wouldn't stop. At one point, I dreamed only of the screams Eve made as she fell to the ground," Sam paused.

Emberly understood. She couldn't count the number of times her baby sister's screams had rung in her ears. "Heartbreaking" was the only way Emberly could explain it. Eve's screams would forever scar her. "I get it. No matter how many times I replay it in my mind, I can never figure out a way to have stopped it from happening. I'm sorry. I wish there was something I could do to help you."

"Why are you sorry? She wasn't my sister. I can't imagine how hard it must be for you. And Zayne. He must be devastated."

Emberly nodded solemnly. She knew Zayne had been trying to hide the truth from her, but devastated was a good word to describe the pain she knew he must be feeling.

"Just try to shake your head next time. It sounds ridiculous, but I do it when I get bad thoughts in my head. It scares them away for a little while."

"Thanks for the advice," Sam said and they became silent. He started stroking Emberly's head and she grew sleepy again. "Why don't you go to sleep?" he suggested as if he could read her mind.

Emberly nodded slightly and laid against the back of the couch. Sam placed a blanket on top both of them then leaned over and kissed her on the cheek. She smiled, and her heart filled with joy.

They fell into a routine as the days passed. They would wake up at six and get ready for work. Emberly and Sam would take the bus together, then part ways for their day. At work, Emberly and Imani worked hard in training and by the end of the first week, they were already memorizing some of the more complicated menu items. At the end of their shift, Emberly would always find Sam waiting outside for her.

Emberly was excited when her first long week of work had finally come to an end. The four of them had decided they would decorate Jaylon's place for Christmas that weekend. Emberly had run into the kitchen that morning, beaming with joy.

"Why are you so happy?" Jaylon asked.

"Why shouldn't I be?" Emberly asked back, as if the answer was obvious.

"Because I've never seen you so happy. And it's kind of creeping me out," Jaylon joked.

"Haha, you're so funny," she mocked him. "I'm happy because today we get to make this house all Christmassy."

Everyone laughed, but Emberly just grabbed her breakfast from the counter and ate it as fast as she could. They would start the day by going shopping for decorations since Jaylon apparently didn't own any. She had searched his house for hours, but the only Christmas thing she had found was a single ornament that Sam had made for Jaylon when they were younger.

Emberly, Sam, and Zayne went to the mall after breakfast. Jaylon had claimed that he had too much work to do and couldn't go with them, but Emberly had a sneaking suspicion that it was more likely that he just didn't want to help carry their purchases. But, so long as she could still go, it didn't bother her. Plus, she'd get him back by making him do more of the decorating.

They walked around the mall for a while and found all kinds of decorations, including a wreath to hang on the front door. They had borrowed money from Jaylon since they still hadn't gotten their first paycheck yet.

Emberly felt like a kid in a candy store. She dashed from store to store while Sam and Zayne trailed behind her, laughing because she looked like a mad woman on a mission. But Emberly did not care. It had been so long since she had been in a store, or even truly celebrated Christmas, that she had promised herself that this year would be different. That there'd be more than just candy hidden about the house like their mom used to do.

And Emberly was determined to see that wish fulfilled.

Their hands were full, but Emberly still had one more store that she wanted to go into, so the three of them walked in and then parted ways. Sam and Zayne went in one direction, presumably to look for a bench to sit on, while Emberly walked towards the other.

As Emberly browsed the items in one of the aisles, she felt someone brush against her back. She turned in the direction, but only saw the back of one of the employees as they continued down the aisle. Emberly followed the woman, hoping she could ask her a question about the sale that was advertised in the store's front window.

She reached the woman and tapped her on the shoulder to get her attention. Emberly's jaw, along with everything she'd been carrying, dropped as the worker slowly turned around.

Emberly couldn't believe it. She wouldn't believe it. She refused to believe it.

"Mom?"

CHAPTER TWENTY-SEVEN

Emberly rubbed her eyes, trying to clear her vision. It couldn't be possible. Her mom was dead.

"It's really me, Emberly," she told her, trying to console her daughter whose brain had yet to connect the dots. She tried to put her hand on Emberly's shoulder, but Emberly took two steps back to avoid the hand of the ghost. Or at least, someone who should have been a ghost.

"How...why..." Emberly's brain and mouth wouldn't operate together. "You're not dead?" Emberly was finally able to ask.

"No, honey. I'm not," she smiled.

But instead of providing the comfort her mom had intended, her smile brought up layers of anger, hurt, and resent. Emberly squinted in rage, "Don't call me honey, and don't you dare smile about this. You were dead. We were told that you had died! Yet somehow, here you are. So, if you think this is just some big joke, tell me now so I can leave and pretend this never happened."

Her mom's smile faded, giving Emberly the courage to hold her resolve.

"This isn't a joke, Emberly. I'm really alive."

"How, I—" Emberly looked at her mom then suddenly remembered who else was currently in the mall, in this very store—Zayne.

"Stay right here. We need to talk," Emberly bent to retrieve her fallen bags from the floor. "And don't even think about running away," she shot a look of disgust at her mom as she added, "again."

Then she left to look for Sam and Zayne. She found them on the opposite side of the large store, looking at candles. They seemed so at ease that Emberly didn't want to interrupt them. But no matter how much fun they were having, they needed to leave. Emberly yanked Sam on the shirt and almost made him drop a candle. Luckily, he managed to pass it to Zayne before he could.

"You guys need to leave," she told him.

"What, why?"

"Just do it," she pleaded.

His expression turned serious, "What's wrong? Did something happen?"

"Something came up that I need to...deal with it. I'll explain later, but for now, just please get Zayne out of here. I'll meet you both at home as soon as I can."

Sam looked deep into her eyes for a few moments, taking in the troubled expression on her face, "Okay. Okay, I'll take Zayne home right now. But promise me that you'll call if you need me."

"I promise. And here," she said as she shoved her bags at him, "take these too."

He just barely had enough time to grab them before she turned around to search for her mom again.

As she walked, she wondered for a brief moment if her mom had perhaps decided to leave instead of waiting to talk, but she ended up finding her in the same aisle that Emberly had left her in. Her mom told Emberly to follow her and reluctantly she did.

Her mom led her through aisles of clothing to a door that read 'Employees Only'. They pushed past the door and walked down the almost deserted hallway until they arrived at one lone office at the very back. Her mom took a seat at the desk and motioned for Emberly to sit down.

"No, I think I'll stand for this," Emberly just said, then added. "Can anyone hear us back here?"

"No. It's far away from the front of the store and it's not even close to break time, so we should have privacy."

"Good. Then, are you kidding me?!" she yelled. "How the hell could you just up and leave us like that? What, did you just say to yourself, 'I'm done with my kids, who I really had nothing to do with from the beginning' and decided you'd have more fun without us, *in Canada?*"

She waited for her mom to respond but all her mom did was tell her to sit down again.

"I don't need to sit down, *Mom,* thank you very much," she replied in a harsh tone as she started pace the floor in anger.

"You don't get it, Emberly. I had to go."

"I don't buy that for a second. No one just 'has' to leave their kids. But maybe I'd better understand your reasoning for ditching us if you'd bother to explain it to me."

Her mom sighed, "Fine. I suppose I owe you the truth."

Emberly just gave her a "Yeah, ya think" look in response.

"A long time ago I had made a deal with this...'group of people' we'll call them. The details of the deal don't matter, but when they went to jail—"

"Jail? Who...?" Emberly questioned.

Her mom sighed, "It was the Marley Terrance gang."

Emberly's mind raced back to a night from so long ago. The night before the twins' birthday—the last night they had spent together as a family, watching the news. Emberly had thought her mom seemed bothered by the mention of the gang members escaping from jail, but her mom had brushed it off at the time. *Apparently*, Emberly thought bitterly, t*hat was yet another lie in a long list of lies her mom was so well-versed in.*

Seeing that Emberly understood, her mom continued, "I thought I was free of the deal, so I broke it thinking they wouldn't find out. Unfortunately, a few years ago they did. I got a letter from someone they had contact with that said that once they got out, I would be the first to pay. I was scared because I saw what they had done to your father and how they killed him—"

"Wait," Emberly interrupted, "you told me dad died of a heart attack the day before the twins were born," Emberly was becoming even more furious. *What other parts of her childhood were an utter lie?*

"Didn't you ever wonder why it was so sudden and odd of him to have a heart attack when your dad was healthy and had no medical conditions?"

"No, mom, I was *seven*...so excuse me if I didn't really think too hard about the details of dad's death," Emberly spat.

"Fair enough. Well, anyways, your father had also made a deal with them, years before he died. That's actually how we had met in the first place."

*How romantic*, Emberly thought sarcastically.

"I don't know exactly what all happened, but when your father failed to live up to his end of the deal, they killed him. Horrifically too. I was terrified when I saw what they were capable of doing. Worried that the same thing would happen to me, especially after I broke my deal with them. So, when I heard they had escaped from jail, I ran. I'd already planned out my escape years in advance, just in case," she smiled as though proud of herself.

"How are you proud of that? You shouldn't be proud of having a plan to abandon your kids. Why didn't you tell us? You put us through *hell* you know. From the second the policeman, who at this point I am now realizing was a fake, came to our door, to now. You didn't even know what was going to happen to us when you left."

"Yes, I did. I had it all figured out. The policeman, Mrs. Vander and Mr. Zeros all worked with me and your father, before he was killed. The context of our job in dangerous for you to know and totally unimportant." Emberly begged to differ, but let her mom continue. "And those books I gave the twins were clues on how to get to Canada. And your necklace was a constant reminder for you to keep going. Everything I showed you in the last couple days of my real life were to push you in the right direction. Which is why I had you going to Ms. Margot's foster home. A lady I knew would work you to the bone and make you want to escape," she smiled at her ingenious plan but Emberly just scowled at her, trying to control the urge to start screaming at her mom.

"Let's get two things straight here. Number one, Ms. Margot didn't just work us hard, she abused us. She hit us every day, no matter how hard we worked. She gave me this scar after I yelled at her for slapping Eve," Emberly pointed to the scar on her face. Her mom went silent. Emberly guessed she hadn't noticed the scar yet.

"And number two, I don't care how many damn clues you gave us, or how certain you were that we would find you, you abandoned us. You thought only of yourself, and couldn't be bothered to tell us, let alone take us with you. You didn't even care enough to send us a letter."

"What if someone read it?"

"Would it have mattered? We were your children! You should have done whatever it took to protect us, or at the very least, not let us think that our mom had died! You left us and didn't give two shits whether we were okay or not," Emberly screamed.

They sat in silence for a while as Emberly seethed over the information that had been flung at her. So many questioned circulated in her mind.

How was it possible?

What deal with the gang had her mom broke?

Why was her mom such a coward?

Emberly couldn't think straight. Finally, she just had to say something, "How do you think we got here?" she genuinely wanted to know if her mom's plan had worked.

"Well, I knew Zayne was obsessed with the *My Journey North* book I had given him on his birthday, so I assumed you would have run away from Hampton and hopped on a train to head to Toronto, thinking you had no more family alive."

Emberly looked at her mom and burst out in laughter, "That's what you thought?" she wheezed. "See, now that's funny. Do you want to hear the real story? So, you're right, we did escape, but we didn't go south. We went north, because that's where Canada is." Then Emberly explained everything about finding Sam, the thefts, Zayne getting sick, the police station, the hunters chasing them with their guns, and the seemingly never-ending torture and pain of walking for months without knowing when it would end. Emberly explained everything, except for one detail that she thought deserved more of a spotlight on.

"That's not what I expected. But at least it worked out, and you're all safe," her mom mistakenly thought of Emberly's pause.

Emberly shook her head in disappointment, "Well, that's the thing. Those hunters came after us a second time, and not only did they hold me and everyone else at gunpoint, they shot Eve in the back, and she died. So, no, we're not 'all safe'."

Her mom's lips quivered and she covered her mouth as tears welled in her eyes.

But Emberly wouldn't have it. She slammed her hand on the desk. Her mom's head shot up in surprise.

"No, you do not get to cry," she said with her teeth pressed together in rage, "You do not deserve to mourn the loss of Eve. You didn't even know her. And how could you? You were never there. I was seven when dad died, and yet I was expected to somehow take care of my baby siblings because you chose to give up. I know you lost your husband, but I lost my dad. And when I lost my dad, I lost my mom too.

"It was up to me to raise the twins and this is how you thank me? By telling me that my dad was killed by a gang, and that you, my cowardly mother, faked your own death and abandoned your children. My sister is *dead* because of the choices you made!"

Tears poured down Emberly's cheeks. Her face was hot with anger and her words were choked by tears, "Because of your ignorance, I will never get to see my sister again. I'll never get to see her smile, or hear her laugh. I won't get to watch her grow up into the amazing woman she would have become. And Zayne, he lost part of his soul the day she died. All because of you!"

She couldn't take it anymore. The saltiness of her tears added to the already bitter taste in her mouth. She grabbed her mom's arrow necklace that was still around her neck and ripped it off and threw it on the ground.

"There," Emberly choked out. She used her shirt sleeve to wipe the tears from her eyes. "You better keep that as a reminder, because this will be the last time you ever see me again. We didn't need you in our lives then and we sure as hell don't need you now."

Emberly wiped the tears from her eyes and stormed out of the office. She ran down the long hallway, sobbing as she ran. She felt suffocated in the windowless, narrow corridor, and she had to catch herself a few times before she fell to a heap on the ground.

Finally, she reached the door that led back to the store. She burst through and leaned against a nearby wall for support. Emberly put her head down and hoped no one would stop her as she walked out of the store.

She practically ran through the mall, flinging the front doors open as she made her escape. The fresh air hit her tear-soaked face and cooled the hot tears.

Emberly sat alone at the back of the bus watching the sky darken and wondering what Zayne would think of all of this. She never wanted to see her mom again, but she wasn't so sure what he'd think. She was torn over whether she should tell him about seeing and talking to their mom. The last thing Emberly wanted was to cause Zayne any type of pain. But by the time the bus pulled up to her stop, she had made her decision. She wouldn't hide the truth from him. She wasn't her mom. Zayne deserved to know.

She walked up the slippery sidewalk to their house. Emberly could hear music coming from within. She looked in the window and saw Zayne and Sam putting the Christmas tree up. They were both laughing and having a good time. Apparently, Jaylon's lie about not going to the mall with them was really a cover so he could go and surprised them with a tree. Her heart warmed at the gesture. Emberly somehow found the courage to open the door.

Inside smelled of cookies and hot chocolate and despite everything that just happened, it almost seemed perfect. She closed the door quietly and hung her coat on the rack and placed her mittens and toque in the bin near the door. She ran to the kitchen, hoping to stay hidden from the boys for just a little bit longer.

But of course, Sam had seen her. She heard him tell Zayne to organize the decorations as he followed Emberly to the kitchen. On the counter was a cup of hot chocolate that had been set out for Emberly, but she didn't take it. Instead, she sat at the dining room table and buried her head in her hands.

"Emberly what happened to you?" Sam asked.

She lifted her head, and he could see her red eyes and splotchy cheeks, and he immediately went to close the door to the kitchen. "Emberly," he said as he walked back over to her and placed a hand on her knee for comfort, "you're scaring me. Tell me what happened."

She took a deep breath as she worked up the strength to tell the story, "My mom's not dead," Emberly whispered. The sound of the words coming out of her mouth was enough to make her want to puke.

Sam's eyes went wide and he covered his mouth with his hand, "Wait...what?"

"She's not dead. She faked her death," the bitterness of the words made it come out a little too loud. Luckily Zayne hadn't heard.

Emberly then told Sam everything that her mom had told her. As she spoke, tears rolled down her cheeks. They weren't tears of sadness or disappointment. They were tears of rage and anger. By the end of her story, Emberly couldn't take it anymore, and she laid her head on the table and wept. She was heartbroken and devastated. But most of all, she wanted to punch something. Or someone.

Sam left her for a second but then returned with the cup of hot chocolate and placed it by her hand. Then he placed a soothing hand on her back. She sat with her head on the table for a few more breaths, until the flow of tears stopped.

She looked up at Sam. She knew that her face was wet with tears and that her eyes were stained red. But crying, as she had learned from Sam, was not a definition of strength or weakness. Emberly's greatest weakness as it turned out was thinking that you could never show any emotion.

That was a lesson she had learned from her mom who chose only to express her emotions in the comfort of her room—never in front of her kids. So that was what Emberly had learned to do. But why should she hide it any longer? Why should she lie about how she was feeling? Her mother had lied. Her mother had been a coward, and Emberly wanted to be nothing like her.

"I have to tell Zayne, but I'm worried about how he's going to take it," she admitted.

"He's a tough kid. You just need to be honest with him."

Emberly nodded, knowing that Sam was right. So, before she could second guess herself, she got up and walked to the living room. Zayne was there and was almost done taking all the decorations out of their plastic wrappings and putting them in rows on the ground.

Emberly took a deep breath and decided to rip the bandage off, "Zayne, Mom's not dead," she told him. Zayne whipped his head around, and Sam elbowed Emberly in the rib.

"Probably not the best way to tell him," Sam whispered under his breath, but Emberly just ignored him.

Zayne's face was confused and twisted. Emberly sat beside Zayne on the ground and explained everything. Nothing was left unsaid, because that's what Zayne deserved. The complete and utter truth.

When Emberly finished telling him everything, he stared at her, "So, Mom's not dead, and she lives here in Toronto as well?"

Emberly nodded.

"And you told her that we would never see her again, right?"

"Well, I said that I would never see her again. I wasn't sure how you'd feel about it all, and I didn't want to take that choice away from you," she responded.

Then Zayne did the exact opposite of what she thought he would do. He threw his arms around her and hugged her so tight, "Well, I want nothing to do with her either," he said firmly.

Emberly pulled him back to look at him, "You're sure?" she asked.

"I'm sure," he nodded. "She was selfish and abandoned us. She doesn't deserve us. Plus, it makes me realize how hard you worked for us. You're less than half her age and you always put family first, even when things were terrible."

Sam joined them on the ground and wrapped his arms around them. They all held tight.

After a while, they decided to get up and watch the sun set from the backyard. They settled down on the grass and gazed up at the blanket of stars that protected them once again.

The worst had passed. Emberly was sure of it.

# EPILOGUE

*13 years and 6 months later*

E MBERLY WALKED TO THE bedroom where her two-year-old daughter, Evie, slept. Emberly crept in and quietly made her way to her daughter's bed, where she was still sleeping peacefully.

Emberly watched as her daughter's chest rose up and down with every breath. Evie's black hair was plastered to the side of her face she slept on, and a hint of a smile was spread across her face as she dreamt.

Emberly hated that she had to wake the sleeping child, but today would be an important one, and they couldn't be late. She gently shook Evie's shoulder. She tossed a bit before popping open her bright blue ocean eyes. Evie smiled when she saw her mom, and it made Emberly's heart fill with joy. Emberly reached down and picked her daughter up then balanced her on her hip to kiss her cheek.

"Did you sleep well, Pookie?" Emberly asked as she tapped Evie on the nose. Evie started giggling as if it were the funniest thing in the world. Emberly couldn't resist the joyful sound of her daughter's laugh, so she started laughing as well. They walked out of the room, with Evie still balanced on Emberly's hip and made their way to the kitchen. The smell of bacon and pancakes teased Emberly's nose as they made their way to the kitchen table.

Sam stood at the stove with a spatula in one hand and a plate in the other. An apron was tied to his waist but not in the right fashion; it was looped and twisted and one of the strings was flung over his right shoulder. To top it off, he wore striped pajama bottoms and some sort of golf shirt he had bought years ago. Sam was good at many things, but fashion and somehow tying knots still weren't among them. Emberly couldn't help but laugh aloud at the sight, "Nice outfit."

Sam turned around and scoffed, "Hey, you have no room to talk, Miss 'I'm changing into sweats for the reception of my best friend's wedding.'"

Emberly threw her head back and laughed. She figured he wouldn't let that go. She had felt pretty in the bridesmaid dress she wore at Imani's wedding but only for the hour she had to wear it. After that, Imani practically had to bribe Emberly to keep the dress on for the entire night.

She set Evie down in one of the chairs, then went to give Sam a quick kiss on the cheek before heading back with two plates of pancakes. Evie, much unlike her namesake, was waiting patiently in her chair for Emberly to return with the food. Sam soon joined them, and they had a nice breakfast as a family.

Emberly relished these moments. They reminded her so much of the happy times she'd spent with the twins when she was younger, and she promised herself that when she started a family of her own, they'd continue the tradition of family dinners. She and Sam had decided not to get married, even after having Evie, mainly because neither of them had wanted to be. Both had learned from their pasts that being married didn't mean you were a family. Family was who you chose to surround yourself with, and they didn't need a ceremony to confirm that.

Emberly's eyes wandered around their house as she ate. It was still relatively new. They had bought it just over two years ago, right before Evie was born, with the money they had saved up along with a little help from Jaylon. The grey walls were accented by the occasional forest green wall and oak furniture. And it was easily double the size of the house Emberly had lived in as a kid, yet it felt cozier, as if the love within was what gave it the warmth that had been missing from her childhood house. It felt like a true home to Emberly, and that was why she loved it so much.

After breakfast, Emberly took Evie to get changed. She picked out a pair of black pants and a white shirt, then added a cute sweater overtop of the shirt. That sweater wasn't coming off until just before the afternoon's events were to start. The white shirt she wore wouldn't stay white any longer than an hour if she was anything like her clumsy father.

Emberly followed Evie out of her room, as she scampered to go play with her toys. Emberly met Sam in the kitchen just as he was finishing the dishes.

"Are you ready for tonight?" Sam asked.

Emberly yawned in response. She was exhausted. Her job as a paramedic was tiring, but Emberly loved every minute of it. Some days were harder than others. Like the days where someone would cry over the loss of their sister or brother, or when a mother or father worried if their child would make it through. Those were the days she was reminded of Eve. Those were the days that were hardest. But no matter how hard they were, Eve found pride in being able to help give others the fighting chance that had been taken from Eve.

"Yeah. I just need to do something. Can you watch Evie while I go get some stuff ready for tonight?"

"Yes, she's my daughter. I think I'm more than capable to take care of her," he joked.

Emberly joking rolled her eyes then went to get ready to leave the house.

The warm spring air and the scent of roses from their window planters hit her face as she stepped out of her house. *Today was going to be a good day,* she promised herself. He deserved it.

Emberly's first stop was to pick up the present she had ordered online at a local book store close to her house. Luckily it had arrived on time. The day pressed on better than she had hoped and Emberly was flying through her to-do list. She had gone to the liquor store and the grocery store to get some last-minute items Sam had forgotten when he had gone the day before.

Right before her last stop of the day, Emberly popped into her favourite coffee shop to grab something to drink. She was greeted by Tatiana and Arleta's bright personalities as soon as she walked in.

As promised, Emberly had called Arleta when they arrived in Toronto. Not knowing when Arleta would officially be released from prison, Emberly had called the number she'd been given every day until someone finally picked up. Emberly filled Arleta in on everything, her past, their adventure, and their plan for Toronto. Then she invited Arleta to join them in Toronto. Days later, Arleta showed up on her doorstep. Only a few days after that, Emberly introduced her to Tatiana, and Arleta fell in love with more than just the city.

The two of them ran over and gave Emberly a huge hug, almost knocking her over. Emberly laughed and enjoyed their comforting embrace.

"It's been ages since we've seen you!" Arleta said.

"We've missed you," Tatiana added.

"I've missed you guys too! I realized it had been too long since I was last here, so I thought I would pop in to see you today while I was shopping."

"And to get a drink," Arleta joked. "The usual?"

Emberly laughed, "Please!"

Arleta went to the counter to fix Emberly an iced coffee, while Emberly turned to Tatiana, "You two are still coming to the party tonight, right?"

"We are," Tatiana confirmed.

Arleta returned with Emberly's drink and an envelope, "Another letter came in the mail for you today," she said, handing Emberly the envelope.

Emberly rolled her eyes. She didn't need to see the return address to know exactly who it was from. Her mom had apparently done some digging after seeing Emberly in the mall and had found where Emberly worked. Ever since, she'd send letters to the coffee shop on every holiday, hoping Emberly or Zayne would send something back.

They never did, and they never intended on doing so.

"We can throw it away here if you want?" Tatianna offered.

"No, that's okay. Zayne should read it since it'll be for him. Then I'll throw it away...or maybe even burn it."

The girls chuckled and said goodbye to Emberly as she left the shop.

The bakery was Emberly's last stop. She walked to the counter and picked up her order. She lifted the lid of the white box and read the writing on the cake. The words "Happy Birthday" stared up at her in blue icing. Emberly smiled then thanked the kind owner and made her way back home.

Emberly looked at the clock on their living room wall as she walked back into the house. One o'clock. Not much longer until people started to show up at the house. She needed to hurry to finish prepping for Zayne's party.

Emberly placed the cake on the snack table Sam had set up while she was gone, then took the card from her mom out of her purse. She fought the urge to rip it to shreds, and instead, added it to the pile of birthday cards for Zayne. She'd let it be his choice to open it or not.

She found Evie sitting on the floor, completely immersed on building a castle out of her colourful blocks. Emberly kissed her daughter on the head then went to help Sam out in the kitchen.

Emberly was focused on cutting vegetables, instead of her hand, when she heard a knock on the door. She raced to open it and greeted her old friends.

Amilia, Wyatt, Verity, and Verity's girlfriend, Aria, barreled through the door first. They were followed by Imani, her husband, and their baby daughter, April, who was the same age as Evie and the best of friends, just like their moms. Emberly gave them all hugs as they entered and directed April to where Evie and her pile of blocks were.

Since Imani's husband was taller like Sam, the two of them set up the higher decorations on the walls and hung streamers from the roof, while the remainder of the adults sat on the ground blowing up balloons. And not long after, Tatiana and Arleta showed up with some snacks from the coffee shop and helped with the remainder of the party decorations.

Zayne and his fiancé, Louis, wouldn't be there for at least another hour. But even though Emberly had given Louis explicit instructions to take his time, she still wanted to make sure everything was done before they arrived.

Just as the hour mark was nearing, Jaylon burst through the front door, "Zay... Zayne and..." he couldn't catch his breath.

"Jaylon, are you okay?" she asked him.

He nodded as he stood up straight, "Okay, good," she slapped his arm. "Why are you late? You know that Zayne and Louis are supposed to be here at any minute."

Jaylon rubbed at his arm, "That's what I was trying to say before you slapped my arm. As I was running to the house, I saw Zayne and Louis walking from the other direction. They're pretty close."

Chaos arose.

Imani grabbed both kids and handed Evie to Sam. Emberly grabbed Jaylon by the arm and dragged him away from the window. Wyatt flipped off the lights, and everyone dove to hide.

As the room fell silent, Emberly fumbled her phone and texted Louis that they were ready, then she held her breath as the front door swung open.

She heard the quiet mumbling of the two of them and then heard Zayne ask, "Why are the lights off?"

"Surprise!" everyone yelled as they jumped out at the same time. Zayne stumbled backwards in shock and knocked over a lamp. Luckily, Louis caught it before it hit the floor.

Once Zayne realized what was going on and who was there, his face lit up like a million stars. Emberly smiled from ear to ear knowing he was completely surprised.

Zayne ran over and gave her a huge hug.

"Thank you so much, Em," he whispered.

"It was my pleasure, buddy."

Zayne let go and turned to thank and visit with everyone else in the room. Someone turned the music on and another proclaimed it was time for drinks.

Emberly stood up from the kitchen table and cleared her throat. Everyone's conversations ceased as they turned their eyes from their empty dinner plates to her.

"I wanted to thank everyone for coming. It means so much to me—to us," she gestured to Zayne. "That you were all able to clear your schedules to spend an evening together. We've all been through so much and have sacrificed so much just to get to this point, and it really is the family you choose that is the greatest blessing."

Everyone smiled warmly at each other.

"Unfortunately, not all of us could be here in person today," Emberly grabbed onto Zayne's hand and squeezed tight. "Eve would have loved this party. She was always so happy and full of life, and though I wish we could have seen her grow up, she'll forever remain in our hearts."

Emberly's eyes met Zayne's. His were equally filled with tears—as were everyone's.

"Eve would have loved this," he smiled. Then he stood up and gave his big sister hug.

The rest of the night went on with tears of joy. Zayne opened his gifts, then some people walked over to the living room to watch the basketball game while others remained at the table and talked.

And when the sun started to set, Emberly decided it was finally time to bring out the cake. Everyone gathered back around the kitchen table while she and Sam brought out the cake. They were extra careful not to drop it, since Emberly had decided to put twenty-two candles on the cake. Sure, it might have been a bit excessive to light that many, but it was more fun that way.

Emberly started singing, and soon everyone joined in.

Happy birthday to you,

Happy birthday to you,

Happy birthday, Zayne and Eve,

Happy birthday to you.

Zayne looked at the cake then back at Emberly. She smiled at her little brother whose tears glistened in the candlelight.

"Go ahead. Blow them out," she encouraged him.

Everyone watched him, excitement on their faces.

Zayne looked at Emberly one more time and smiled. Then he turned back to his cake and blew out the candles for him and Eve.

# ACKNOWLEDGEMENTS

This acknowledgment has been honestly so hard to write because of how many people have helped make this experience so incredible. Everyone I've told about my book has been supportive and beyond excited about my novel. But there are a few people who need more than a general message.

Although she probably hated it, my sister Julia sat and listened to me talk about my book for hours. Did I have to bribe her sometimes? Maybe, but she still did it and that's why she was the first person I let read my book after the editing process. Her love of animals and creativity had a strong impact on the creation of Eve Clove and the story in general!

I'd also like to thank my parents who put up with me for months while I worked through this. Thank you to my mom who forced me to read as a young kid and helped me to fall in love with words. Without Junie B. Jones and our Christmas Book Countdown, I wouldn't have been able to begin writing this story. My dad, even though he doesn't like to read, helped me so much by teaching me how to form a proper business e-mail and edit my documents correctly. Not only that, he pushed me at points when I was too frustrated to move on. Thank you both so much.

Of course, I couldn't make this acknowledgment without mentioning the one person who I've been attached to since grade one. Elena has listened to me rant about the plot of my book for hours at a time and she's responded to my paragraph-long texts late into the night. I couldn't have finished this book without her support and I'm so glad she's stuck by me for so long.

Another one of my great friends, Lauryn, worked so hard on creating the beautiful painting which is printed at the front of the book. I've always been a big fan of Lauryn's art so I thought it would be a good idea to ask if she wanted to paint a piece for my book. A few drafts later she finished and after showing me, I couldn't stop smiling. She captured the mood of my story perfectly.

A big thanks goes out to my editor, Lacy. I went into this process completely confused and she helped me and taught me so much. She walked me through every aspect of editing and publishing my book and you wouldn't be reading this right now if it wasn't for her guidance.

I'd also like to thank Heidi for all her help. Without her, my book would not look as beautiful as it does.

I know I had a few requests, but she took them and made it better than I ever hoped it could be.

Lastly, I'd like to thank the person who I will give the most credit out of everyone. They were my inspiration for this story and I couldn't have done it without them. Love you forever and ever.

## ABOUT THE AUTHOR

AJ Milnthorp is an up-and-coming young teen author who has newly published her first book, A Blanket of Stars. She began writing at the age of 13 and finally self-publishing her first book at 15. She currently goes to high school in Saskatoon SK where she plays basketball on her school team. After school, you can usually find AJ running around to dance class or basketball practice. She is very excited about the launch of her book and hopes you enjoy it!

CPSIA information can be obtained
at www.ICGtesting.com
Printed in the USA
BVHW050620090223
657947BV00001B/1